Annabel watched him

Carter scraped up the pancakes and slapped them onto the plate. He didn't say a word, just poured out more puddles of batter.

She watched him, intrigued, wondering...

Was she having the same effect on him that he had on her? Was he as attracted to her as she was to him?

If so, were they ever going to be able to get on with their lives unless they got past it?

A younger Annabel wouldn't have done it.

A less frantic Annabel would never have dared.

But this Annabel was thirty-six and wanted her sanity back. She wanted her sense of focus and direction, her calm and peaceful life.

"Carter," she said to his back, "do you think maybe we should just forget the pancakes and go to bed?"

ABOUT THE AUTHOR

For Anne McAllister, ideas for stories are everywhere. She has found inspiration in a variety of sources—a childhood memory, a phone book, even a fortune cookie. In all her stories she writes about relationships—how they grow and how they challenge the people who share them. Here in *MacKenzie's Baby*, Anne reprises the role of Carter MacKenzie, whom readers will remember from *I Thee Wed*. Anne makes her home in the Midwest with her husband and their four children.

Books by Anne McAllister

HARLEQUIN AMERICAN ROMANCE

ANNE McALLISTER

MACKENZIE'S BABY

Harlequin Books

TORONTO • NEW YORK • LONDON
AMSTERDAM • PARIS • SYDNEY • HAMBURG
STOCKHOLM • ATHENS • TOKYO • MILAN
MADRID • WARSAW • BUDAPEST • AUCKLAND

For Patrick, with love

Published October 1992

ISBN 0-373-16459-9

MACKENZIE'S BABY

Printed in U.S.A.

Prologue

"Jason Neillands?" The pediatric nurse scanned the sea of parents and offspring in the overcrowded waiting room.

Thank God, Carter thought. He'd never given much thought to the notion of purgatory, but after forty minutes, a waiting room in a pediatrician's office seemed about as close as one could get.

He scooped his nine-month-old charge away from the magazine he was shredding and followed the nurse down the corridor.

The nurse marched them into one of the examining rooms and turned, pencil poised, to look expectantly at Carter. "And what seems to be the trouble with Jason today?"

"Er, sore throat. Can't sleep. I—he...lies awake all night."

"Does he cry?"

"Uh, no. Not a lot, I mean. Sometimes. He's a baby, for heaven's sake."

The nurse tapped her pencil on Jason's chart, then gave Carter a skeptical look. "Does he have a temperature, Mr. Neillands?"

"I...don't think so." He didn't think he'd tell her he wasn't Mr. Neillands, either. Let Jack's reputation suffer a little. Do him good.

He could tell that it was all she could do not to roll her eyes at his incompetence. She contented herself with pursing her lips. "Undress him down to his diaper. Doctor will be in shortly." She went out, shutting the door with a decided thump behind her.

Doctor had damned well better be in shortly, Carter thought as he perched on the edge of the examining table. It was already almost noon. He'd picked Jason up at ten. Frances was going to wonder where the hell he'd got to with her kid. When Carter'd taken him, he'd said he was only going for a walk in the park, that they'd be back in maybe an hour.

"You won't tell her, will you, chum?" he asked the baby who stood holding Carter's fingers and balancing on his knee.

Jason gave him a dimpled grin and leaned forward to gum Carter's shoulder.

The door opened, and a silvery-blond woman in a plaid shirt and brown corduroy slacks appeared, frowning down at Jason's chart as she did so. Only her stethoscope gave her away, Carter thought with amusement.

"Well, Jason," she said briskly, "what's the troub— *Carter?*"

"Hi, Sis." He gave her a sheepish grin.

She shut the door firmly behind her. "What are you doing here? Where's Frances? Where's Jack? That *is* Jason?"

The baby, hearing his name, turned and grinned at her, then wobbled precariously and grabbed a handful of Carter's hair to steady himself.

"Ouch. Hey, easy, fella." Carter shifted the child in his arms, turning him to sit and bounce on his blue-jeans clad knee. "Of course it's Jason. What'd you think?"

Millicent MacKenzie Moore regarded her older brother with eyes of long experience. Her expression was even more skeptical than the nurse's. "And Frances sent him to the doctor with you?"

Carter shrugged. "It . . . isn't him. It's me."

"Carter."

"I've been having these sore throats, Milly. Long sleepless nights."

"Carter, I'm a pediatrician."

"You're a doctor. Columbia Phi Beta Kappa. Yale Med." He grimaced. "Don't think Dad kept it a secret."

Millicent sighed. Their father's pride in her accomplishments had only been equaled by his disgust with Carter's lack of them. Not that Carter had ever cared. "You could have called your regular doctor."

"He says there's nothing wrong."

"Maybe there isn't."

"Then why can't I sleep?"

Milly's brow arched. "Guilty conscience?"

He rubbed a hand across his face. "Don't I wish."

Milly cocked her head. "Pure as driven snow, are you?"

"Close," Carter admitted. "Since Diane I haven't—" He stopped and shook his head. Even with Diane he never had.

He and Diane Bauer had been friends, never lovers. But he'd loved her. At least *he* thought he had. Diane had said he didn't. She'd said he didn't know what true love was.

What the hell did she know? he thought grimly. She'd only had eyes for Nick. Three months ago she'd married him.

"I feel lousy," he said plaintively now. "I lie awake all night. Remember when I used to have croup as a kid?"

"You don't have croup, Carter."

"Maybe I have mono."

"Didn't your doctor do lab tests?"

"Yeah, but—"

"Were they negative?"

"Yeah, but—"

"Then I doubt if you have mono."

"But there's gotta be something wrong with me. I can't sleep. I work for hours. I don't date."

Milly, heading for the door to usher him out, stopped dead and stared, nonplussed. "Why not?"

"What's the point? All the women look the same...."

"Maybe you are sick." She backtracked and reached for a tongue depressor. "Stick out your tongue and say *ah.*"

"*Ahhhhhhhh-gggghhh!* Cripes, Mil, what're you trying to do, gag me?"

She gave him a sweet smile. "Could I?"

He glowered. Jason bounced up and down and clapped his hands.

"Your throat looks fine, Carter." She checked his nose, his ears, his eyes. "Nose, eyes and ears are fine, too. Take off your shirt."

She held Jason while Carter stripped off his dark green T-shirt, then handed the baby back and laid the stethoscope against his chest.

"It's cold," Carter complained.

"Hang tough, big guy," Milly said with her typical lack of sympathy, and moved to listen to his back.

When she was done she pinched his quarter inch of spare tire and gave him one of her Mary Sunshine smiles. "I hate to tell you this, brother dear, but I think you're going to live."

Carter tugged the shirt back on, then looked up to scowl at her. "That's all you're going to do?"

"Well, I could take your temperature, I suppose."

Carter opened his mouth and waited.

Milly just looked at him, then at the thermometer in her hand. "It's rectal, Carter," she said gently.

He bounded off the examining table. "Forget it."

She caught him by the belt loop before he could get the door open. "Hold it a minute."

"You said I'm fine."

But she didn't let go until he turned around to face her. "Physically I think you are," Milly said seriously. "Mentally, emotionally... I wouldn't be so sure."

Carter's mouth twisted. "Go see a shrink, you mean?"

"You could. But I don't think you need to unless it gets worse."

"What do you think?"

"That maybe you need a break. Since Diane got engaged and since Dad died—"

"He doesn't have anything to do with this."

"But it's only been five months." It had been a shock to them both when their robust, healthy father had dropped dead on a Bermuda golf course last April.

"It might have been years for all the contact we had."

Millicent sighed. She'd grown up a bystander to the ongoing battle between Carter William MacKenzie III and his black-sheep son. She'd hoped it might end last April. It hadn't yet. "He tried, Carter."

"He was the most trying son of a bitch I ever knew!"

"Carter!"

"He was. He had my whole life mapped out for me. Tried to tell me every damned thing to do from the time I first took a breath. And whatever it was, I never did it well enough, did I? If he was still around, I'll bet you he'd be telling me I won't die as well as he did, either!" Carter dropped his voice in a damningly accurate imitation of the elder MacKenzie. "'I died after sinking a birdie. You'll probably go out after a double bogey, you young fool.'"

"He's dead, Carter," she said quietly. "He can't tell you anything now."

"And thank God for that," Carter muttered. He bent his head, concentrated on watching Jason's chubby feet dance along the tops of his jeans-clad thighs. He didn't want to talk about his father. He never wanted to talk about his father.

Milly tapped the stethoscope against the table. "I still think you need a break. If all you've done since Diane got engaged is work—"

"I play, too," Carter said quickly. "Don't forget that."

"I thought you weren't dating."

"I'm not. Now. I did. After Diane got engaged, and...and later, I—I...went out a lot." An understatement if there ever was one. He'd felt a sense of panic, desperation for months, as if he were on some sort of merry-go-round, reaching for the brass ring and missing, then missing again. As if his life was going faster and faster, spinning away from him. He couldn't explain it, didn't try.

"But now you don't?"

He shook his head.

"What do you do?"

"Order soybeans. Shelve bags of bulgar and barley. Pack peanut butter. Inventory ninety-million varieties of organic shampoo. Keep the steel-cut oats from mating with the regular milled." He managed a grin.

Millicent tweaked his nose. "Work, in other words."

"Yeah."

"Maybe you've been working too hard."

Carter snorted. "Tell that to the old man."

Milly ignored him. "Do you want a prescription?" she asked him slowly.

Carter's brows lifted. "I thought you said I wasn't sick."

"Not that kind of a prescription."

Jason was squirming in his arms, trying to get down. Carter swung him around and settled the baby onto his shoulders. "What kind?" he asked warily.

He couldn't think of a thing he hadn't tried. Work. Play. Wine, women and song.

New York City wasn't short on stimulation of any sort. What he hadn't thought of, Jack or Frances had. Even Nick and Diane, once they'd come back from their honeymoon, had gone out of their way to keep him busy and to include him in their life.

Carter hated it. After a few attempts at dragging wholly unsuitable women along on outings with his friends or, worse, going alone as a third wheel, he stopped going at all. Being the adjunct to everyone else's happiness was worse than burying himself in soybean invoices until three in the morning.

"I think," Milly said now, considering him the way she did things under a microscope, "you need a change of scene."

"I went skiing in Jackson Hole last January. I went to Nassau in April and to Hawaii in July. I was out fishing at the folks' place in Jersey just last weekend."

"Not just a week or a weekend," Milly said. "More. A lot more."

He frowned. "You mean move?"

"Maybe not permanently." She smiled at him, blue eyes guileless. "I wouldn't want you gone forever, you know. But for a few months, why not?"

"The store, for one thing. I know Dad didn't take it seriously, but I thought you might at least." He knew damned well his very own Jack Sprat's Health and Wellness Store was small potatoes compared to the Idaho-size business conglomerates his father had run. He hadn't expected the old man to respect it. He'd hoped for a little more from Milly.

"Of course I do," his sister said quickly. "But don't you have an assistant manager?"

"Yeah, but—"

"And isn't he competent?"

"She, but—"

"She," Milly said firmly, "is probably itching for the chance to show what she can do." One blond brow arched. "Isn't she?"

"Yeah, but—"

"You don't want to give her the chance?"

"Of course I do. It's just that..."

"That if you leave you might have to get down to the nitty-gritty of what's bothering you?" Milly's eyes were gentle and knowing as they met his.

Carter sighed. If there was a virtue to being so damnably transparent, he didn't know what it was. Jason thumped him on the head.

"You haven't been off the treadmill for more than a week since you came back from Berkeley how many years ago?" Milly asked.

"Eleven," he said heavily.

"A long time," Milly mused. "Eleven years ago I was a college sophomore majoring in partying. Times have changed, Carter. You've changed. Maybe your body is telling you something your mind should listen to. Maybe you ought to try something new, get a different perspective. Figure out what's missing, what you really want out of life."

"And then I'll be back to normal?"

Milly grinned. "Heaven forbid." Then her grin faded. "Seriously, I think you should try it."

Carter rubbed a hand across his face. "Where would I go?"

Milly looked at him for a long moment, then cast aside the last vestiges of her professional persona and became fully and completely the sister who'd always adored him. She put her arms around him and gave him a hug.

"That's up to you, Carter. You'll know it when you see it. I'm sure you will. And then—" she reached up to pat his cheek "—you'll go wherever the spirit leads you. And when you get there, you'll realize what you need."

Chapter One

Boone's Corner, Vermont?

God help him, yes. That was what the sign said, and he'd been here before so he knew it was true.

But he hadn't been here to stay before. Never that. Two or three days over Thanksgiving. An evening's visit with Jack and Frances on his way to Killington. That weekend last January when they'd all come up for Jason's baptism. A couple of days this past August when he and Jack played hooky and came up to go fishing.

Short, restorative visits.

Visits that—however short—had always seemed plenty long. Unlike this one—two weeks—which promised to make eternal rest seem like a two-hour nap.

Why in heaven's name had he said he'd come?

Frances hadn't expected him to. She'd simply mentioned the problem last week as they sat on the grass in Central Park, munching corn chips, playing with Jason and watching Jack play softball.

"Cripes, you'd think it was the Series," Carter had said, watching as Jack slid headfirst into second base.

"With Jack it might as well be." Frances looked at her husband with an indulgent smile. "My husband the competitor. He's not happy that he'll miss the play-offs."

Carter raised a brow. "Where's he off to this time? I thought he was sticking pretty close to home."

He damned well would be if he were Jack. When Jack had married Frances almost two years before, Carter had thought his friend was losing his mind. As a much-sought-after, highly paid model, Jack frequently found himself in exotic parts of the globe propping up some of the world's most beautiful women.

"Nice work if you can get it," Carter had often griped. And at the time he couldn't see giving that sort of life up for anyone or anything.

Now he wasn't sure.

He found himself waking up at night, staring at the ceiling, tossing and turning in his wide lonely bed and, by this time, he'd given up wondering what luscious young woman he could call to share it with him. Now he got up and prowled around, working crosswords and playing solitaire, then picking out songs on the battered old guitar he hadn't touched since his college days. And the songs he remembered...all those lost love, hit-the-road-again, life-is-passing-me-by songs.

"*He's* not going anywhere. *We* are going up to Vermont next week," Frances was saying. "We're having a new roof put on the house."

"You're moving?" Carter felt a moment's panic at her words. Jack and Frances were his best friends. While he didn't see them as often as he once had, sometimes didn't even talk to them for a week or two, he always knew they were six blocks away. Like the Chrysler Building or the Statue of Liberty, they were a part of the landscape that he knew he could count on.

If they left...

"Not immediately," Frances said, brushing her long hair out of her face. "But we're talking about it. Jack won't be modeling forever, you know, and we would rather raise Jason in the country.'' She gave her son, busily chewing her purse strap, a fond smile. ''In any case, we need a new roof. The old one leaks. And with winter coming, we need to get it on soon. It practically took an act of God to get Benton Brothers to fit us in, and then it turned out to be during Jack's play-offs. I said I'd go alone to oversee, but he says that wouldn't be fair, that I won't be able to get enough writing done if I'm the only one taking care of Jason.''

''I'll go.''

Frances blinked, then laughed. ''With me? Somehow I don't think even Jack is that generous.''

''Not with you,'' Carter said. ''Though,'' he added with a grin, ''if I thought he would...'' He waggled his eyebrows at her and relished his ability to make her blush. ''I meant I'll go for you.''

Frances just looked at him.

''Why not? I could use a vacation. My sister's been telling me I need one. A change of perspective, she said.''

Frances's gaze narrowed. She cocked her head, looking at him. The directness of her gaze unnerved him.

He shifted uncomfortably, then looked away, reaching out to snag Jason up into his arms and nuzzle the little boy's soft dark hair.

Frances clicked her tongue. ''Ah, Carter,'' she chided gently, ''you're such a soft touch.''

''So what do you think?'' he asked her, his tone gruff. He slanted her a glance.

''That you need one of your own.''

''One what? House in Vermont?''

''No. Child.'' Frances's eyes were gentle as she smiled at him.

"Yeah, sure. But last time I checked Bloomingdale's, they were all out."

Frances punched his arm.

"Ow." Carter rubbed his arm and did his best imitation of a pout.

Frances laughed. "Poor Carter."

He scowled at her. He didn't want her pity, and as far as he could see, that's exactly what it was.

Her smile faded slowly and she cocked her head. "You mean it, don't you? About going to Vermont?"

It was a perfect chance to back out, to say he'd been kidding, that of course he didn't want to spend half of October moldering away in backwoods New England.

But Milly's advice kept echoing in his ears. "You need to sort out your life, find out what's missing. You'll know it when you see it."

Boone's Corner, Vermont, sounded as good a place as any to start.

But now, turning into Frances's lane and looking around at the steeply wooded hills, the narrow roads, recalling the town he'd cruised through in ninety seconds flat just ten minutes ago, Carter wasn't so sure.

He was a city boy, for heaven's sake. He'd been raised right smack in the middle of one of the biggest in the world.

And while there was no doubt that he was plenty savvy when it came to New York street smarts, in thirty-six years his entire experience with the wilderness could be summed up in six weeks at summer camp when he was ten, a dozen or so fishing expeditions mostly in his parents' New Jersey backyard, a score of ski trips where the self-service lodge dining room was as close as he'd come to roughing it, and six years in Berkeley, California, which, if it wasn't precisely rural, certainly had a wildness all its own.

"You'll be fine," Frances had assured him when he'd expressed second thoughts yesterday morning. "We have hot-and-cold running water, indoor plumbing, windows, doors. All of life's necessities—except a new roof."

But as far as Carter could see now, there wasn't a Chinese takeout or a barbecue joint for miles, nobody named Ray sold pizza and, if he wasn't mistaken, that was a goat munching grass in the middle of Frances's lane.

He shut his eyes, then opened them again in the hope that he had been hallucinating.

The goat regarded him indifferently, then went back to munching.

Carter leaned his forearms on the steering wheel and considered his options.

He could hit the goat, drive around the goat or turn tail and head back from whence he'd come. There was always the chance that the goat would move, of course, but Carter didn't put much faith in that. He sighed and stretched, trying to ease the kinks from the five-hour drive, trying to give the goat the opportunity to move.

The goat ignored him.

Frances hadn't mentioned goats. While he knew that she used to have some before her marriage, he'd assumed they were gone. After all, she and Jack spent most of their time these days in New York. Surely the goats couldn't run things by themselves.

If they could, they could have supervised the installation of the new roof.

The goat took a step, then bent its head again and continued cropping. Carter sighed, then tapped the horn. The goat lifted its head, looked at him once briefly, then went on with its meal.

Carter knew dogs. He knew cats. He'd even had a guinea pig once. But goats were a mystery. One he didn't really want to solve.

"If you need anything, and I mean anything at all," Frances had told him when he was leaving, "call Annabel."

Her friend, she meant. Annabel Archer she meant. The Quintessential Earth Mother Of The Western World, she meant.

Purposeful, no-nonsense Annabel, who could wither grown men with a stare—and did—would doubtless know exactly how to deal with a goat.

Carter was damned if he was going to ask her.

He would have to see her later this afternoon to deliver Frances's birthday greetings, but that was it.

Carter edged the car forward. This time the goat didn't even look up.

Carter sighed, stopped, opened the door, got out and leaned against the side of the car.

The goat munched on. It was brown and white and spindly legged, with two curving horns that made it look almost top-heavy when it lifted its head. When *he* lifted *his* head, Carter corrected himself. There was no doubt from this distance about the sex of the animal.

He straightened, narrowed his eyes and began to walk toward the goat.

"Get out of the road," he said.

"Shoo," he said.

"Go on. Get out of here before I nail your rear with the toe of my boot," he said.

The goat must have thought Carter was a soft touch, too. He didn't move anything except his eyes, which watched Carter ever more warily the closer he came.

Carter cleared his throat. "Listen, Billy, you—"

But he got no further. The goat abruptly lifted his head, stiffened, then plunged forward, hurtling straight at him.

One minute Carter was standing in the lane, the next he was flat on his back in the dust.

"Wha' the—" He spat out a mouthful of good Vermont gravel and grimaced. It was a change in perspective, all right.

He hauled himself to his feet. The goat uttered a sound somewhere between a belch and a chuckle, ambled on down the lane and went back to his meal.

"Welcome to Vermont," Carter muttered.

He brushed off the seat of his jeans and examined the torn elbow of his shirt. It was going to be a long two weeks, he thought.

But at least the goat was standing on the verge now. The lane was empty. Carter decided he'd take his victories wherever he could find them.

FOR HER THIRTY-SIXTH birthday Annabel Archer was baking herself a cake.

She hummed to herself as she did it, crushing the all-spice and grinding the nutmeg and cinnamon, then sifting them into the flour with the old hand-crank sifter she'd got at the auction in Old Man Milliken's barn last January.

In the background, on the tape her children didn't know she had, a nasal masculine twang carried on about being done wrong by and surviving.

Annabel mouthed the lyrics along with the twang. She knew them by heart, though her children thought she listened to nothing less exalted than Bach—J.S., J.C., C.P.E. and, at her most lowbrow, P.D.Q.

Libby and Leif would drop over dead if they knew their mother spent stolen moments with Waylon, Willie and their ilk. But there was something supremely self-indulgent about the whine of a steel guitar no matter whose voice accompanied it, and anyway, it was her birthday. She had a right to listen to whatever she wanted. Besides, when it came to being done wrong by and surviving, Annabel was an expert.

She added the eggs one by one, stopping between each to do a snappy soft-shoe shuffle between the table and the sink. She wondered how many other women could do it as credibly as she could in a pair of earth shoes.

Libby would have rolled her eyes and groaned, "Oh, Mom," if she'd seen it. As far as seventeen-year-old Libby was concerned, her mother could be a great source of embarrassment these days.

Life with teenagers wasn't what everyone had ever predicted that it would be. It was worse.

Not that Annabel didn't enjoy Libby and Leif. They were, despite their ages and their current despair of her, the light of her life. But sometimes it seemed as if overnight they had turned from steady, reliable sixty-watt beams into psychedelic flashing neon.

"I'm getting old," she said to the cat. "Aging, like a fine wine."

The cat smirked.

Annabel tweaked his ear. "Or a moldy fruitcake. I know. I know."

She and the cat, a formerly stray Maine Coon that Leif had found huddled in Frances's barn and had dragged home and named Goliath—which suited him—often had conversations like this. He was the only one who didn't argue with her anymore.

She picked him up and danced him around the room. He let out a moan of long-suffering protest, but he didn't struggle until the phone rang. Then he practically leapt out of her arms onto the counter where he stalked behind the mixing bowls and sat down to regard her with offended dignity.

Annabel shook her head at him. "I suppose you think you were saved by the bell," she chided as she reached for the phone. "Hello?"

"I bet you thought we forgot."

"Frances!" Annabel's face broke into a grin and she pushed a strand of hair out of her face. "No, I know you better than that. You wouldn't have the decency to let me grow old without reminding me."

"You're not old."

"Tell that to Libby."

Frances snorted. "What does Libby know? She's a mere child."

It was Annabel's turn to snort. "You haven't seen her in a while, then. You'll get a rude awakening when you do. I thought you'd be here by now. Aren't Bentons doing the roof this week?"

"They are. But we're not coming."

"Well, I can't say I won't miss seeing you, but I'll keep an eye on things."

"Not necessary. Carter's on his way."

The world seemed suddenly to tilt.

"Carter? Carter MacKenzie?" Annabel couldn't quite hide the disbelief in her voice. She hoped she did a better job with the dismay. "You're kidding."

"Not a bit."

"He wouldn't come up here. Not voluntarily. What'd you do, doctor his martinis?" There was no other way Annabel could imagine a clever, smart-ass big-city boy like Carter MacKenzie agreeing to spend two days, much less two weeks, in the wilds of Vermont.

"He said he wanted a vacation."

"He's run out of Club Meds?"

"I think he wants a different sort of vacation this time."

Annabel doubted that.

"Why is it I get the feeling you don't like Carter?" Frances teased.

"Use your imagination," Annabel said gruffly. "He has all the depth of a mirror and all the sincerity of a used-car salesman."

Frances laughed. "He's not that bad."

Annabel made a doubtful noise.

"Truly," Frances said. "I don't know of a better friend. He's loyal and kind and he thinks Jason is the cat's meow."

"Jason is the cat's meow," Annabel said. "It doesn't take much insight to see that."

"You're just prejudiced. Really, Annabel, give him a chance."

"I probably won't even see him."

"He's delivering your birthday present."

Frances was famous for her gifts. She always put such thought into them. Annabel supposed it was because Frances was a writer that she had such a gift for empathy. But her presents were always so clever and apt that Annabel often wondered what she was revealing to her perceptive friend.

Last year, for example, Frances and Jack had simply moved in for the weekend, pressing into her hand a plane ticket to New York, the key to their apartment and an envelope full of tickets to the best New York shows. Annabel had protested.

"It's too much. I don't need this," she'd said, even as they'd bundled her onto the plane that night.

"You do," Frances had said implacably. "More than you'll ever know."

And Annabel, coming back five days later revived and refreshed, had admitted that Frances was right. "It was sort of fun really," she'd allowed, which didn't begin to cover how much she'd enjoyed the solitary bliss and cultural immersion they'd provided for her.

Frances didn't say, I told you so.

"You're sending my birthday present with Carter?" Annabel didn't know if she liked that. "What is it?"

"You'll see."

"You got them to put me on the cover of your latest book?" Annabel teased. Frances wrote historical romances, which Annabel only read because her best friend wrote them. It was a bone of contention between them. "It doesn't hurt to dream," Frances would say. But Annabel didn't agree. "I don't need dreams," she would reply. "I like my reality just fine."

"Whoops, gotta run," Frances said now. "I promised Jack I'd meet him for a quick bite before his game and Jason's still sleeping. Talk to you later." And she was gone.

Annabel stood with the receiver against her ear for another half a minute before she slowly set it down again. What would it be this time?

Something discreet, she hoped. The last person she wanted sharing in her birthday surprise was Carter MacKenzie.

She'd spent only a few hours in his company. They were more than enough. He was everything she'd told Frances he was, plus he had the charm of a toad.

How, she'd asked Frances more than once, could a man own and run a health-food store when he spent most of his waking hours eating junk food?

"He strives for balance in his life," Frances had told her, grinning.

Balance? Annabel doubted he knew the meaning of the word.

He certainly went to excess when it came to women. Every time Annabel had seen him, it had been in the company of a different one. All of them beautiful.

"I suppose he strives for variety, too," she'd groused.

"His time will come," Frances had said confidently during the summer. "He's ready for it to happen. I really thought it had with Diane."

Annabel had only met Diane Granatelli née Bauer once, at Thanksgiving a year ago. She didn't know her well, but what she did know, she liked. Diane was the one woman she'd seen Carter with who seemed to have a brain in her head.

She wasn't at all surprised when Diane married someone else. She told Frances so.

Frances had clucked her disapproval and said that Annabel didn't understand him. Annabel was willing to concede that. She had no desire to, either.

She finished stirring the cake and popped it into the oven, then sat down at the table and began to poke cloves into the first of a half a dozen oranges.

Every pomander she made now would buy one shingle when she resided her house next summer. That was a lot of pomanders, granted, but she had wreaths and dried flower arrangements and herbal teas to sell to make up the difference, and anyway, equating pomanders with shingles was an incentive. It made what seemed an impossible task possible. Annabel had learned long ago to take things one step at a time.

It would be an hour before Leif got home from school, and Libby wouldn't breeze in until six because of cheerleading practice. She could at least finish this one before things got too hectic.

The doorbell rang. She grimaced, then sighed and jabbed one last clove into the orange, then went to answer the door.

It was Carter, all right. But after that, all bets were off.

Certainly he wasn't standing there looking lean and clean and sexy with his usual cocky grin on his face. On the contrary, he was dirty, disheveled and grim.

"Is that your goat?"

Annabel blinked, then looked in the direction in which he'd jerked his head.

There in the lane beyond the grassy yard, tethered to the bumper of his car, was a reluctant, defiant, noticeably irritable goat. Not just any goat, either.

"Arnold!"

"Ah." Now she caught a glimpse of his smile, albeit the sardonic one. "You do know him." The smile twisted. "Somehow I thought you might."

"Where did you get him? Why do you have him tied onto your car? What have you done to him?" Annabel's voice rose as she pushed past him and hurried down the steps into the yard.

"What have *I* done to *him?*" Carter was following her, breathing down her neck. "That goat damned near killed me! First he blocked the lane, then he mowed me down, then he ran in front of the car and I practically squashed him. Then he followed me all the way to Frances's house. He got up on the porch and wouldn't let me in the damned door!"

Annabel would have liked to have seen that. She smothered a smile as she realized the reason behind Carter's dusty jeans and torn shirt, the smudge of dirt on his cheek and the glint of fire in his eyes.

"He thinks he's a guard goat."

Carter's eyes narrowed as if he thought she might be making fun of him. Annabel tried to look demure. She couldn't recall the last time she'd managed it—probably twenty-five years at least.

"Well, keep him tied up from now on," he said gruffly. "If I get him in my sights again, I won't think twice about flattening him."

At that Annabel did laugh. "You? The same man who wouldn't eat the turkey last Thanksgiving because he saw it beforehand still wearing feathers?"

Carter scowled. "I'm not planning on eating your damned goat."

"And a good thing, too," Annabel said fiercely. "Come on, Arnie." She reached for the rope and began untying it. "Let's get you settled."

She led him around the back of the house toward the small hillside pasture where he belonged, making a mental note to tell Leif to latch the gate—at least for the next two weeks.

Arnie was used to running free between her house and Frances's, and he didn't bother people he knew. But he was particular about strangers, and Annabel didn't want him being the excuse for Carter MacKenzie landing on her doorstep time and time again.

She shut the gate with a flourish and latched it carefully, then turned and gave Carter a smile. "There. Satisfied?"

He looked from her to the goat, then back again. It was pretty clear to Annabel that he didn't have a much higher opinion of her than of the goat. He grunted and turned back toward his car.

Annabel followed him, wanting to get her birthday present. "Frances says you're staying for a couple of weeks," she said politely, more because she knew Frances would expect it of her than because she wanted to make conversation.

"Just while they get the new roof." Carter sounded irritable and put-upon, and Annabel wondered again why he'd allowed Frances to talk him into coming in the first place. He headed straight for his car and opened the door, starting to get in.

"Wait!"

Carter turned. "Wait?"

Annabel's mouth opened and closed. She felt like an idiot. "A-aren't . . . aren't you . . . forgetting something?"

Where's my birthday present? she wanted to say, and felt like a veritable child for wanting to say it.

She wouldn't care about it if it weren't from Frances. Who got excited about receiving a dog-eared copy of *1001 Knock-Knock Jokes* or the fuzzy yellow sweater in the window at Beecham's that was, coincidentally, also just Libby's size?

But Frances never gave those sorts of gifts. Hers were special. Knowing. Aimed directly at the woman Annabel was. They came with full forethought and no strings attached.

"Forgetting?" Carter's brows were pulling together.

Annabel's fingers knotted into fists. "Frances said...er, you were . . . er, bringing my . . . birthday gift?"

Carter scowled. "She told you?" He sounded horrified.

Annabel drew herself up stiffly. "Well, I don't see that it's any skin off your nose," she said irritably. "She only asked you to bring it, didn't she?"

The look he gave her was wary. Finally he shrugged and took the two long strides that covered the distance between them.

"She said to give you this," he muttered and, taking her by the shoulders, he pulled her close and brought his mouth down over hers.

"YOU DID *WHAT*?" Jack Neillands stared at his wife in amazement.

Frances shrugged equably. "Told him to give her a kiss."

"Carter? Kiss Annabel?" Jack started to laugh.

"What's wrong with that?"

"Mother Earth and the Big Bad Wolf?"

Frances looked affronted. "A lot you know. They're perfect for each other."

Jack just looked at her, stupefied. "You're out of your mind."

"Marriage has gone to my head," Frances agreed, putting her arms around him. "I want everyone to be as happy as we are."

Jack kissed her. It was a long, lingering kiss, but when he looked up, he was shaking his head. "Yeah, sure. But Carter and Annabel? This isn't one of your books, you know."

"I know," Frances said serenely.

Jack cocked his head and looked at her. "Come on, Fran. What did you really give Annabel for her birthday?"

Frances smiled. "She'll know."

Chapter Two

She knew. She was aghast. No, that was too mild. She was fuming. Furious. Frantic.

She was punching out Frances's phone number almost before Carter had driven down the hill and turned off the lane onto the highway.

Frances wasn't home.

Annabel banged the phone down, made a tiny sound of suppressed rage and flung herself about the kitchen, practically caroming off the walls.

Damn Frances anyway! How dared she? And Carter! Heavens above, why, of all men, Carter?

A kiss was bad enough. She could still, even now, feel the hard, warm touch of his lips on hers! But it wasn't just the kiss, and Annabel knew it.

It had to do with Frances's last book, with a kiss her hero had given her heroine—the kiss that awakened her to love. And Annabel had rolled her eyes.

"Spare me," she'd said.

But Frances had simply laughed at her. "It happens."

"Sure." Annabel had scoffed. "Like it happened to you."

"Well, no. It took Jack a bit longer to convince me. But that doesn't mean it can't happen."

Annabel had shaken her head. "I'll believe it when I see it."

And now Frances had sent Carter to kiss her! To fall in love with her? And she with him?

And how did she think it was going to happen? Like magic?

Oh, damn Frances anyway.

The door banged. "Hi, Mom!" Leif tossed his backpack onto one of the chairs, sniffed the air, then beamed. "Cool. Birthday cake. What kind?"

"Hmm? Oh, spice." Annabel ran a hand through her hair, knocking out the pins distractedly.

"When can we have some? Can I have the bowl when you make the frosting? I got a B on my math test and Mrs. Street says I do too understand ratios, but I don't think so. How come Arnie was in the pasture? I let him out."

Used to this sort of after-school conversational barrage, Annabel let Leif's questions and comments flow over her in a wave, none of them penetrating except the last.

"You what?" she yelped. "You let him out? Oh, hell." She went flying toward the door, leaving Leif staring after her.

"What's wrong?"

"MacKenzie," Annabel threw over her shoulder. That was what was wrong. In spades.

Damn it, where was that goat? Her eyes darted back and forth, taking in the empty pasture, the small barn and shed, the ominously silent garden. Where on earth had he gone?

Where did he always go? she asked herself with resignation.

Her shoulders slumped. Arnie, like all males, was a victim of his hormones. Where else would he go but where he could find a bit of female goat companionship? To Frances's. She shut her eyes.

"What's goin' on, Mom?" Leif wanted to know. He was practically running to keep up with her.

"That miserable Carter MacKenzie is staying at Frances's until the roof is on," she told him, even as she headed out through the woods toward Frances's place. "He had a run-in with Arnold earlier today." And if he had another one, he'd be back.

"Carter? Here? Really?" Leif was clearly delighted. There was nothing miserable about Carter as far as he was concerned.

Annabel shot him a baleful, over-the-shoulder glance. "He said he'd flatten Arnold if he got in his way again."

"Naw, he wouldn't do that," Leif said with the same assurance she'd felt. "Carter's a good guy."

Annabel's lip curled into a snarl. "Fine," she said. "If you think so, you go get him back."

"Sure." Leif gave an equable shrug and headed off toward the trail that led over the hill to Frances's house. "No problem."

Annabel watched him go, shaking her head. No problem? That's what he thought.

What on earth had Frances told Carter besides that he should give her a kiss?

Had she confided in him? Surely not.

Carter would no more allow himself to be a target of Frances's misguided matchmaking—especially with Annabel Archer—than she would.

And there was no doubt in Annabel's mind that matchmaking was what Frances intended.

And Annabel, in her naiveté, had actually asked for it!

"Where's my birthday present?" she'd asked him. She wanted to sink through the floor at the very thought. She was glad Leif was home to go get Arnold. The last thing she wanted today was another encounter with Carter MacKenzie. Though she didn't see how another could possibly be worse than the last one!

She watched Leif disappear over the top of the hill, then turned and went back into the house. Leaning against the door, she pressed her fist against her lips, trying to forget the feel of Carter's lips.

This was her haven, the two-story log house with wide plank floors and tiny-paned windows that she and Mark had found all those years ago—the abandoned building, which she had made into a home with hand-hooked rugs and homemade pottery and loads and loads of love.

It had seen her work and seen her play, seen her laugh and seen her cry. But always she had loved it, always she had felt warm and safe here, protected against the vicissitudes of a capricious world.

Now, with the tingle of Carter's lips still vivid in her mind, suddenly it didn't feel quite so safe at all.

THE GOAT WAS BACK.

Carter, about to go outside again and get into the car to head into Boone's Corner for groceries, took one look and stopped dead in the doorway.

There was no way he was going out to tangle with that cloven-footed ruffian again today. When he'd taken it back to Annabel, he'd glossed over his experiences with it.

He hadn't mentioned the way it had flattened him twice, the way it had followed him up on the porch, nosing its way in while he was unloading the car, how he'd gone upstairs and come back down to find it in the kitchen, how he'd had the devil's own time getting it out.

He'd never told her it had stood on the porch and butted its head against the front door so hard he'd finally had to come out and chase it through the woods to capture it. And he certainly hadn't mentioned the way it had nailed him in the rear end the minute he turned his back on it even after he'd tied it to the bumper of his car.

He wasn't about to admit any of that—especially to Annabel Archer.

It was bad enough he'd had to kiss her.

Ordinarily Carter liked kissing women. In his top ten favorite things to do, it was right up there in the top two. But not, for heaven's sake, Annabel Archer!

She'd made him feel like some gawky schoolboy who, on a dare, had allowed himself to be talked into stealing a kiss from the disapproving spinster teacher.

He rubbed a hand across his mouth, wishing he could forget the touch of his lips on hers. Her mouth had been surprisingly soft. Her lips had been slightly parted, from surprise, not encouragement, but still he'd felt a split second's temptation to slip his tongue between them.

And get it bit off, no doubt.

He was lucky to have escaped with his life. What on earth could Frances have been thinking of? Of all the women she could have asked him to kiss...!

And what in the hell sort of birthday present was that? Or was it just a joke? Probably her real gift was in the mail.

It must be living with Jack that was making Frances so feisty, he thought grimly. She had to know that he and Annabel Archer were like fire and ice. The less they had to do with each other, the better.

But Annabel was not his immediate problem. He raked a hand through his hair and contemplated the goat. Arnold.

Who in their right mind would name a goat Arnold? Mephistopheles, more like. Or Satan.

Perhaps Annabel Archer was a witch and Arnold was her familiar.

Never a violent man, Carter found himself wishing for a shotgun now. How the hell was he going to get out to his car and get groceries with that damned goat patrolling the place?

"Arrrr-neeee!"

Carter's head jerked up, his eyes flicking away from the goat toward the wooded hillside. He spied a small figure wearing jeans and a lumberjack shirt trotting down the trail.

"Arrrr-neeee!"

He grinned. A savior. And by the grace of God, not Annabel, either.

He waved at the boy loping down the trail toward him. "He's here, Leif," he shouted from the doorway. "I've got him."

A small exaggeration and perfectly excusable under the circumstances, Carter decided. He gave another wave and walked out onto the porch.

Arnold lifted his head and met Carter's gaze straight on.

"Arnie!" Leif admonished, skidding to a stop next to the goat.

"Watch out," Carter warned.

"Don't worry," Leif said, looping a lead around the goat's neck and giving him a hug. "It's all right. Arnie wouldn't hurt a flea."

Carter opened his mouth, but no sound came out. Arnie? Harmless? Impossible.

But wasn't that Arnold, right this very minute, nuzzling Leif's cheek, rubbing his head against Leif's hair?

Carter tucked his hands into the back pockets of his jeans, wincing against the bruises his palms touched. Arnold nibbled playfully at Leif's ear. Leif rubbed noses with him, then looked over at Carter and flashed him a grin.

"Ma said you were gonna flatten him if you found him loose again. But you didn't. I knew you wouldn't. You wouldn't ever do that, would you, Carter?"

Carter's fingers, still in his pockets, crossed. "Er, no. Of course not." It wasn't precisely a lie. He probably couldn't flatten Arnold if he tried. He didn't say he wouldn't try.

Leif beamed. "I didn't think so. Ma exaggerates," he confided and gave Arnold another hug.

"Mmm."

"But if you really don't want him around, I guess we can put him in the pasture." Leif looked at Carter hopefully.

Carter, uncurling his fingers and easing them out of his pockets, winced again. "I kind of think you ought to," he ventured. "I'm not used to goats being on the road, you see. I might...accidentally...run over him. Or something."

Leif looked suddenly worried. "I guess we should, then, huh? Till you're gone, I mean."

Carter's smile was one of profound relief. "I'd appreciate it. I'd hate to be the one to do old Arnold in."

"You wouldn't," Leif said confidently. "How long you gonna be here?"

"Till the roof is on. A couple of weeks, I guess."

"Swell. You wanta come to the spaghetti supper at school next Friday?"

"I—"

"It's a good cause. We're supporting the swim team. Me an' Libby aren't on it, but Mom says if you live in a small community, you gotta do these things. Besides, it's sorta fun."

"Well, I—"

"Tickets are only four dollars. How many times can you get a good meal with seconds for only four dollars?"

Carter gave Leif a sidelong look. He looked for all the world like Oliver Twist hopefully holding out an empty gruel bowl. "You aren't by chance getting a cut from each ticket you sell, are you?"

"Me?" Leif looked momentarily guilty, then grinned unrepentantly. "No. Not unless you count that whoever sells the most gets two tickets to the last Red Sox game of the season."

"Ah. In that case, I don't see how I can refuse."

"Me, neither," Leif said cheerfully. He fished in his pocket and came up with a slightly crumpled sheaf of tickets. He peeled off one. "I don't suppose you'd like to take a date?"

"Who? Arnold?"

Leif shrugged. "I dunno. Ma, maybe?"

Carter's stomach gave a lurch. "I don't think—"

"Naw. You can't take her," Leif said. "She's already got a ticket. Besides, she's going with Aaron."

Carter frowned. "Who's Aaron?"

"He's a friend. He's the county ag agent."

"Ag?"

"Agricultural." Leif enunciated the word carefully, as if Carter might never have heard it before. "Jack calls him the sheep-shit expert."

Carter grinned. Now he remembered where he'd heard the name before. Aaron had once, in Jack's estimation, been a contender for Frances's affections. Clearly, even having won, Jack wasn't being a gracious winner.

Carter was prepared to be, especially if it meant he didn't have to squire Annabel Archer to a spaghetti supper. He took out his wallet to pay Leif the four dollars, but that meant getting within butting distance of Arnold. Halfway down the steps he stopped.

"It's okay," Leif said. "I won't let him hurt you."

"I thought you said he wouldn't hurt a flea," Carter reminded him darkly.

"He wouldn't. But he has opinions, y'know." Leif tugged hard on the rope, pulling a reluctant Arnold back as Carter came forward warily. "An' sometimes he doesn't have good ones."

"Neither do I," Carter said sourly. He held out the money, took the ticket and backed away.

"Thanks. Don't go. Let Arnie get to know you."

Carter gave Leif a skeptical look.

The boy shrugged disingenuously. "How's he gonna learn to like you if you run every time you get close to him?"

"I wasn't running," Carter said somewhat stiffly.

"I know that," Leif said quickly. "But don'tcha want to make friends with him?"

Making friends with a goat was not high on Carter's list of priorities, but if it would allow him free passage to and from his car, there was perhaps something to be said for it. He took a cautious step forward.

Arnold lunged.

"Hey!" Leif, goggle-eyed, hauled back on the rope with all his strength. "Cool it, Arnie. Hey, old fella. Be nice."

Nice? Carter felt a sardonic laugh coming on. "Maybe we should forget it."

But Leif shook his head. "Naw. I got him now. Stick out your hand and let him get to know you."

With about as much enthusiasm as he had mustered when he'd had to kiss Annabel, Carter held out his hand.

Arnold stared at him suspiciously.

"You oughta give him a treat. You got anything to eat on you?"

Carter shook his head.

"In the house?"

"I was just going to go for groceries when you came."

Leif lifted his shoulders. "Ah, well, maybe he'll like your shirt cuff or something."

Carter hoped not. He wouldn't have been surprised, though. Arnold was still watching him warily. The feeling, Carter could have told him, was mutual.

"Go on," Leif urged the goat. "Give him a nibble, Arnie."

Carter's teeth came together gently but firmly. He held his breath. Shut his eyes. Waited.

All at once there was a cold, wet slurp, a tiny nip. His eyes flew open.

"See! I told you! He likes you! I knew he'd like you!" Leif hugged Arnold. "Do it again!"

Carter wiped his hand on the seat of his jeans. "Let's don't overdo it, huh? Give him time."

Leif sighed. "Yeah. I guess you're right." He gave the goat another enthusiastic hug. "Good boy, Arnie," he praised.

"Good boy," Carter echoed faintly, then began to move toward his car. "See you later. I've got to get some groceries now."

"You can eat with us."

"No!"

Leif's eyes widened at the force of Carter's tone.

"I mean, no, I wouldn't want to put you to any trouble."

"It's no trouble," Leif said magnanimously.

"You aren't cooking the dinner. Are you?"

"No, Ma is. But she's always inviting people. The more the merrier, she always says."

"I don't think she means me. Your mother and I . . ." How, Carter wondered, could he explain the more or less instant antipathy he and Annabel Archer had obviously felt?

"It's her birthday. She made a cake, and . . ."

"*She* made a cake? She made her own birthday cake?" Even for Annabel Archer that seemed somehow unfair.

Leif shrugged. "She makes better cakes than Libby 'n' me. I made her a paper-towel holder in shop class. Solid walnut."

"A paper-towel holder?"

"It was that or a three-legged stool."

"You made the better choice."

"I thought so. Anyway, she'd want you to come. If I tell her I invited you and you refused, her feelings will be hurt. And if you're worried, 'cause there might not be enough, don't. There's plenty. Ma's cooking Chinese. Chicken Almond Yuck or something. Come on, Carter. What do you say?"

He wasn't going to get away with saying no; he knew that much. He also knew Annabel wasn't going to be any more thrilled than he was that he was coming to her birthday dinner. He sighed.

"I'll even put Arnold in the pasture till you go back home."

A corner of Carter's mouth quirked. "Is that your final offer?"

Leif considered for a moment. "You can have my fortune cookie. We eat at six. Libby's home from practice by then. You'll come."

It wasn't a question. They both knew he would.

"*DINNER?* You invited him to *dinner?*"

"Don't yell, Ma. I only did what you're always do-ing—taking pity on the poor and homeless...."

"Carter MacKenzie is neither poor, nor homeless. Far from it!" Annabel was still yelling, even though she was making a distinct effort not to.

It was true, what Leif was saying: she did drag home strays for dinner; she did exhort her children to care for the less fortunate; she did stress neighborliness and helpful-ness as admirable virtues.

But Carter MacKenzie? Coming to dinner? On her *birthday?*

"Very funny, Frances," she muttered, turning away. What sort of direct line to God did Frances have that she could pull such strings? Annabel gritted her teeth.

"What?" Leif asked. Cherubic, solemn eyes followed her.

"Nothing." Annabel opened the silverware drawer with a crash. "You'd better add another place setting then," she said with bad grace.

"Okay." Leif gathered up chopsticks and a plate, then frowned at the table already set for three. "What about Ernie and Bert and Eb? Aren't they coming?"

Ernie and Bert were really Sisters Ernestine and Bertha, the remnant congregation of a once-thriving convent whose nonretired members had gone off to save souls in more populous areas. Bert and Ernie had, with a little help from Jack and the Holy Spirit, turned the convent into one of the most sought after bed-and-breakfast establish-ments in all Vermont.

It was a rare birthday that they didn't help celebrate. And the same was true of Ebenezer Toot, owner of Boone's Corner's general store.

"Bert and Ernie have a houseful of stressed-out businessmen. And Eb had a root canal this morning. He says he may never eat again." Annabel was feeling much the same way, and it had nothing at all to do with root canals.

Leif dug his toe into the braid of the rug. "I s'pose I could go back an' tell him not to come."

Oh, right, Annabel thought, *and have him think I'm an even bigger witch than he already does.* She sighed and raked her fingers through her hair. "No. That's all right. I was just...unprepared, that's all."

"How come you don't like Carter?"

"It isn't that I don't like him," Annabel began, then remembered that besides exhorting them to feed the less fortunate and doing so herself, she also exhorted them not to lie. "Well, you're right, I don't like him," she admitted. "He...makes me uncomfortable."

Leif cocked his head. "Why?"

How to explain that without going into things she had no intention of going into tonight or any other time? "He's...unpredictable."

From the very first moment she'd seen him, she'd been wrong about him. It was exactly what she'd told Frances—she didn't understand Carter MacKenzie, could never get a handle on how he would behave.

Most men were an open book to her. There were the strong, silent types. The tough, macho types, the bookish, earnest types, the devil-may-care types. There were even, few and far between, the to-die-for romantic-hero types like Jack.

And there was Carter MacKenzie.

She'd never met a man she couldn't pigeonhole. Until him. Cocky. Calm. Quiet. Quick. Cool. Charming. He had more applicable adjectives than the minister's cat, and all of them contradictory.

And sometimes he looked at her as if . . .

No. She shook her head firmly. He couldn't remember.

She barely remembered herself. It was years ago. Aeons. Another lifetime. They had been other people then. At least, *she* had been.

About Carter she wasn't sure.

Deliberately Annabel sighed. "Never mind. Everything will be fine," she said when Leif still looked worried. "I'm just fussing. Mothers do."

"Not you," Leif said.

"Perhaps I'll start."

"No." Leif shook his head.

"Thanks for the vote of confidence."

Leif wrinkled his nose. "What's that?"

She smiled and ruffled his hair. "Your faith in me. Come on." She opened the refrigerator. "If we're going to have company, I'm going to need some help. You can slice the mushrooms."

IT'S ONLY DINNER, Annabel thought as six o'clock arrived and with it, Carter. How difficult could it be?

She'd forgotten about Murphy's Law. And Libby.

If anything that could go wrong, would, in the normal course of events, how much more likely was it to do so if one took an already trying situation and introduced into it one's seventeen-year-old daughter?

Not precisely, Annabel realized almost the moment Libby walked in the door to find Carter leaning against the kitchen counter, a rhetorical question.

If she'd thought the fifteen minutes she'd spent making small talk with Carter before Libby's arrival had been fraught with tension, it was nothing compared to the increase she felt when the door banged open and Libby appeared on the threshold.

"Carter?" It was very nearly a squeal. Libby's normally flushed cheeks took on an even rosier glow and she flew straight across the room, shedding books and jacket as she went, to fling her arms around him.

Carter, to give him credit, didn't fling his arms around her. But he didn't look displeased at the attention, either. He was grinning as he caught Libby by her upper arms and held her out to look her up and down.

"My God, a woman! You've become a woman." His grin grew even wider. "And what a woman, too." There was just the right amount of male appreciation in his tone to make Libby glow.

Annabel's teeth came together with a snap.

"Wash your hands, Liberty," she said and returned her daughter's steely glare with one of her own. "You're late."

Libby shrugged unapologetically. "Old Puterbaugh kept us late. If I'd known Carter was going to be here, I'd have skipped practice and come straight home."

She linked her arm in his and looked up to give him an adoring smile and bat mascara-encrusted lashes at him.

"I thought you wouldn't miss a cheerleading practice for God or the orthodontist," Annabel said dryly, recalling a conversation she and Libby had had less than a week before.

Libby gave an airy wave. "Oh, well, you know...for Carter..."

Annabel rolled her eyes. "Come on," she said before things deteriorated further. "Let's eat."

At least, she told herself, she didn't have to worry about keeping the conversational ball rolling. Libby and Leif took care of that, regaling Carter with tales from school, anecdotes about their friends, their follies, their fun. And Carter seemed as willing as she was to sit back and let the kids take the lead.

Did he know what Frances was plotting? she wondered. He couldn't, Annabel was certain. If he had, she doubted whether he would be within ten miles of here.

Poor thing, Annabel thought, then promptly squelched the thought. She wouldn't waste any sympathy on Carter MacKenzie.

She slanted him a wary glance but, perversely, she found that he seemed to be on his best behavior and, in fact, was as wary of her as she was of him.

He focused entirely on the children, barely sparing her a glance throughout the meal.

Why should he? Annabel thought. Watching Libby make a fool of herself would be enough distraction for anyone.

Her daughter had become no less giddy with the serving of the meal. She was clearly enchanted to find Carter there, and obviously eager to throw herself at him.

"Two weeks? You're going to be here two weeks? Super!" Libby clapped her hands. "You can come watch me cheer."

Carter looked less than enthusiastic.

"Libby, I don't think..." Annabel began dampeningly.

But it did no good, for Libby just shot her a disdainful glance. "I don't expect you to come, Mother. I know how you feel. But not everyone hates football."

"I don't hate—"

"Mother *hates* football," Libby confided to Carter, who raised his brows, turned his head and gave Annabel an assessing look.

Annabel met his gaze defiantly, daring him to say something snide. He didn't say a word.

"She thinks it's a secular manifestation of the aims of the military-industrial complex." Libby recited the words as if they were a direct quote. Annabel's fingers tightened on the chopsticks.

"She thinks I should stick myself out here in the weed patch all day, pottering about with sprouts and things, cultivating my own garden." Another apparent quote. Libby sighed and rolled her eyes. "I might as well be dead."

She might soon be, Annabel thought, her fingers itching to wring Libby's slender neck.

It wasn't that what Libby said was so far from the truth. Annabel was not wild about football. She might, once, have even, in a rash moment, equated it with military strategy. It didn't mean she would prefer her views to be expressed in quite those same terms to the man on the street. Or to Carter MacKenzie, damn it.

What Carter thought of her daughter's pronouncements she had no idea. He simply murmured politely at intervals and kept his head bent over his plate. Only occasionally did she catch him glancing her way. Hastily she averted her own gaze.

"Time for fortune cookies," Leif said at last. He passed them out, handing two to Carter. "You get mine."

Carter handed it back. "One fortune's enough for any man."

Libby was already biting into hers. She pulled out the paper and gave a little squeal. "Look what it says! I'm going to get my heart's desire."

"You're gonna marry Tom Cruise?" Leif asked.

She shot him a withering look and turned to Carter. "What does yours say?"

Carter unfolded his. "Same thing."

Leif came and peered over his shoulder, then ripped into his own. "So does mine."

So did Annabel's. She didn't think it was very likely to happen, however, especially since today hadn't been anywhere close to her heart's desire. "I think we just happened on to a very optimistic fortune-cookie company," she said.

Libby looked crestfallen. Leif said, "We got rooked." Carter looked as if he felt about the day much the same way she did.

Annabel prayed it would end quickly.

Libby rattled on even after the meal had ended, but Annabel wasn't even listening now. She stood at the sink, rinsing off the dishes, breathing a sigh of relief.

It was over. Any minute now he'd leave. She looked hopefully toward the door.

"Time for presents and cake," said Leif.

"Presents? Cake?"

He stared at her aghast. "You forgot it was your birthday?"

"When you get to be her age..." Libby said airily.

Annabel made a strangled sound, coloring furiously at the first glint of Carter's amused grin. "Right. Get the dessert plates, Liberty," she said tightly.

Libby did. She also made a production of decking out Annabel's cake with thirty-six candles.

Leif shut off the light and led them in singing "Happy Birthday."

It was an occasion that frequently made Annabel squirm. She had never really enjoyed being the cynosure of everyone's attention, even when everyone was composed of no one other than her children.

But tonight, when the singing also held the sound of Carter's surprisingly true baritone, she felt even more like ducking beneath the tablecloth.

Still, she apparently hadn't been immune to all those years of proper etiquette that her mother had despaired of having had any effect on her. She managed a creditable smile and a slightly raspy "thank you" at the end.

She even managed to blow out the candles in one determined breath, wishing, as she did so, that Frances would get what was coming to her.

"What'd you wish, Ma?" Leif demanded.

Annabel shook her head. "Never mind. It won't come true if I tell you."

"I know what I'd wish," Libby said, batting her lashes and giving Carter a come-on smile that made Annabel's teeth ache.

"Cut the cake, Libby," she said and slapped the knife handle into her daughter's hand.

Libby cut the cake. Leif scooped ice cream onto the top of each piece. Annabel handed a piece to Carter without even looking at him. She had always sensed a certain ironic amusement in his eyes whenever he had seen her and her children in the past. She could just imagine what he must think of them after this evening.

The cake would have been good if she'd been able to taste it. As it was, she choked it down, keeping her eyes on her plate the entire time.

"Time for presents," Leif said the moment they were done with the cake.

Annabel would have protested, but he was already on his way to the closet by the front door. She simply waited, willing herself not to make a fool of herself, when he came back with the small stack of gaily wrapped packages.

"Open this one first," Leif said, thrusting a big rectangular box at her.

Obediently Annabel did and exclaimed with enthusiasm over the dark-stained walnut paper-towel holder she found inside. "It's wonderful," she said, smiling at her son. "Just what I needed."

"I know. Libby made a dumb bookshelf. An' she kept it," he added loftily. "But I knew you'd like this."

"I do." Annabel leaned over quickly and kissed him, and Leif, blushing, ducked his head and shot a quick glance at Carter, then shrugged and kissed her.

Libby rolled her eyes. But seconds later she proffered the next box on the pile. Annabel took it. It wasn't nearly as heavy as Leif's box and when she shook it gently, she heard only a soft rustling sound.

"You know what it is, don't you?" Libby demanded, her eyes alight with excitement.

Annabel shook her head and began to unstick the tape and ease off the paper.

"Rip it, Ma," Leif urged.

But Annabel wouldn't. She took her time removing the paper, then folded it and set it aside before slipping the lid from the box. Inside was a pair of wildly flowered jeans remarkably like the ones that Libby's best friend, Alice, had been wearing recently—the ones Libby had practically swooned over.

"Heavens." Annabel cleared her throat.

"Aren't they great?" Libby's eyes sparkled. "Don'tcha just love them?"

"They're . . . really something." Annabel took them out and, smiling brightly, held them up against her. "They might," she ventured, "be a tad on the small side."

Libby's face fell. "Do you think so? It was the only size they had left. But if you can't wear an eight . . ."

Annabel couldn't ever remember wearing an eight. "I'm sure they'll be fine," she told her daughter. "And if they shrink—" she shrugged "—perhaps you can still wear them even if I can't."

"Do you think so?" Libby's eyes shone. She gave her mother a hug. "Thanks, Mom. But I will take 'em back if you want."

And Annabel, hugging her back, shook her head. "No, Lib. They're fine. Just fine. I love them."

And when Carter gave what for all the world sounded like a muffled snort, she looked over Libby's shoulder and glared at him.

"Come on," Leif said now. "You got one more." He shoved another good-size, lightweight box into her hands.

She frowned at it. "I told Ernie and Bert not to get me anything this year."

"It isn't from Ernie and Bert, Ma," Leif told her. "It's from Carter."

Annabel's head came up with a snap. Her stare collided with Carter's.

"*Carter* brought you a present?" Libby sounded as amazed as Annabel felt. Her gaze traveled from her mother to Carter and back again. She frowned, too.

Annabel shook the box gently, as if too energetic a motion might set it off. She heard only a soft rustling sound. Crumpled newspaper, probably. Wrapped around a bag of herbal tea leaves, no doubt. That was the best construction she could put on it. What if he'd gift wrapped a random selection of Arnold's goat droppings? She wouldn't have put it past him.

"So open it," Leif demanded, clearly not smitten with any similar fears.

Annabel sighed. Bending her head, focusing strictly on the box, she began to peel the paper away. Her fingers weren't nearly as adept as when she'd unwrapped Libby's. She tore the paper almost at once, then, fumbling, nearly dropped the box. At last the paper was disposed of and she sat with the box on her lap. Carefully, unsure what to expect, she lifted the lid.

It was a shawl. A shawl in vibrant blues and greens, knitted of the finest angora. Her fingers curled into its softness, kneading it, then lifting it to rub against her cheek. She was speechless at the unexpectedness of the gift.

For all her practicality, Annabel could still appreciate beauty, and when the two were united, she couldn't resist.

"Oh, wow!" Libby exclaimed.

"Cool," said Leif. "Try it on."

Self-conscious, Annabel stood and unfurled the shawl, then settled it around her shoulders and struck a dramatic pose, her cheeks burning. "There. What do you think?" She looked at her children, not at Carter.

"Fantastic," Libby said.

"Great," agreed Leif.

In the silence that followed, Annabel had to look at Carter. He was still sitting in the wing chair, his loafer-clad feet crossed at the ankles, his long legs stretched out, his fingers laced across his flat belly. He was leaning back, looking up at her from beneath hooded lids. Annabel, meeting his gaze, felt as if she were wearing less clothes, not more.

"Well?" she demanded irritably.

A corner of his mouth lifted at last. "Yes," he said.

It wasn't a query, it was a pronouncement. It was approval. The smile reached the other corner of his mouth. He hauled himself to his feet and took the three long steps he needed to stand in front of her.

"Happy birthday, Annabel Archer." He bent his head and kissed her on the lips and this time, for an instant, his tongue did touch hers.

Then he was striding toward the door. It opened and he was gone.

"ANNABEL CALLED while you were gone," Jack said to his wife.

Frances's brows lifted. "Oh?"

"She said, thank you."

Frances looked at him suspiciously. "She said, *thank you?* And that's all?" In her wildest dreams Frances had never thought it would be that easy.

"No." Jack spooned a mouthful of mashed bananas into his waiting son's mouth. "She said the shawl was beautiful."

"What shawl?"

"That's what I said. And she said, the shawl we gave her."

"But we didn't give her a shawl."

"I told her that."

"And what did she say?"

"Nothing. She stammered around a bit, then hung up."

"Did she mention Carter?"

"Not once."

"Curious," Frances said. "Curiouser and curiouser."

IT DIDN'T MAKE SENSE. It only made sense if Jack and Frances had given her the shawl, had sent it with Carter to be delivered at dinner . . . if the kiss given earlier had been given only to tease, to annoy, to throw her off. It was a beautiful shawl. She'd loved it on sight, had known it was "her," exactly the way Frances, seeing it, would have known it was her and bought it for her birthday.

But she hadn't.

Carter had.

Presumably.

Which meant what?

Lying awake, restless and remembering as she stared up at the shadows that splashed across the ceiling of her moonlit bedroom, Annabel wished she knew.

Chapter Three

It didn't make sense.

Kissing Annabel Archer *once* because Frances had asked him to, well, all right. Carter had always helped out his friends. A guy did what a guy had to do.

But *twice?*

Carter thought he needed his head examined.

He was clearly in far worse shape than he'd thought.

He lay back against the pillows, his arms folded under his head, and stared at the ceiling, remembering his folly, remembering the warm, sweet taste of Annabel Archer's mouth.

It had nothing to do with Annabel Archer per se, of course. It was just that he'd been far too long without a woman. He could have felt that sharp, insistent hunger with any woman. He *would* have, he was certain.

And, he thought savagely, with any other woman, chances were he could have satisfied that hunger by now.

Instead of which he was lying here alone, supremely *dis*satisfied, with only the sound of a barn owl and the occasional bleat of a sheep in the pasture beyond the window to keep him company.

"Thanks, Milly," he muttered. "Thanks a whole hell of a lot."

He rolled over and punched his pillow, tried to sleep. But his eyes refused to close. In the moonlight he could see the photos on the dresser. Three of them.

One was an unposed blowup of Jack and Frances at their wedding, with Jack looking as if he couldn't believe his good fortune and Frances positively glowing with her love for him. The second was of Jason at six months, already in possession of the cocky grin and masculine charm that would doubtless make him a lady-killer in his prime. Carter's mouth twisted in rueful acknowledgement of his godson's inherent talent.

If anyone had told him a year ago that he would be absolutely nuts about a nine-month-old baby, Carter would have laughed in his face. But it was true.

Granted, he'd spent plenty of time doing what he'd told Milly he'd done—chasing women. But he'd spent a damn sight more time playing with Jason, going for walks with Jason, giving piggyback rides to Jason. And when he was with Jason, he wasn't even thinking about finding a woman to replace Diane in his life. He was far too consumed with the moment.

He'd never thought he'd be a good father. Heaven knew he'd had a bad enough example from his own. C.W. had had lots of expectations for his son, but very little time. The only way to get his attention had been to annoy him. Carter had perfected the art. He couldn't see that it had done him a damned bit of good.

In the first few years of his own meager attempt at entrepreneurship in New York, Carter sometimes fantasized that his father would walk into Jack Sprat's Health and Wellness Store, look around and smile. He dreamed that C.W. would nod his head and say, "Yes. This is sane. This is manageable. It's not a conglomerate, but I like it. You could teach me a thing or two, son."

He never had. Then Carter had allowed himself one or two brief fantasies in which he and C.W. ironed out their differences at the end. A sort of sappy deathbed reconciliation scene that would prove to him once and for all that, in spite of everything, his father had loved him.

He hadn't got that, either.

He didn't know what he did have, except a lot of misbegotten dreams and fantasies, a thriving health-food store that he cared about more than he wanted to admit and a few good friends whose lives were changing and deepening and who seemed to be rapidly leaving him behind.

He wanted a child. A wife. He wanted commitments. Responsibilities.

Things that had terrified him less than a year ago were now at the top of his list of priorities.

And, God help him, today he had kissed Annabel Archer. Twice.

He punched his pillow again, rolled over again. Sighed. Rolled back over and contemplated the third picture.

It was another enlarged snapshot, taken on the afternoon of Jason's baptism. They were standing just inside the church, Jack and Frances hovering behind, looking nervously at the couple staring down at the infant they held between them. He and Annabel Archer.

At the time it had been all he could do to bring himself to stand next to Annabel Archer, to smile politely at her, to slip away at the earliest opportunity before she could fix him with her basilisk stare or impale him with a cutting remark, before he succumbed to the urge to knife her with a remark or two of his own.

He didn't know what it was about Annabel that brought out the worst in him. He didn't know what it was about Annabel that brought out anything in him!

The need to give her something for her birthday, for example. He certainly hadn't intended to.

But while he was in town getting the groceries, he'd seen the shawl. He'd been thinking about Leif's paper-towel holder, about her baking her own cake, and he'd found himself wondering, for the first time, what life must be like for Annabel.

She'd always seemed as tough as old boots to him. He'd told Frances he was afraid to give her a kiss.

"Afraid?" Frances had scoffed. "Of a softy like Annabel? Oh, good grief."

But Carter had never considered her a softy, and he'd said so.

"She's had to be tough because she's had a tough time," Frances had told him. "But that isn't the real Annabel. Inside she's a marshmallow."

Perhaps it had been to test that marshmallow theory that he'd found himself buying the shawl, wrapping it himself, trying to guess what her reaction would be. He'd imagined scorn, disdain, a perfunctory "How nice" before she set it aside.

He'd never dreamed she'd curl her fingers into the wool and rub it against her cheek, never imagined her color would heighten so much that her freckles would fade into the general rosiness and that her wide hazel eyes would actually sparkle.

It had been a hell of a shock.

Such a shock that he had kissed her. Again.

"I KNOW WHAT you're up to," Annabel said to Frances the next morning.

"*Moi?* Up to?"

"And it won't work," Annabel went right on determinedly. She had scarcely slept all night, but she wasn't admitting it to Frances.

"Don't get so testy," Frances said. "It doesn't become you."

"And Carter MacKenzie does?" Annabel retorted.

"I think he might."

Annabel felt as if steam were coming out of her ears. "Didn't you ever listen to anything I said? I don't want a man in my life. I don't need a man in my life."

"That's what *I* said," Frances reminded her. "You told me I ought to reconsider."

"Well, you should have, and I'm glad you did. Jack is right for you."

"Yes. And if you give Carter a chance, I think you may find that he's right for you."

Annabel made an inarticulate muttering sound. "I told you yesterday, I think he's as shallow as a plate. And he doesn't have any better an opinion of me."

"Carter needs a woman—"

"Fine. I'll find him a woman, just so long as I don't have to be it."

"The *right* woman," Frances said patiently.

"Don't worry. I can do it."

"Oh, Annabel." Frances sounded sad.

"Leave it to me," Annabel said and rang off before Frances could come up with anything else.

The best defense, Annabel knew—and not from watching Monday Night Football—was a good offense.

And that meant finding Carter a woman. Not precisely an easy task in a town the size of Boone's Corner, Vermont. And even if she expanded her sights to include Gaithersburg to the north and Pock's Hollow to the south, she didn't have a much bigger selection. But it was cer-

tainly preferable to waiting and seeing what other tricks
Frances had up her sleeve.

She sat down at the table and began to make a list.

In three hours she managed to come up with four names:
Patty Willits, Tracey Forrester, Beth Hayes and Marilee
Newman.

And even that was stretching it a bit. Patty was the vet's
assistant. She tended to check the teeth of anything
breathing, which Carter might or might not find entertaining. She was also rather young. Barely twenty-two.
And still a bit spotty, come to that. Carter, used to women
as lovely as Diane Granatelli, wouldn't hesitate to turn up
his nose.

Annabel crossed Patty off the list.

Tracey Forrester was even younger, also chubbier,
though less spotty. She worked at the grocery in Gaithersburg, where she chewed bubble gum and talked a mile a
minute, both at the same time. When she wasn't talking,
she still managed a sunny smile to greet every winter
snowstorm and every station wagon full of summer tour-
ists.

If Annabel smiled that much, she was sure her jaws
would ache.

She tried to imagine Carter with Tracey.

She crossed Tracey off the list.

Beth Hayes wasn't a Tracey Forrester. She taught geometry at Libby's school. She was single and spare and as
socially square as the angles she taught. As far as Annabel knew, she'd never been married or had a date. Even
Aaron Leggett hadn't shown the slightest interest.

If Aaron didn't, how could she expect Carter to?

Another pencil slash.

Marilee Newman. Tall. Even taller than Annabel. With
long, bleached-blond tresses that reached almost to her

waist and a tan that would make Miss California seem pale. Marilee was an associate at Winterwood and Walden, Attorneys at Law, Gaithersburg's only legal firm.

Annabel didn't know if she'd been married or not. She frankly couldn't imagine "not" being a possibility given Marilee's attractiveness to the opposite sex, but she didn't know Marilee well enough to have found out.

Marilee had moved to the area only a year before, and since she had no kids Annabel's kids' ages, nor any inclination to move beyond the circle of friends she met at Toastmasters and the AAUW, she and Annabel had rarely met.

Annabel had no idea if she would appeal to Carter or not. Physically, Annabel thought, she stood a good chance. Beyond that, who knew?

And how was Annabel supposed to effect an introduction, anyway? She somehow couldn't imagine Carter taking her meddling well. She began to regret ever telling Frances she'd find him a woman.

Let him find his own woman, Annabel thought irritably.

Or perhaps Frances wasn't infallible, after all. Maybe he wasn't even interested in finding one. And if he was, so what? She didn't care. As long as he wasn't interested in her, he could have any woman he liked.

CARTER SPENT THE DAY by himself.

There was, he was pleased to note, no Arnold to contend with—which meant that there was no Annabel, either. He was even more pleased about that since he still hadn't figured out how to deal with her.

There was also no sign of Bentons. He was less happy about that. A phone call netted him an answering-machine message that said to call back after five or to leave his number and someone would return his call. He did the latter, and he would have done the former, but shortly after three his frenzied pacing was broken up by a knock at the front door.

"Hi!" It was Libby. She wore a happy-face grin and her long dark hair was windblown. She looked so young and fresh and vibrant that Carter couldn't help smiling back.

"Hi, yourself. I thought you'd be cheering." He stepped back and allowed Libby to pass through into the living room, glad for a friendly face. Libby, unlike her mother, had never been a problem.

She tossed her book bag onto the table and draped herself casually on the sofa and smiled expectantly up at him. "Oh, no, not every day."

"My mistake." He waited for her to explain what had brought her calling, but she didn't. She just smiled. "Can I get you something to drink? Milk? Er—" he tried to think of something appropriate "—soda?"

"I suppose it is a little early for a beer." Her nonchalance made Carter blink. "So I guess I'll have a cup of coffee. If you don't mind?" Her voice dropped a note or two, became husky. Seductive?

Surely not.

Carter swallowed. "Coming right up." He headed toward the kitchen to look for the coffee. Libby got to it before him.

She gave him a wide smile and a pat on the cheek. "I'll fix it. You sit down. You've probably been working hard. What did you do all day?"

She knew exactly where the coffee filters were, too. And the measuring spoon.

Carter, helpless in the face of such efficiency, still feeling the warmth of her palm against his cheek and wondering if it could possibly mean what he thought it meant, sat.

No, he thought. It couldn't.

He tried frantically to remember what Jack had told him about Libby. It didn't seem to be nearly enough all of a sudden.

She was thinner than her mother, coltish almost. No hips to speak of, and what breasts she had were camouflaged under a baggy green Celtics sweatshirt. A sweatshirt wouldn't hide Annabel's breasts, Carter was certain.

Annoyed at the direction of his thoughts, he turned them abruptly, concentrating on the girl at hand and the question she'd just asked.

"I went to town," he told her. "Looked around. Visited with Ernie and Bert. Stopped in and talked to Eb."

"How exciting," Libby drawled.

Carter shrugged. "He's a character."

Libby wrinkled her nose. "But he never goes anywhere, does anything. Nobody does here. It's all so *boooooring*. You know what I mean?"

Carter didn't completely agree. But then he thought about his own reaction to Boone's Corner when he'd arrived yesterday. He tried to imagine what it must be like for Libby, who, as far as he knew, had spent her life here. He remembered his own rebelliousness at her age and he'd grown up in the most exciting city in the world. "I know what you mean."

"I knew you'd understand," Libby confided. "Mom doesn't. She thinks Boone's Corner is the Hub Of The Western Cultural World."

Carter could well believe that. He laughed.

Libby thumped the coffeemaker together, adding the coffee and setting it on the stove. "She *loooooves* it here. She won't even go to Boston."

"Well, if you aren't used to them, haven't been in them—"

"Mom was *born* in Boston."

That surprised him. There was no big-city sophistication about Annabel Archer. At least, he'd never seen any. He shrugged. "Maybe she got fed up."

Libby snorted. "Maybe? She won't even talk about it. It's like I'm speaking Martian whenever I ask. But it couldn't have been very exciting, could it? I mean, not with my mother."

"Probably not," Carter said in all truthfulness.

"So, tell me about New York. Is it wonderful?" Her eyes glittered eagerly. "I want to go there so bad."

"It's okay. Plenty to do. Most of the time, at least." He wasn't about to share his current aimlessness with Libby. She wouldn't be able to understand it in a million years.

"I bet it's super. Next summer Frances says I can come down and visit them, if Mom lets me."

"Why wouldn't she?"

Libby rolled her eyes. "Contamination."

"Well, yeah, the pollution can be pretty bad some days, but—"

"Not *air* pollution, Carter. Mind pollution. You know—" Libby's voice broke into a singsong chant "— how's she gonna keep me down on the farm after I've seen NYC?" She gave him a stunning smile. For a second he could see Annabel in her again. Something in her eyes. Not the smile. He wondered if Annabel had ever in her life smiled at anyone like that.

She must have, he thought, if she'd managed to marry someone and have two kids. Or maybe not. Maybe she had simply intimidated some poor sod into marrying her.

The latter seemed a damned sight more likely, Carter decided.

"What do you take in your coffee?" Libby asked him.

"Nothing."

"Me, neither," she said giving him a conspiratorial smile. She handed him his mug and took a healthy gulp of her own. Her eyes bugged. Her adam's apple bobbed frantically and she lurched over to spit it into the sink.

"Too hot?" Carter asked.

"Ah...just a little." Libby waved her hand in front of her mouth and gave a sheepish little grin. "I guess I...forgot."

"Mmm." More likely she never drank the stuff.

"I just have more important things on my mind today," she said, sipping carefully this time. She set down the mug, looked at him and batted her eyelashes.

She didn't look at all like her mother when she did that! Carter couldn't imagine Annabel batting her eyelashes at anyone. Not in a million years.

He fought down a smile and took refuge behind his coffee mug. "More important things?" he prompted.

"Like seeing you again."

It was Carter's turn to choke on the coffee.

Hastily Libby patted him on the back. "Are you all right?"

Eyes watering, throat burning, he nodded his head. "Fine," he croaked.

"Good." She gave him one more long sultry look, then settled down at the kitchen table so that their elbows nearly touched. Her knee nudged his thigh.

Abruptly he stood up and set the mug down with a thump. "You gotta go."

"What?"

"I mean, I don't want to keep you. Your mother will worry. It's getting late."

"It's a quarter to four."

"Right. You shouldn't be late for supper."

Libby sighed. "I normally don't get home from practice till six, Carter."

"I thought you said you didn't practice every day."

"Well, er, not all days. But..." The two of them stared
at each other. It was hard to say which of them was the
more flustered now.

"Well, *I* ought to put together some supper even if you
don't." He headed straight for the cupboard and began
setting cans on the counter.

It was far too early to start fixing anything from a can
unless he wanted to eat with the proverbial chickens, but
what else could he do? He sure as hell wasn't going to sit
there and let a seventeen-year-old flirt with him.

He might consider himself hard up—he might even be
looking to get involved—but he sure as hell wasn't looking to get involved with Libby! And have Annabel Archer
as a prospective mother-in-law?

God help him.

Libby was at his side in a moment. "I love to cook."

"So do I," he lied.

"Great. We have something else in common."

Carter shut his eyes. Swell. "I can manage." But she
wasn't taking no for an answer. It was going to be easier to
let her cook than to get rid of her, and it might be safer.

"Be my guest," he said and retreated to the table again.

"There's chili, applesauce, soup, canned spaghetti,
tuna, rice, noodles...." She turned and smiled at him.
"What would you like?"

The way she was looking at him and the soft, seductive
tone of her voice made him wonder if she was talking
about dinner. He wasn't about to ask.

"How about chili and rice. It's a complete protein."

Libby made a face. "You sound like my mother."

Just what he wanted to hear.

Libby set about preparing the meal, sashaying her non-existent hips to and fro past him at eye level, slipping behind him to get a pot for the rice and letting her breasts brush against his back, then leaning across the table in front of him to reach the saltshaker.

Carter edged forward, then back, all the while trying to make intelligent responses to her running commentary about the misery of living in rural Vermont and the supposed joys of the big city.

He began to think dealing with Arnold might be preferable.

Ten minutes later when the doorbell rang, he practically ran to answer it.

It was Leif. Carter nearly dragged him into the living room.

"I can't come in," the boy said. "I just stopped to warn you. I had to bring Arnold down."

Carter wondered if perhaps he was becoming psychic. If he decided he'd prefer an earthquake or some other magnificent natural disaster, would it happen?

"You *had* to bring him? Why?"

"It's fall."

Carter shook his head, uncomprehending.

Leif gave him a patient, long-suffering look. "He makes babies in the fall, Carter. You know, has sex," he added when Carter still stared at him in stupefied silence.

"I know what you mean," Carter managed at last, strangling on the word. He jammed his hands into his pockets. Visions of Arnold among the nannies filled his head. His own months of frustration loomed to haunt him. He shook his head desperately. "Yeah, fine. You go ahead. Do whatever you want."

Leif grinned. "It's not me. It's Arnie."

"I *know* that!"

Leif glanced into the kitchen and frowned. "What's Libby doing here? How come she's not cheering?"

"She says she doesn't have to."

"She does," Leif told him matter-of-factly. He cocked his head and considered first his sister, then Carter. "Ho, boy, Carter," he said, grinning as he turned to go back down the steps. "You better watch out. You could be in big trouble!"

Carter grabbed him. "What's that supposed to mean?"

"You know." Leif was still grinning.

Carter was afraid he did. "She wanted to cook," he growled. "So I let her. Big deal."

"For her," Leif agreed solemnly.

"It doesn't mean a thing."

"Tell her that."

Carter raked a hand through his hair. "Get out of here, you little monster!"

Leif laughed and scampered down the steps.

Libby appeared in the kitchen doorway. She wore an apron now, which, Carter supposed, was intended to make her look even more domestically appealing. She shoved a strand of hair back away from her face. "Dinner's nearly ready. I've made a salad, too."

She'd also set the table, and it was immediately clear to Carter that he wouldn't be dining alone. "You shouldn't have gone to so much trouble."

She smiled. "Oh, it was no trouble. I'll do it every day if you like."

"No, that's okay," he said hastily. "I wouldn't want to take advantage—"

"You wouldn't be taking advantage. I'd love to do it. I need to practice cooking."

Carter shook his head adamantly. "So do I."

Libby paused. "Well, then, maybe you can cook for me sometime."

Carter felt as if the neckline of his T-shirt had become suddenly tight. "Maybe...sometime."

Before Frances, Jack had at times complained about the way women hovered around him, breathed on him, batted their lashes at him. Carter had been singularly unsympathetic. Until now.

Libby was looking at him expectantly, obviously waiting for him to sit down. Seeing no alternative, Carter sat.

Over the course of the last twenty years, Carter had had dinner with plenty of females. He had danced his share of duty dances, gone on his share of disastrous blind dates. And he could never remember having been more uncomfortable or trying to be more careful not to show it.

There was ingenuousness to Libby's attentions that made him worry terribly about the possibility of hurting her.

Not that he wanted to encourage her, for heaven's sake. But he didn't want to shut her down rudely, either. She was so young, so untouched.

He got the definite sense that she was trying out wiles on him that, if he reacted wrongly, could have an adverse effect on all her future relationships with the opposite sex.

A conscience, Carter? he chided himself. *At your age?*

But that was, in fact, what it must be. He couldn't imagine that he would have behaved with such avuncular circumspection a few months ago.

God, he must be getting old!

ANNABEL WAS GETTING frantic and she suspected it showed. "What do you mean, she didn't go to practice?" she demanded into the telephone. "Libby always goes to practice. She hasn't missed a cheerleading opportunity since she was born."

"Well, she missed this one, Ms. Archer. Just said she wasn't coming and took off. I think she took the school bus home." Libby's best friend Alice sounded earnest and absolutely truthful. She was also, as Annabel's inquisition went on, beginning to sound upset.

Not half as upset as Annabel. It was seven o'clock and she hadn't seen hide nor hair of her daughter.

"Well, if she'd taken the school bus, she'd have come home, wouldn't she?" Annabel asked. It seemed like a reasonable assumption to her.

"I guess so, Ms. Archer," Alice said miserably.

"She didn't say where she was going?"

"No."

"Or what she had to do?"

"No. Nothing. She acted sort of mysterious."

Mysterious? What did that mean? "If she comes by, you tell her to call me at once," Annabel instructed and hung up.

What, Annabel wondered as she stood staring out the window into the darkness, could have been suddenly more important to Libby than cheerleading?

She spotted Leif coming across the yard with Arnold and let out a sigh of relief. At least one of her children was accounted for. And her goat. She hadn't wanted Leif to take Arnie up there at all, but Leif had been adamant.

"I gotta," he'd said. "I need 'em for 4H."

So Annabel had let him go. "Don't bother Carter," she'd warned.

And Leif had nodded. "I never bother Carter. We just talk and stuff. I'll explain about Arnie."

Annabel thought she would have liked to hear that.

Leif banged in through the door. "Mmm. Smells good. Am I late?"

"No later than Libby," Annabel said distractedly. "Damn that girl. She didn't go cheerleading. She didn't come home. She probably went shopping in Gaithersburg with Mary Kate and didn't tell me. I'll wring her neck if she has."

"She's at Carter's."

"What?"

He turned then and shrugged, drying his hands, grinning at her. "She's with Carter. She cooked him dinner!"

Annabel felt her mouth opening and closing like a fish.

"She's in love with him," Leif said. "What an idiot."

"In love with—? She didn't go to practice so she could go cook dinner for Carter MacKenzie?" Annabel knew her voice was on a steady rise. She knew she practically ended the sentence at a shout. She didn't care.

Libby? Her darling, defenseless daughter? And *Carter MacKenzie?*

Oh, God. Please God, I didn't mean it. I didn't mean he could have any woman if he'd leave me alone. He can't have Libby!

She pulled on a jacket and was heading out the door almost before she knew what she was doing. Halfway up the hill she stopped.

What was she going to do? Bang on Carter's door and demand Libby's release?

He was hardly holding her prisoner. Annabel wasn't entirely certain about Carter's role in the afternoon's events, but she wasn't a complete fool. She knew that Libby wouldn't be there if she didn't want to be.

And barging in and making demands was the surest way to alienate her daughter that Annabel could think of.

Oh, damn, she thought. Why was parenting always so difficult?

She stood on the hillside, weighing her alternatives.

Her eyes went to the top of the hill, to where the path led down the other side toward Frances's house, to Libby. To Carter. Her mind fast-forwarded to how big a fool she could make of herself if she went that way.

Her gaze turned back toward her own snug log home where Leif stood in the lit doorway, watching her. She could be a fool if she went that way, too.

She raised her eyes to the heavens. It was a vast black canopy sprinkled with stars, immense but not unfriendly. Looking at it, Annabel felt the years roll away. She felt as she had at twenty, at twenty-five, young and vulnerable and uncertain.

When she was young, back when Libby was in first grade and Leif only a toddler, Annabel had often come up to sit on the hillside in the evening when the children were asleep to get a better perspective on her life.

It seemed as though all she had time for during the day was to work like a demon. But at night she would climb the hill to sit quietly and reflect, albeit briefly, on her day. She would think about what was—and then about what might have been.

And at the end, before getting to her feet and going back to her everyday life, she would raise her eyes skyward to find that star somewhere to the right of the Big Dipper, the one she used to wish on as a child, the one she knew better than to wish on anymore.

It was always there, constant and reliable. When she no longer had her parents, when she no longer had Mark, she still had the star.

She didn't know its name, its constellation, its astronomical significance. She only knew it focused her, steadied her, kept her from making a fool of herself. It had always been there to balance her when she hadn't been sure if she could cope, when she'd contemplated throwing in the towel and running back home to Daddy.

She hadn't looked for it in a long time.

As the children got older, as what might have been faded into a simple determined acceptance of what was, as she grew up, she'd stayed in her kitchen at night, reading, working, humming to herself. Satisfied. Comfortable.

She wasn't comfortable tonight.

She hugged her arms across her chest and stared upward, finding the star. It gleamed faintly in the night sky, steady and reassuring.

"Now what?" she asked softly, though whether she was talking to the star or to God or simply to herself, she wasn't certain.

She tucked her hands into the pockets of her jacket and stood still, watching, waiting.

There was a sudden crackling behind her. She spun around to see two shapes moving down the hillside toward her.

"Libby!"

"Mom? What are you doing up here?"

Annabel, seeing the second shape materialize into Carter, took a slow, careful breath. "Enjoying the evening. Looking at the sky."

"That's all?" Libby sounded suspicious.

Annabel gave her daughter a look of wide-eyed guilelessness. "What else would I be doing?"

Libby flicked an instant's gaze over her shoulder at the man who'd stopped just behind her. "N-nothing, I guess," she said brightly. "I . . . I suppose maybe I should have called to tell you. I was at Carter's."

"Leif said. And yes, I would have appreciated a call."

"I fixed dinner," Libby went on. "And we did the washing up together. Then we took a walk. Around by Milliken's old place. You know? The trail that crosses the bridge."

Annabel nodded. She knew. She and Mark had often lingered, kissing, on that bridge. Her eyes narrowed as she looked at Carter. Had he been kissing her daughter?

"Then he said he'd walk me home," Libby went on. She glanced at Carter again. She was smiling. Swooning.

Near to melting, Annabel thought, annoyed. "How thoughtful," she said tonelessly.

"My pleasure," Carter said.

She looked at him sharply. He sounded pleased. She gave him a steely glare.

Carter met her gaze with a stubborn one of his own. "Would you rather she'd walked alone?"

"This isn't New York City. But I appreciate your concern." She took Libby by the arm and began herding her down the hill. "Thank you for seeing her home, Mr. MacKenzie."

"I enjoyed it, Ms. Archer," he drawled, then after a moment, "Come again, Libby."

Over my dead body, Annabel thought.

"Tomorrow," Libby promised, blowing him a kiss.

Chapter Four

There was no help for it. As much of an idiot as it made her feel to do so, Annabel had to intervene.

It was one thing to have Carter MacKenzie preying on her—not that he was, of course. It was entirely another to find him lusting after her seventeen-year-old daughter! He might not like the selection of local ladies, but he was going to have to make do.

She didn't say anything more to Libby. She simply sat stonelike in the living room and listened while Libby babbled on for the remainder of the evening, extolling Carter's manly virtues. His muscular arms. His strong jaw.

His hairy chest?

Annabel clenched her teeth. Just how Libby knew he had a hairy chest, she managed not to inquire.

She even mustered up a smile when Libby said how glad she was that he'd come and wasn't he such a good friend to Jack and Frances for doing so.

"Indeed."

"Don't you think he's handsome?"

She hadn't, if the truth were known, given it a lot of consideration. The less she thought about Carter MacKenzie, the better. "I suppose he's turned out well enough."

Libby gave a little squeal. "Did you see a picture of him when he was little?"

"No. I did not."

"But—"

Annabel flapped her hands. "It's just a matter of expression, Libby. For heaven's sake, stop pestering me. Go do your homework."

"I did it."

Annabel's hands came to a halt in midair. "All of it? Without being told? When?"

"At Carter's. He helped me."

"You asked Carter to help you with your homework?"

"Oh, no. I didn't really want to bother him with it. But... well, he offered. We had this rotten long trig assignment and he helped me with it all."

Having done so, he rose in Annabel's estimation a tiny bit. Or he did until she realized that he might merely have done so to give Libby a reasonable excuse for coming there in the future, some plausible reason to offer her mother for spending time with him.

"You needn't bother him with your homework."

"I'd better bother somebody," Libby said, "or I'm going to flunk trig."

And heaven knew, Annabel wasn't going to be able to prevent that. As far back as ninth grade, Annabel had begun opting out of anything having to do with numbers.

It wasn't that she couldn't do them; it was simply that she hated them. And once she'd finished geometry, she'd said, "That's it," and had never looked back.

Her father had told her it was a huge mistake. But almost everything she did was, according to Edward Lodge Archer, a huge mistake. Annabel hadn't thought ignoring mathematics was one of them. Until tonight.

"Well, there must be someone else who can help you . . . Eb? Ernie?"

"Ma," Libby said patiently, "they didn't have trig when Eb was a kid. And I don't think math is Ernie's thing."

"Well, what about Aaron?"

Libby cocked her head. "Oh, good idea. And he can come over every evening to help me."

"Sarcasm does not become you, Liberty."

"You suggested it."

"My mistake. Is Carter really good at it?" She couldn't imagine it, somehow. It seemed too much like work for Carter to excel at it.

"Yeah, he is. And he explains it well, too. Lots better than old Morrissey at school."

"Why'd he have his shirt off?"

Libby blinked. "What?"

Annabel could have torn out her tongue. "Never mind." She tried to leave it alone. She couldn't. "You said he had a hairy chest."

"He does."

"How do you know?"

"I did his laundry."

"And he *undressed?*"

"I . . . accidentally spattered some chili on his shirt when I was cleaning up, so he took it off and I said I would wash it."

Annabel's gaze narrowed. She looked at her daughter carefully. Accidentally? she wondered.

Libby looked away, reaching out to snag her backpack off the table. She rustled inside it for her math book and pulled it out.

"See?" She waved a neatly set out paper full of equations in front of her mother. "He knew everything about the law of cosine and all that business about secants and cosecants.''

Annabel, who knew about as much about cosines and secants as she did about lateral forward passes was reluctantly impressed. ''And you understand it now?''

''Oh, yes.'' Libby nodded her head enthusiastically. ''He should be a teacher. He was amazing.''

''Good.'' Annabel wasn't really sure if it was good or not. It was perhaps, at best, a mixed blessing. She wondered if God looked more kindly on men who taught girls trigonometry as they seduced them. She didn't think mothers did.

Still, he clearly hadn't seduced Libby yet, though, she suspected, not from Libby's lack of trying. With luck, perhaps she could forestall it before it became a sure thing.

''Very nice,'' she said briskly. ''Now, since you're such a whiz at laundry, you can bring your dirty clothes downstairs so I can get an early start tomorrow.''

Libby looked as if she might have argued, then, as if she was considering all the other avenues the conversation could have taken.

''Right,'' she said and, giving Annabel a sunny smile, she bounded up the stairs.

''WHAT DO YOU MEAN, you won't be able to get here this week?'' Carter scowled at the telephone in his hand, listened to the droning explanation on the other end, sighed and rubbed a hand around the back of his neck.

He'd got up this morning to another ominous silence. But this time he'd managed to do more than exchange messages with the elusive Benton Brothers. In fact, he had Luther Benton right at that very moment on the other end of the line.

"You told Mr. Neillands you'd be here this week," he said when Luther's excuses finally ground to a halt.

"Can't. All that rain we had couple of weeks ago, it set us back."

"And you couldn't have called and told him?"

"It's long-distance," Luther said, as if that was all the explanation necessary.

"I bloody know that!" Carter exploded. "It took me five hours to get up here!"

"We can be there next week, I reckon."

"You reckon?"

"Well, ain't nobody can say what the weather's gonna do, can they?"

"No," Carter muttered. "Ain't nobody can do that."

"Well, then," Luther said, "you see what I mean. Next week, week after. Don't fret. We'll be there 'fore the snow falls."

"It's the rain, not the snow they're trying to keep out."

"Ayuh. That, too."

Carter quietly strangled the phone in his hands, then took a deep breath and made up his mind. "You've got the roofing shingles in stock?"

"We're roofers, ain't we?"

"Fine. I'll be down this morning to pick them up. I'll put on the roof myself."

His decision wasn't as altruistic as it might appear at first glance. It was basically self-preservation.

"Tomorrow," Libby had said in response to the invitation he'd issued simply to annoy her mother. He'd known damned well what Annabel was doing on that hillside, and it wasn't looking at the stars. She was afraid he was after her daughter.

The truth was, her daughter was after him! And he didn't know how many more visits from Libby he would be able to handle as well as he'd handled the first one. Through dinner and washing up, he'd held her off. The question about her studies that had resulted in their foray into trigonometry had been pure blind luck. The walk had been less lucky. He could see real dangers lurking in the moonlit path, the old stone bridge, the now-deserted but still-comfortable farmhouse. It was not a place to go with Libby.

Seductive teenagers were a mystery to him—a mystery he wanted to preserve forever. Being on the roof, he thought, might give him the edge he needed.

Bentons were surprisingly cordial when he showed up. Probably, he thought sourly, because they fully expected him to call them up to rescue him in the midst of his folly a few days hence.

They smiled and snickered behind their hands, helped him load all the shingles into the back of his Blazer and sent him on his way with a hearty "Good luck, fella."

If they didn't actually add, "You'll need it," it didn't matter. Carter could hear the words echoing off the mountainsides as he drove home.

He needed it sooner than he thought.

There, sitting on the front step, waiting for him, was Annabel Archer. Bloody hell.

He parked the car beside the barn and got out. She had watched him drive without moving at all. But when he began walking toward the house, she stood up and came toward him slowly across the yard.

Like gunslingers, Carter thought.

He felt decidedly unarmed. He wasn't sure what she wanted, but he was willing to bet it had something to do with Libby. She obviously didn't trust him an inch.

"Here," she said and thrust a paper into his hand.

He took it, frowning. "What's this?"

"A list of local eligible women."

His head jerked up. He stared at her, amazed. "You're joking."

"I'm not. This one is a vet's assistant." Her finger jabbed at one name on the page. "This one teaches. This one works in a supermarket down the way. The last one's a lawyer. Not many, I realize. But old enough—" her voice hit the word *old* with a definite authority "—and certainly a better bet."

He cocked his head, regarding her carefully. "Than Libby, you mean?"

She looked momentarily taken aback that he would be so blunt. Then, "Yes," she hissed.

She reminded him of a mother cat defending its offspring. Her cheeks were flushed; her eyes flashed fire. She looked ready to burst into flame in a moment. Even her gingery hair seemed to glow.

He couldn't help grinning. "But Libby's lovely," he teased.

"Libby is seventeen!"

"She'll be eighteen in four months."

"She told you that?" Annabel looked horrified.

Carter shrugged equably, beginning to enjoy himself now. "Who else?"

Annabel's mouth opened. And shut. He could almost see her making the effort to calm herself. He wanted to tell her it wouldn't work.

"Damn it!" She exploded. "It won't work!"

"What won't work? Me and Libby?" He tried to keep the smile off his face.

"That, too," Annabel snapped. "But I meant me, trying to be rational. Trying to appeal to your good nature, your sensitivity, your common sense! I should have known!'' She was almost shouting now. ''You don't have any common sense!''

''How clever of you to have noticed,'' Carter said mildly.

''Damn,'' Annabel muttered under her breath. ''I shouldn't even have come.'' She spun away and started to stalk across the gravel toward the trail.

He caught her arm and spun her back to face him. ''Hold on.''

''Why should I? It was a mistake to come.''

''You're sure of that?''

Fire flashed in those amber eyes again. ''What do you think?'' she asked scornfully.

''I think I'm in big trouble if the only woman in the world who supposedly appeals to me is seventeen.''

Annabel just stared at him, but her gaze went from angry to merely suspicious. ''Meaning?'' she asked after a moment.

''Meaning I'm not after your precious daughter.''

'' 'Come again, Libby,' '' she quoted in a deliberately seductive singsong voice. ''That wasn't you?''

Carter laughed a little self-consciously. ''Not in that tone of voice.''

''But you invited her back.''

''I was being neighborly. What'd you expect me to do, throw her off the property? Sorry, lady, that's your forte, not mine.''

The color in Annabel's cheeks grew even deeper. ''I try to be neighborly, too,'' she said in a grudging tone. ''Maybe I haven't been very pleasant . . . to you.''

''Yeah, well, I sort of said it to annoy you, too,'' Carter admitted.

Annabel's brows arched.

''You looked so disapproving.''

"I was. I *am*," Annabel said.

"Well, stop worrying. Libby's safe with me."

Annabel shifted from one foot to the other. "Thanks," she muttered. Then, "I'm sorry if she bothered you."

"No bother," Carter said quickly. "She's a good kid."

"But she is a kid," Annabel said firmly.

"I know that," he said. "But she's very nearly an adult, you know. She isn't going to be a little girl forever."

"Do tell."

He grinned. "I thought you'd probably already figured that out."

"I'll try to keep her away," Annabel promised.

"It won't work."

"Why not? You can't be that wonderful." The moment she said it, her face flamed.

Carter gave her an amused look. "I haven't had many complaints."

"I didn't mean that," Annabel said tightly. She tried to pull her wrist out of his grasp but he didn't let go.

"I know what you meant," he said easily. "It's just that—" he shrugged "—I enjoy baiting you."

She scowled. "Why?"

"You get so mad. And it makes me feel a little better," Carter added after a moment. "Most of the time you're damned intimidating."

Annabel's grin was like sunshine, dazzling enough to make Carter blink.

"I think I've created a monster," he muttered. "It isn't becoming, you know."

Annabel smiled. "Who wants to be 'becoming'?"

Not her, obviously. And just as well, too, he thought. When she smiled Annabel Archer was really surprisingly pretty. It made him want to kiss her again.

"Let's see this list," he said.

She intimidated *him?*

She didn't know whether to believe him or not. It was a mark of her basic lunacy that she even had to think about it, Annabel decided. When had Carter MacKenzie ever stood there and told her the simple, honest truth?

But heaven knew she wanted to believe him. It would make life so much easier to feel she had a foothold on the slippery cliff of their relationship.

What relationship? she asked herself.

A few days ago she would have denied the possibility of ever even having one.

But after the past few days...after his cordiality toward Leif, after his gift of the shawl, after his soothing of her fears about his interest in Libby...there might, she conceded, be a remote possibility.

She spent the rest of the afternoon winding Spanish moss around heart-shaped wire forms, trying to think about how she was going to decorate them. Instead she thought about Carter.

She thought about his impish grins, his outrageous comments, his deliberate teasing. She thought about his lean, whipcord body and the way his hair flopped across his forehead and the way he had to shove it back.

Not a good idea, thinking about things like that.

She thought instead about the list she had given him. Was he, even at this moment, consulting it?

He'd certainly snatched it quick enough. It just went to prove that Frances was right about him wanting a woman.

That was all right, Annabel told herself, as long as the woman wasn't Libby. Or her.

That last thought, long suppressed, definitely unbidden, came out of the blue and hit her squarely between the eyes.

No, she thought. Oh, no. She couldn't be so stupid as to entertain such a ridiculous possibility as herself and Carter together, could she?

She sat quite still, staring down at the creation in her hands. A heart. Wire and moss, tiny dried roses, baby's breath and a bow. Delicate. Fragile. But sturdier than it looked. Far, far sturdier than the heart of an adolescent girl had been years ago.

No, of course she couldn't consider it. She wouldn't let herself.

Once had definitely been enough.

HE TOOK PATTY WILLITS to a movie. She laughed in all the wrong places. She was censorious about his penchant for junk food. He got the feeling that every time he opened his mouth, she was checking his teeth.

He took Tracey Forrester to the spaghetti supper. She giggled. Incessantly. She hung on his arm. Her presence seemed to have the effect of making Libby scowl at him all evening. But what was worse, he had the dubious pleasure of watching while Annabel, obviously ignoring him, smiled and laughed with Aaron on the other side of the room.

He made it a point to go over and speak to her. She was cordial, welcoming even, as if she had mended her ways after he'd commented on them. But it didn't feel real or as if she meant it.

Perversely he found he liked it better when she sniped at him. He was so irritated by her polite words and cool welcome that when he got home at ten, he went up on the roof and, with the flashlight in his teeth, pounded in an entire row of shingles. Then he took a long walk, a cold shower and went to bed.

He didn't get a lot of sleep. At first his mind was filled with thoughts of Patty and Tracey and Libby. But once he fell asleep, they vanished and Annabel Archer haunted his dreams. She sicced her goat on him, then metamorphosed into Libby and batted her eyelashes at him. But when he made a move on her, she walked away.

In the morning, shortly past six, he called Milly to complain.

"It's not working," he said the moment she picked up the phone.

"Carter?" She sounded sleep muddled and confused. "Is that you? What didn't work? Where are you?"

"Godforsaken Corner, Vermont, trying to get some perspective on my life. What you said I should do. And it's not working. At all!"

There was a silence while Milly sorted through that. "What happened?"

"Nothing. Everything. There's this woman—she haunts me. And her daughter—"

"Both?" Milly sounded more awake now.

"No! Not both. The daughter's after me. She's a kid, for heaven's sake! And the woman doesn't want anything to do with me. I just damned well see her everywhere and I think about her and...and I...I..." His voice trailed off.

"You what, Carter?"

"I don't know," he muttered, anguished.

"Sounds like it's working to me," Milly said quietly. "Tell me about this woman."

"She's a witch."

"Really? That sounds promising."

Carter snorted. "She's Frances's friend. Frances made me kiss her."

"Made you kiss her? Heavens."

"Oh, shut up."

Milly giggled softly. "Sounds like she's really getting to you, big brother."

"She made me a list of eligible women," he grumbled.

"Did she? How enterprising. Why?"

"She's afraid for her daughter. Thinks I'll seduce her."

"Did you come on to her?"

"Of course not! I'm not a cradle robber."

"Then why would she think . . . ?"

"She just doesn't like me."

"Why not?"

"How the hell should I know? Maybe she's got it in for tall, handsome guys. I don't know. She's unnerving as hell."

Milly laughed.

"It isn't funny. The way she looks down her nose at me, glares at me, gives me these disapproving stares all the time—she's just like Dad."

Milly sighed. "I doubt if she's at all like Dad, Carter."

"You haven't met her," he said darkly.

"I'd like to. Did you ever think she might be giving you the names of these women because she's equally unnerved by you?"

"That'll be the day."

"You might be surprised."

"Yeah. Sure."

"You're such a skeptic, Carter," Milly chided. "I think it's great."

"What's great?"

"That you're interested in her."

"Interested? In her?" he practically yelped.

"Who else? She's all you've talked about."

"Not because I'm interested. I told you, she hates me. And I don't like her, either. Why would I want to get involved with someone who reminds me of Dad?"

"You tell me," Milly said quietly.

Carter scowled at the phone. "It's not like that," he muttered.

"And I'm telling you, I don't believe it. Tell me more. Have I met her? Is she young and single and eminently eligible?"

"No, you haven't. And she's middle-aged and widowed. With two kids," he reported dampeningly. "Not my type at all. I told you that."

"But she still has the power to torment you? My, my."

"You're a sadist, Milly."

"I'm a sister."

"Same thing."

"Poor Carter."

"Poor Carter is right. I came up here for rest and relaxation, and all day long I'm plagued by kids and goats and a woman who hates my guts, plus I'm putting on a new roof, for heaven's sake."

"Are you?" Milly sounded impressed. "Well, that's one way to get a new perspective."

"Very funny."

"Not funny. Good. You sound livelier, Carter. Something must be happening."

Something was, but Carter wasn't sure he liked it. He wasn't even sure he believed in it. God knew he didn't want to.

"What's her name?"

There was no use pretending he didn't know who Milly was talking about. "Annabel. Annabel Archer."

"Sounds vaguely familiar."

"You probably heard Jack or Frances mention her."

"Maybe." There was a pause, then, "Oh, cripes. I've got to get going. I have rounds at the hospital this morning. Call me soon?"

"Sure."

"And, Carter? Think about what I said—about your Annabel maybe feeling a bit intimidated, too."

"She's not *my* Annabel."

"Yet."

Chapter Five

His Annabel.

Lord, what a thought.

It made him want to pull the pillow right over his head. It made him want to turn tail and run as fast as he could.

It was true, he realized as he lay there in bed and stared up at the ceiling, what he'd told Milly about her reminding him of his father.

While clearly there wasn't much of a physical resemblance to the hawk-nosed, barrel-chested steamroller who'd sired him, she and C.W. had a lot of other things in common. They certainly seemed to share the same disdain of him, the same minimal bored tolerance for his antics, the same penchant for cool dismissal.

And he felt the same about them: he wanted to rattle them, unnerve them, get under their skin.

It had been easy with his father. All he'd had to do was go his own way, do what he liked, disparage the power and the glory that came with the MacKenzie name, and C.W. was ready to strangle him. Even when he made an effort to keep the old man happy, it was to no avail.

Carter had found that out quite early.

"It's a good school. It was *my* school," his father had trumpeted as he'd sent Carter off to Kenwood Prep at the age of thirteen. "They respect MacKenzies there."

They threw Carter out in less than two months.

"Smoking?" his father had roared. "Shinnying up the flagpole in your underwear? What in hell were you thinking of, you young fool?" C.W. had bellowed at him when he was sent home in disgrace.

Carter, as stubborn as his old man, didn't reply.

There was no way he could explain that still-immature thirteen-year-olds didn't command the respect that company CEOs did, no way that he could tell his father the only way a skinny little kid could earn it from his peers was to take foolish risks, act tough, never show the slightest fear. He had tried . . . had done the best he could.

For C.W., Carter's best was never good enough. Not in school, not in football, not in dating. He was told so time and time again. So, to his father's face, he always simply pretended he didn't care.

So did C.W. Having a son like Carter—who didn't command immediate respect by his size and authority, who not only didn't make first-team quarterback, but who actually rarely got to play, who never dated the right girls— was irritating in the extreme.

As time went on, C.W. did his best to ignore the son who bore his name.

Carter resented that even more than he resented his father's fury.

So he did things to get the old man's attention. Things designed to infuriate and annoy. Things that would get a rise out of him and which would prove to Carter that his father was at least aware of his existence, even if he didn't love him.

For some reason Annabel Archer made him feel much the same way.

He didn't understand why she disliked him. He didn't expect adulation from every woman he ever met. But he could be charming. He could be fun. He was good for a few laughs, a night on the town, a roll in the hay.

And if they weren't interested in that, he knew it instinctively and was quite willing to be a good friend.

But not with Annabel Archer?

He'd sensed her disapproval from the moment they'd met. She'd given him a stiff smile and a snooty stare when Frances had first introduced them.

He'd commented on it, teasing her—or trying to. But that had only made her stiffer and snootier. She'd uttered a bare monosyllable, then walked away.

She might as well have thrown down the gauntlet.

He'd never learned not to accept a dare.

Every time they'd met after that, he'd done his best to say outrageous things to her, to tease or harass her. It had become a minor goal in his life to discomfit Annabel Archer.

And until recently that had certainly been enough.

It was all Frances's fault, he thought morosely. If she hadn't had to redo her damned roof, he wouldn't be up here. He wouldn't be thinking about Annabel, dreaming about her.

He was willing to bet Annabel never dreamed about him.

He thought about what Milly had suggested, about the possibility of Annabel being intimidated by him.

"Not bloody likely." He gave a bitter laugh. Annabel wouldn't be intimidated by a tank.

She's no better than the old man. Forget her, he told himself.

But how could he forget her when she lived just over the hill? When her children were at his door? When her goat was in his pasture? When her cool, deliberate antagonism irritated the hell out of him? When her smile made the sun come out?

CARTER MADE IT A POINT to meet Beth Hayes. He'd asked Ernie and Bert about her. They said she was sweet, lovely, intelligent, kind. Good, he thought. She sounded a perfect antidote to his fixation on Annabel Archer. After the first two he began to wonder if Annabel hadn't been setting him up.

He skulked around the school parking lot for two hours to casually run into Beth as she walked to her car. And she seemed surprised at his story about Frances having mentioned her and telling him to be sure to look her up.

"I scarcely know Frances Neillands," she protested. She looked at Carter doubtfully.

"She knows you. Says you're a great teacher. I suppose one of the kids in your classes must've said it. Libby Campbell, I think."

"Libby? She got a *D* in geometry."

"Oh, well . . . maybe it wasn't Libby then." Carter began to wish he'd thought up another story. "Anyway, I was wondering if you'd like to go out Friday night."

"Well, I . . . There's school, you know? A football game and . . ."

"Swell. How about going to the game?"

She sighed. "I . . . suppose we could do that."

She might be sweet and lovely and kind, but she sure as hell wasn't enthusiastic. Carter feared he was making a mistake. But he could hardly retract the invitation. Besides, Libby was coming out of the building just then, and he didn't want her input into this conversation.

"Come on," Carter urged. "It'll be fun. I'll pick you up at six. We can have a bite of supper first."

Beth Hayes sighed. "I suppose."

IF PATTY HAD GUFFAWED all through the movie and Tracey had chattered and giggled all the way through the spaghetti supper, Beth Hayes never cracked a smile.

She rarely spoke, either. Carter did his best to be charming, but if he couldn't metamorphose into a geometric figure, he reckoned he didn't have a chance.

He hoped things would improve when they got to the football game. Libby had told him she was cheering, had been delighted to hear he was coming, had even accepted his coming with Beth Hayes with equanimity.

"Oh, her," was all she'd said.

But despite Libby's dismissal, he still held out hopes. Beth was svelte and elegant looking. And even if she didn't laugh and talk, her very presence would let Annabel know that he wasn't repulsive to other women.

His plans, though, went awry from the first. Even when they got to the game, Beth scarcely said a word. Worse, she kept a good two feet away from him all the time. It was cold enough to merit having someone to snuggle up next to, but when Carter tried, she quickly edged away, tucked her duffle coat more tightly around her and gave him a frosty look. "I am a teacher."

The look he gave her must have made his bafflement obvious. She managed a slight smile. "I'm sorry, but it wouldn't do, you know. I must set a good example for my students."

Carter glanced around at the students, most of whom were huddled so close together that it was hard to tell where one began and the other left off.

"Right," he muttered.

Beth gave him a prim smile. "I knew you'd understand."

He understood, all right. He understood it was going to be a long night. He stared back down at the field, hunching his shoulders against the wind, and wondered if Annabel was laughing at him.

He had been looking for her since they'd arrived. He'd looked for her right down front where she could see Libby cheering, but he didn't find her there. And though he periodically craned his neck and scanned the rest of the bleacher crowd, he didn't find her there, either.

"Hi. Can I sit with you?"

Carter turned to find Leif standing behind him, grinning.

"If you don't want me to, that's okay," Leif said quickly when Carter didn't answer at once.

"Of course you can sit with us. Why not?"

"Swell." Leif studied the amount of space between Carter and Beth, decided it was sufficient, then clambered down to sit between them. "Cold, isn't it?" He shivered cheerfully, hugging his arms against his chest.

"Yeah." Carter hesitated a moment, then put his arm around the boy, drawing him close. "That help?"

Leif grinned, huddling closer. "Yep."

They sat that way for the rest of the half, snug and warm against the cold north wind. It had been years since Carter had gone to a football game. He couldn't remember one, in fact, that he had gone to for purposes of enjoyment. MacKenzies went, according to C.W., to play. And win.

This was different. Easier. Far more relaxing. Leif asked innumerable questions and Carter surprised himself by knowing the answers. He bought Leif a soft drink and himself a cup of coffee. Beth declined anything.

"You sure you're comfortable?" he asked her now and then.

She always said, "I'm fine," and moved farther down the wooden bench.

At halftime Beth glanced at her watch, then at him, and back at her watch again. "Would you think me terribly rude if I asked to go home? It's not that the game isn't interesting, or... or that you aren't, but..."

"You have a lot of papers to grade?"

She nodded eagerly. "How'd you guess?"

"Instinct. Come on, I'll take you home," Carter said with an alacrity that would have made his socially proper mother wince.

He deposited Beth Hayes on her doorstep, bade her a quick farewell and was back in his car before she shut the front door. He considered, for a moment, not even going back to the game.

It wasn't as if he dearly loved football. Nor was he going to enjoy Annabel's knowing smirks. But Leif was waiting, saving him a seat, and he didn't want to disappoint the boy. Besides, he was enjoying it.

Leif was right where he had left him, but since Beth had left, now he could ask, "Where's your mother?"

Leif blinked, as if the question surprised him. "At Eb's. She always goes to Eb's. Like Libby said, Ma doesn't like football."

"But Libby cheers."

"Yeah. That's Libby's choice. That's what Ma says anyway. That we have to make up our own minds about things, make our own choices in life. She brings us to the game, then she goes and plays checkers with Eb. We call her when the game's almost over and she comes to pick us up."

It was apparently simple and clear-cut to Leif. It boggled Carter's mind. In his own experience, his parents had not encouraged their children to make up their own minds. Exactly the opposite, in fact.

If Carter William MacKenzie III didn't like something, then no one liked it. Period.

Apparently Annabel wasn't completely like his father. She didn't raise her children the same way, at any rate. In fact, he rather admired the way she raised her children. They were nice kids, fun to be with, forthright, eager, charming, funny.

He supposed they might have inherited it all from their father, but honesty compelled him to admit that Annabel might have had something to do with it. It was a disconcerting thought.

He didn't have time to dwell on the notion, though, for right then the Gaithersburg Gators scored a touchdown and Leif dragged him to his feet to cheer.

"Cool!" Leif exclaimed. "Do you think they might win? Do you? They haven't won a game in years."

"Maybe tonight." Carter was grinning, too, feeling the same sort of exhilaration that Leif felt. Eager, joyful, alive. He was glad Beth had left, grateful that Annabel hadn't been there to see her leave.

He sent Leif down to buy popcorn and Snickers bars, then they drank hot spiced-apple cider. Halfway through the fourth quarter Carter found himself explaining the virtues of zone defense, the Gators scored another touchdown, Libby leapt around, cheering madly, Leif said, "You really know a lot about football," with sincere admiration, and Carter felt better than he'd felt in months or, maybe, years.

"Did you go to lots of games with your dad?" Leif asked him.

"Some," Carter said. But they hadn't been fun. Not the way this had been.

He didn't want the game to end. But when it did, he wasn't abandoned to go home to Jack and Frances's alone.

"Come with us," Libby said, hanging on to his arm, grinning up at him. "We always go out after for donuts."

He didn't even stop to think. "I'd like that," he said.

He'd forgotten about Annabel.

When they got out to the parking lot, there she was.

She was wearing his shawl.

The sight of her standing under the lights, her gingery hair windblown, the blue-green sea of the shawl swirling around her, almost took his breath away.

"We won!" Leif yelled. And Libby grabbed her by the hands and swung her around.

Annabel grabbed for the shawl, laughing, looking flustered as she glanced at him. It made Carter smile.

"We missed you," he said.

"I'll bet."

"He brought Ms. Hayes," Leif told her. "She went home at halftime."

Annabel looked at Carter, her brows arched.

He spread his hands. "What can I say? She must have found my charm too much for her."

Annabel's mouth twitched. Then she gave up trying to fight the grin and laughed. "Oh, undoubtedly."

"Come on," Leif said. "I'm starving."

Carter looked at him, horrified. "I fed you popcorn and candy and—"

"Shh!" Leif glared at him. "Not in front of Ma!"

Annabel gave him a mock-stern look. "You know what I think about junk food."

Leif's smile was ingenuous. "We gotta make choices, Ma."

Annabel pretended to strangle him. "What did I ever do to deserve you?"

Leif giggled. "If you don't know, I won't tell you."

Annabel's face flushed. "Come on, then. Let's go."

"Carter, too, Ma," Leif said.

Annabel looked at him. For just an instant their gazes met.

"Carter, too," she said.

ANNABEL HADN'T BEEN prepared for Carter. She'd heard from Ernie and Bert that he'd asked about Beth Hayes. She'd convinced herself he'd have invited Beth to drive toward Rutland to one of the inns for a quiet, romantic meal.

Seeing him coming out of the stadium with Leif and Libby was a shock. If she'd known he'd be there, she wouldn't have been wearing the shawl, for heaven's sake. And she wouldn't have left her hair to hang loose as though she were some sort of hippie. She'd have bundled it back neatly and skewered it in place with a wood-and-leather thong.

But, she told herself as she followed the taillights of Carter's Blazer through the streets of Gaithersburg toward Maggie's Muffin and Doughnut Shoppe, it could always be worse.

He could have invited Libby to go out with him after the game, instead of Libby and Leif inviting him to join them.

Her stubbornly rational side argued that there were better case scenarios, too. He could have declined to join them, could have at least said he'd follow her instead of allowing both kids to act as "navigators" and come with him.

He could, Annabel thought, exasperated, have hung on to his date and not been available at all.

Had Beth Hayes really left him at halftime? Had he really cared as little as he seemed to?

Annabel pulled into Maggie's small gravel parking lot alongside Carter's Blazer with all these thoughts still buzzing in her head.

Leif bounced out of the car immediately. Libby still sat in the front seat, talking animatedly. Carter was listening intently. Annabel wondered what Libby was saying—and what he was thinking.

She got out of her car and slammed the door.

The sound made Carter look over at her. He grinned at her and opened the door of the Blazer. "Come on. We'll have to ask your mother," Annabel heard him say to Libby.

"Okay," Libby replied. "But if you manage, I'll be your slave forever. I'll get your laundry so clean, it will blind you."

Annabel decided to ignore the "slave forever" line. It did not bear discussing. Nor did she say, "Ask me what?"

Seventeen years and eight months of motherhood had taught her that there was no use asking for trouble. Unencouraged, it found her soon enough.

"Carter says he'll take us to Boston a week from Saturday," Leif told her without preamble. "So Libby can go shopping, and after we can go to the Red Sox game. Can we go, Ma? Huh? Can we?"

"Leif!" Libby looked as if she'd like to strangle him.

It wasn't Leif Annabel wanted to strangle. She felt as if she'd taken a blow to the gut.

"Boston?" she said to Carter. "You want to take them to Boston? You asked if they'd like to go with you to Boston?"

"No," Carter corrected mildly. "They want to go to Boston, and they said you don't. I said I'd take them if you like."

Annabel didn't like.

She didn't want her children going into Boston. Not with her, not without her. She was doing her absolute best to raise them the way she thought they ought to be raised, and that didn't include forays into Boston where their heads could be turned by things that didn't matter, where their minds could be swayed by people who didn't have their best interests at heart.

She opened her mouth to say so and knew she couldn't. Not to Carter.

Carter took the greatest pleasure in making mincemeat of her at every opportunity. Carter thought she was a reactionary, granola-crunching leftover hippie. He wouldn't understand. Not a bit.

"Tell you what," he said after a moment when she didn't reply. "Why don't we just go in and have muffins or doughnuts or whatever, and you can think about it."

"Please, Ma?" Leif looked at her with absolute longing in his eyes.

Annabel's jaw clenched.

"Leif." Libby nailed his shin with her toe. "Shut up."

Annabel stood straight and waited for Carter to add his pressure to theirs, waited for all three of them to gang up on her. He didn't speak.

Instead he took her elbow, steering her gently toward the brightly lit shop front. "Come on. Let's eat."

Annabel ate. She sat there, determinedly chewing her muffin, waiting, marshaling her arguments. But while Leif continued to look at her with beseeching intensity, Libby held her tongue, and Carter didn't talk about it at all.

In fact, he seemed to have forgotten all about it. He regaled them with tales of his first attempts to sell muffins at his health-food store. Muffins, he insisted, that were made from grass clippings, soybeans and banana peels.

"Very high in potassium," he told them.

He told the story with such seriousness that Leif and Libby were taken in completely. Annabel sat back, choking on her own muffin, and tried not to laugh.

She shouldn't encourage him, she told herself. He didn't need an appreciative audience. But she didn't think what she did would make any difference. Carter MacKenzie would always do whatever he pleased.

"Even Ma wouldn't eat one of those," Leif said, then looked at her. "Would you, Ma?"

"Oh, I don't know," Annabel said. "I think they sound rather good."

"As good as the one you're eating now?" Carter asked.

"I don't know if I'd say that."

"Let's see." And before she could respond, he reached out and drew her hand with muffin in it toward his mouth. His lips touched her fingers. She felt the faint scrape of his teeth against her hand. She snatched it away at once.

For a second their eyes met, and Annabel was surprised that Carter's eyes slid away as quickly as hers.

"I don't know," he said at length, his voice rough through the mouthful of muffin. "I think I actually like the ones I sold better."

Annabel, fingers still tingling, dropped the rest of hers on her plate, then wiped the crumbs off her hand on the napkin. "I'm not surprised," she said somewhat stiffly.

Leif, who had watched it all with consummate interest, spoke up. "So, Ma, what do you think about—"

"—a bite of a doughnut?" Carter cut in before Leif could finish.

It didn't matter. Annabel knew what he was going to ask. "No, thank you," she said.

"But, Ma—"

Carter dug into his pocket and came up with a couple of quarters. "Go play a video game and let your mother eat her muffin in peace."

Leif started to protest, when suddenly he winced and bent to rub his shin. He shot Libby a hard glance. "Okay," he muttered.

"Oh, look," Libby said with great heartiness. "There're Tina and Vicky."

Tina and Vicky, as far as Annabel could see, had been there since they'd walked in. But Libby pushed back her chair. "I just want to go talk to them for a few minutes." And she was gone.

Carter and Annabel sat at the table alone.

"Very clever," Annabel said. "They know I'll say no to them, so they've conned you into doing the asking."

Carter didn't pretend not to know what she was talking about. "Are you going to say no?" He didn't sound challenging, just curious.

"Of course I am."

He shifted in his chair, leaning back comfortably, one arm resting along the back of the chair Leif had vacated. "Why?"

"Because they don't need to go to Boston!"

"You're right," he said. "They don't." He pushed some pumpkin-muffin crumbs around his plate with his forefinger, then licked his finger.

Annabel watched him irritably. She wanted to eat her own muffin crumbs, but she could still feel the touch of his lips on her hand. There was no way on earth she was bringing that hand up to her mouth. Even if he agreed with her about Libby and Leif and Boston.

"They have everything they need in life right here," she went on as if he'd contradicted her. "There're shops here. Clothes. Tapes. Posters. Everything a teenager could possibly want. And Leif can listen to the game on the radio. Or see it on television."

Carter nodded again.

"It's important for them to learn to bloom where they're planted," Annabel said after a moment, knowing she sounded like a sixties' slogan even as she said it. "Boston isn't necessary!"

"No." He cocked his head and smiled slightly. "But it can be fun."

Annabel glared at him.

"I'd forgotten how much," he said almost wistfully. "It's been ages since I went to a football game. And I always used to hate 'em because I always had to go. But tonight I liked it." He looked up to meet her gaze, and she was surprised by the guilelessness in his eyes. "I'd like to go to a baseball game like that."

"So go," Annabel muttered.

"It'd be more fun to go with someone. Someone who wanted to go. Someone who didn't think I should be the first baseman," he added wryly.

"Someone thought you should have been?"

"My father. He was a sports freak. He was good at it."

Though it remained unspoken, Annabel heard the admission that Carter wasn't. It surprised her.

"I know Boston can be fun," she conceded, out of sorts, remembering in spite of herself exactly how much fun it could be.

On the far side of the room she could hear the zing and ping of Leif playing the video game. Nearer she could hear Libby's eager laughter and Tina's squeal. Her children were fine, right here, both of them.

"I thought you'd be at the game tonight," Carter said after a moment.

"I don't like football."

"Yeah. I remember Libby saying so. But I thought you'd be there anyway because she was cheering."

Annabel straightened, lifted her chin and looked down her nose at him. "Are you implying that I'm a bad mother because I didn't come to a football game?"

He shook his head. "You have the greatest kids I've ever met. They're bright, funny and independent. And I think they owe it all to you. You let them make their own choices in spite of the way you feel."

The video game whizzed and banged, the cash register whirred. Annabel didn't hear a thing. All sound but the echo of his words seemed to stop. She stared at him.

Carter lifted a quizzical brow. He cocked his head and returned her stare.

"Damn," Annabel muttered under her breath.

"What's that?"

"You know very well what I said. I said *damn*." She grimaced wryly. "Isn't this what's known as being hoist by my own petard?"

Carter's mouth quirked into a grin. "And are you?"

She pursed her lips, annoyed, outfoxed, impressed at how neatly he had done it. "What do you think?" she grumbled.

He smiled. "That you're a good mother, Annabel Archer."

"How's the roof?" Jack asked Frances when he got home.

Frances looked up from her computer and gave him a bright smile. "Carter's doing it."

"Give me a break."

"He is. I called this afternoon and talked to him. He was on top of the roof even as we spoke."

"The wonder of cordless telephones," Jack marveled. He kissed her, then crossed the room and flopped down on the sofa, beat. "And was Annabel up there with him?"

"Well, no. But that's hardly unexpected. You can't make wreaths on top of a roof."

"I'll bet he hasn't even seen her since the first night."

"Of course he has. That's why he's doing the roof."

Jack's brows drew together. "Say what?"

"So he has the excuse of staying longer," Frances said patiently. "Honestly, Jack." She shook her head. Sometimes men were so dim.

CARTER KNEW what was missing in his life. He knew what he wanted: Libby and Leif.

He wondered if Annabel would trade him.

Would she consider his stereo a fair swap? Or would he have to throw in his Blazer and the custom-built dining-room set Nick Granatelli had made for him, as well?

He knew they wouldn't come cheap.

He knew, if he was honest, they wouldn't come at all.

Annabel Archer had what he wanted. He didn't stand a prayer of getting them.

He could always marry her, he supposed. That was about the only way he could see getting them.

He wondered what she'd say if he suggested it.

Most likely she wouldn't say anything, just laugh.

Even that wouldn't be so bad, he thought now, hunkering down on the roof, feeling the warmth of an Indian-summer sun on his bare back. He liked Annabel Archer's laugh.

She ought to do it more often. She was far too serious, too intense. Like his father.

No, not really.

She cared about her children, her friends, her pets. She tried to take care of them all. He remembered what Frances had said about her being a marshmallow. He was beginning to believe it.

He wondered what had made her so resilient, so independent, so necessarily tough. He wanted to ask her. He knew she'd never tell him. No more than she'd ever trade her kids for all the accoutrements of his fast-lane life.

"You want kids? Go have your own," she'd tell him.

And he knew she wouldn't be interested in going through all that again. He knew she wouldn't be interested in him.

Hadn't she, for God's sake, given him a list of eligible women?

MARILEE NEWMAN was like a breath of fresh air. Bright, articulate, funny. She left the first three on Annabel's list in the shade.

He called on the pretext of wanting some advice about property he was considering for purchase. It seemed smarter than saying that Frances had raved about her. She was, according to Eb, one of those lawyers who end up owning the county because they have their fingers in every real-estate pie.

The only drawback was, if it was true, his father would have loved her.

They made a date for dinner on the following Sunday. "Let's combine business and pleasure," he said.

Marilee agreed enthusiastically.

Carter looked forward to it avidly. Eb had said she was "a looker," too. He wondered if she liked children, if she had any of her own.

He tried to think about Marilee, about what sort of questions he could ask about real estate that would make him sound knowledgeable. He ended up thinking about how to explain the use of the two-point conversion to Leif and the virtues of subtlety in eye makeup to Libby. He dreamed about their mother.

THE TRIP TO BOSTON was better than he'd dared to hope. Even liking Libby and Leif, even wishing that they were his, he knew he hadn't spent a lot of time with them. Over the long haul he might hate them. They might hate *him*.

It was great.

They were, among other things, a damned sight more entertaining and fun to be with than Tracey or Patty or Beth Hayes. Leif was such an amazing combination of innocence and knowledge, of fact and opinion, that Carter found himself asking question after question just to enjoy that boy's candid responses.

And when Libby forgot she was trying to be a seductive teenage femme fatale and was her normally exuberant naive self, he was equally charmed.

He relaxed in their company, having a far better time with them, he realized, then he'd had not only with Tracey and Patty and Beth, but better than he'd had with any woman he'd dated since Diane.

He took Libby to an area of trendy boutiques, then stepped back and watched her set forth. She dragged both him and Leif from shop to shop, oohing and ahhing, trying first this piece, then that one.

But she wasn't easily parted from her money. She was, he saw quite soon, her mother's daughter. She studied things carefully, examining shirts and sweaters, hats and wallets, necklaces and earrings. She weighed this tape against that one, even asking Leif's opinion once or twice.

"I want to think about it," she said at last. So they went to an arcade where Leif zeroed in on the video games. He and Libby found out one of Carter's weaknesses. He could actually get intense when he played Double Dragon II.

"You're good at it," Leif said, amazed when Carter's initials made it into the top-five high scorers.

"Don't tell your mother," Carter grinned. "Come on." He herded them toward the door. "We've got to make tracks if we're going to get to the game on time."

"Wait!" Libby grabbed his hand. "Let's get our photos taken."

It was one of those four-photos-for-a-dollar machines that spewed them out in a matter of minutes. Carter shrugged. "Why not?"

Libby orchestrated the whole thing, arranging the three of them in the booth, putting in the money, then leaning back between them, all of them grinning and mugging for the camera, then shifting facial expressions with each one.

"I'll wait for them," Carter said when they were finished. "You go back and get what you want."

She ended up with three tapes, two T-shirts and an outrageously floppy felt hat that somehow suited her coltish charm.

"What do you think?" she asked Carter, who walked in with the pictures as she was trying it on.

He gave her a thumbs-up. "You look sensational."

"What about my mom?"

"She'd look sensational, too."

Libby punched him. "You know what I mean."

He did and told her that he was sure her mother would think it was great. But he'd meant what he said. The hat would suit Annabel to a *T*.

They got to the Sox game as the first inning began. Leif was in seventh heaven from the moment they'd arrived.

"Oh, man! Isn't this great?" he said at the first glimpse he caught of the field. And once they'd descended the steps to their seats twelve rows back on the first-base side, he kept turning to Carter, then to Libby, his eyes glowing, his grin enormous. "I'm seein' the Red Sox. Right up front. I can't believe it."

Carter lounged back against his box seat and smiled.

"Carter?" Libby tapped him on the shoulder.

He turned and she handed him a small paper bag.

"I would have wrapped it," she said, "but I didn't have time or the paper."

He stared at the bag. "What is it?"

"Open it."

He did. Carefully. Slowly. Unfolding the bag, then shaking it slightly. The black sport-style wallet Libby had been examining in the shop lay in his hand. He opened it up. In the first pocket she had put one of their pictures.

The three of them, jammed together, grinning their heads off.

They looked like a family. He swallowed hard.

"I just wanted to say thanks," Libby said. She gave him a shy smile.

He looked up, met her gaze, felt his throat tighten and wondered if he gave Annabel fifty-million dollars and his soul whether she'd think it a fair exchange. "Thank you," he said softly. "I'll cherish it."

"It isn't much, but I just wanted to tell you that . . . you remember those fortune cookies? Well, you did it. You gave me my heart's desire."

WHERE WERE THEY?

It was nearly two in the morning. There was no reason—no *good* reason—they shouldn't have been home hours ago. They were supposed to have gone shopping first, then to the Red Sox game, then come home.

Even stopping for dinner on the way, they should have arrived no later than 11:00 p.m.

The game had got over before 5:00. She'd watched the whole thing on television and had ended up with a lopsided wreath as a result. But the lopsided wreath was the least of her worries right now.

Where were they?

She knew it had been a mistake, knew she shouldn't have let them go.

"What can I bring you?" Carter had asked when they'd left this morning at dawn.

"Them," she'd told him. "Safe."

And Carter had said, "Scout's honor." She doubted if Carter had a passing acquaintance with any sort of honor at all.

"Where are they?" she asked Goliath for the umpteenth time.

Goliath chirped mournfully and wove between her legs, rubbing his head on her calf. Annabel reached down and plucked him up into her arms, crooning along with Waylon, who had been keeping her company for the past hour and a half.

He wasn't doing as good a job as he usually did. It was one thing to have been done wrong by and to survive. It was quite another to feel so helpless, so alone.

Libby and Leif were all she had in the world. And they were missing.

"They aren't missing," she told herself aloud. "They're just late."

But being late was enough. It scared her. They were the center of her universe, the reason for her being.

After Mark's death she'd had to fight her instincts every time one of them wanted to go out of her sight. If they were close by she'd believed she could protect them. But in her heart she'd known that wasn't true.

She hadn't been able to save Mark. She'd been right there, less than twenty feet from him, and she hadn't been able to save him.

No one could have—except the man who'd been drinking the day he'd roared down the highway on the wrong side of the road. If only he hadn't come around the curve just then.... If only Mark hadn't seen that nest of baby cardinals and wanted a closer look.

Annabel had been over all those "if onlys" a hundred times—a thousand times—before. She couldn't change the past. She had learned to live with it.

She just didn't think she could stand to live with it ever happening again.

"Please, God, no," she whispered now, a sudden awful vision of another such driver out on the road tonight, of Carter momentarily distracted, of...

She fought the vision, fought her memories. She felt cold, her hands clammy, her throat constricted.

A flicker of light swept across the living room.

Headlights.

Annabel ran to the door and flung it open as the Blazer came to a stop in front of the house.

"Where have you been?" Even with relief flooding her, Annabel still couldn't mask the sound of panic in her voice. She practically flew toward the car.

Carter looked surprised. "We stopped to eat. We got to talking...."

"Talking? I thought you were dead!"

"I told you I'd take care of them. We weren't in a big hurry. You didn't say..."

"I should have said," Annabel said tersely. She peered past him in the dark. She could see Leif sound asleep in the front seat. Libby was curled in the back, totally oblivious.

"Come on," she said to them now. "Lib! Leif! You're home! Let's go. Say thank you to Mr. MacKenzie and come in the house!"

They came awake slowly, muttering and stretching. Libby uncurled slowly. Carter stood rigidly by the door.

"Mr. MacKenzie?" His voice was low and hard, questioning her.

Annabel ignored him. "Leif! Come on!"

Leif groaned and opened the door. He looked at her blearily and stumbled out. Libby followed, gathering bags in her arms as she went.

"Thank you, Carter," she said and hugged him around the packages in her arms. "It was the most wonderful day of my life. It really was."

"Mine, too," Leif said. And even he reached out and gave Carter a hug.

Annabel stared at them. She remembered her fears and felt a pain deep within, a loss, a panicky sense of not being in control. "Go on to bed," she said sharply.

She waited to speak until the front door had shut behind them. Then she turned to Carter. "Thank you for taking them." She kept her voice steady and well modulated, her furious panic controlled. "Good night."

He took three steps, caught her arm and pulled her back around to face him. "You were frightened."

Annabel tried to pull away from him. He held on. "It's late. It's very late."

"We were having a good time. We stopped for dinner in Hanover. We got to talking. They're great kids." His mouth curved in a wistful smile. "The best."

"Yes." She didn't want to discuss it. It was over. They were safe. Her world was intact. She managed a thin smile. "Thank you for taking them." She turned to go, but he didn't let her loose.

"Why were you so scared?"

"I told you. It got to be so late. I envisioned disasters. It's a part of the package that comes with parenthood. Protectiveness. Panic. All the best parents do it. I suppose I'm a bit worse than most. They're all I have." She looked away, embarrassed by her confession.

"I understand. I'm sorry."

She looked up at him, startled. She hadn't expected an apology. Not from him.

"I was having too good a time to bring them back," he confessed. "Look." He pulled out the wallet and showed it to her, opening it so she could see the picture. "Libby gave it to me."

Annabel just stared at it. It was so warm, so unposed, so natural. The three of them—Carter and Libby and Leif—with their arms around each other and big grins on their faces. She closed her eyes.

She wanted . . .

No. She didn't. She couldn't.

"Very nice," she managed.

"Thanks for sharing them with me," Carter said quietly.

She smiled slightly. "You're welcome."

"I really am sorry."

"It's all right. You didn't realize. . . ."

"No."

"You will." Her eyes met his. "When you have a child."

WHEN YOU HAVE A CHILD. . . .

And there was wishful thinking for you, Carter thought as he lay in bed and stared at the ceiling.

He thought about Libby and about Leif. He thought about Jason. He thought about the joys and trials of parenthood. He thought about his own father and what a consummate mess that had been.

For years he hadn't wanted a child, hadn't wanted to wish his sort of childhood on anyone.

But now...

He thought about Diane marrying Nick and about all his dreams that had shattered along the way.

He thought about Tracey Thingummy and Patty Whosits. He thought about Beth Hayes and, before then, the legions of women he'd dated with no thought beyond a night's fun and games.

He thought about Milly telling him that he needed to figure out what was missing.

"Oh, yeah, Mil," he said softly into the darkness as he rolled over onto his side and hugged a pillow against his chest. "I know."

But what good did it do?

IT WAS BARELY LIGHT when something woke him.

A sound.

Not birds. Not a truck changing gears on the hill. Not Arnold having his way with a nanny.

Something high-pitched. Intermittent at first. Then louder. Stronger.

Carter frowned, stretched and sat up. "What the hell?" he muttered, rubbing his eyes, raking his fingers through his hair. He glanced at the clock. It was 6:30.

He got to his feet, pulled on a pair of the briefs Libby had so painstakingly laundered for him, then a pair of cord jeans.

He stumbled barefoot and shirtless down the stairs.

It was louder now. Furious. Turning into a full-blown wail.

Wail?

Carter flung open the front door.

There was a baby in a box on the porch.

Chapter Six

Carter blinked. Shook his head. Closed his eyes and opened them again.

There was a baby in a box on the porch.

Yelling its head off.

Waving its arms in the air.

Not a hell of a bad idea, Carter thought.

He edged closer, half expecting it to vanish. It didn't. It screamed on.

He was right next to it now, peering down into its red, enraged face, marveling at the noise that broke the stillness of the morning.

"Hey," he said softly, hunkering down beside the box, rocking it gently. Then, more loudly, "Hey, baby. Hey, it's okay."

But clearly, from the baby's perspective, things were far from okay. It screwed up its tiny face and continued to scream.

"Come on, now," Carter said, fumbling with its blankets, trying to get a secure grip on it before he lifted it into his arms. He thanked God for all the times he'd held Jason, rocked him, soothed him.

If it weren't for Jack and Frances's son, he'd have no idea at all what to do with a screaming infant.

The moment he lifted the child, there was silence, then a faint hiccuping sob. Dark eyes opened to regard him curiously. And looking down into them, Carter smiled.

"It's okay," he said again, hugging the blanket-wrapped baby gently against his bare chest, rocking back and forth on his heels, swaying slightly. "Shh, now. Everything's going to be fine. I don't know who you are or what the devil you're doing camping out on the porch, but we'll figure it out. Don't you worry. Everything's going to be fine."

The baby was totally still while he was speaking. The moment the words dried up, the crying began again.

Carter muttered under his breath. "You're hungry, aren't you? Starving probably." Still holding the baby close with one hand, he squatted again, and groped around in the box, which had been padded with blankets into a sort of makeshift bassinet. He found a bottle, happily still somewhat full, and a piece of paper.

There was rather a lot of writing on it. Loopy and girlish from the look of it, and far too much to do more than glance at in the dimness of the early-morning light. He stuffed it into the waistband of his jeans.

The baby began another long wail.

"Hang on, kiddo." He noted two paper bags sitting on the porch swing, which, he hoped, would hold the rest of the child's worldly possessions. He'd find out later. First things first. Tucking the bottle under his chin and wrestling the box under his one free arm, he carried the baby, the box and the bottle into the house.

There he dumped the box unceremoniously to the floor, then carried the baby and the bottle over to the rocker. He sank down into it, nestled the baby securely in the curve of his arm and offered it the bottle.

Blessed silence—broken only by the occasional whimpery hiccup and a soft slurp-slurp.

"There now, that's better, isn't it?" He smiled down at the unblinking dark eyes regarding him. "Told you so, didn't I?"

There was another soft hic . . . a tiny sniff.

"Right. Now let's read this and see if we can find out who you are and how you got into this mess."

He pulled the paper out and spread it on his thigh. Then, reaching over, he flipped on the table lamp, bathing them in soft light.

He was right about the handwriting. Whoever had written it even used tiny circles to dot her *i*'s and swooping curves crossed all the *t*'s. "Dear Frances," he read. "This is Conan."

He looked down doubtfully at the child in his arms. "Conan?"

The baby gave an audible sniff, then sucked on.

Carter considered the tiny hands, the cherubic cheeks, the dark downy hair. Well, maybe, he conceded. Even with a name like Conan, you had to start somewhere.

"Okay, Conan," he said. "Now we know who you are and who was expected to receive you. Let's see what else we can find out." He read on. "He was born May 24th. He's the most wonderful baby in the world, and that's why I'm bringing him to you." Carter doubted that Frances would agree. Jason was the most wonderful baby in the world to her. He kept reading. "You remember me telling you about Jerry Higgins? He's Conan's father."

Carter looked down at the baby again. "Conan *Higgins?*"

Conan blinked solemnly.

"Oh, brother." He continued reading. "Him and me are trying to work things out, but it isn't easy. He just got laid off and he took off on me. I can't take care of Conan by myself. I work all day as a waitress and at night I am an usher at a theater. Even with tips, I can't hardly make enough for Conan and me to live on. I can't pay anybody to take care of him. My mother would of, but she got sick last month. You know how bad the rest of my family is, so you know I got nobody else. Just you. I'm trying to find Jerry. When we get settled, I'll come and get Conan. I will miss him just awful but I know he will be happy with you. Love, Maeve. P.S. I have listed what Conan can eat on the other side. I will love you forever for taking him."

Carter glanced at the other side, then let the paper fall from his fingers. He considered the words, the child, the implications.

"God," he breathed. It was pure prayer. Nothing else.

He eased the blanket farther away from the baby's face and looked down at the child in his arms, so tiny, so trusting.

Conan Higgins. A child with more baggage than it seemed possible for a four-month-old to have—a child who was supposed to be loved and cared for by Frances who was hundreds of miles away; a child who, at the moment at least, was totally and completely dependent upon him.

"Be careful what you pray for," he remembered his father threatening when he was a child. "You just might get it."

The old man was probably laughing his head off right now.

But Carter didn't have any time to spare thoughts for his father. "What do you think, Conan?" he asked the baby. "You think we can batch it till your mom gets back?"

Conan looked at him, reached out a hand and waved it uncertainly toward Carter's face. Then it fell again, coming to rest against Carter's hand, wrapping around Carter's fingers. Holding on.

For two hours and twelve minutes, give or take a second or two, Carter reigned in supreme and confident pseudo-fatherhood, smiling down at the infant in his lap.

Then Conan woke up.

"I know you're wet," Carter said to the screaming infant. It was basic psychology, right? Acknowledge the problem. It was no great deduction. Conan had leaked right through diaper, sleeper and blanket to leave a warm wet spot on Carter's lap.

Carter scratched at the spot, adjusting his jeans as best he could. Then he carried the baby upstairs and hunted frantically through Jason's bedroom for something to remedy Conan's situation, finding, at last and to his great relief, half a dozen disposable diapers in a bag at the bottom of the closet.

"All's well," he told Conan. "Supplies have been uncovered."

He thanked heaven—and Jack and Frances—for his knowledge about diapering babies. In scant moments Conan was clean and dry. A quick search of the bags on the porch revealed clean, dry sleepers and playsuits. With slightly less dexterity he wrestled Conan into one of them.

"Now," he told the baby, "you wait here while I change." He laid Conan on his back in Jason's crib. Conan screamed.

"All right. Never mind. Come with me."

Conan didn't scream when Carter put him down in the middle of the unmade bed. He looked around curiously, then let his gaze follow Carter as he rummaged through the neat stacks of laundry Libby had arranged on top of Jack's dresser.

Carter stripped off his jeans and briefs, washed off, dressed again, this time adding a sweatshirt before he sat down next to the baby to put on his socks and shoes.

"So what do you think?" he said. "Should we call Frances and tell her?"

But even as he said it, he knew he wouldn't. Not yet.

There was nothing Frances could do. Oh, perhaps she could reach this Maeve girl. Now that he thought about it, Carter seemed to recall having met her once. She was one of several girls Frances had known during her teaching days in Boston, girls she'd stayed in touch with, had tried to give some options to.

Obviously Maeve had made her own choices.

It was equally obvious that Maeve wasn't where she could be reached yet, even if she were headed back to Boston. And she might not be. For all Carter knew she could be headed in the opposite direction entirely—hot in pursuit of the peripatetic Jerry Higgins, with whom she hoped to "work things out."

"We'll just hang loose a little while, buddy," Carter told the baby, picking him up and laying him on his own knees so that they faced each other. "Maybe you can help me with the roof. 'Never too young to learn the ropes,'" he quoted in a tone so like his own father's it made him cringe. "But you don't have to be a roofer if you don't want to be," he added and bent to kiss the baby's nose.

There was no way, Carter soon discovered, to put the baby in his box on the roof. There was also no way he could leave Conan on the ground in his box while he proceeded with the shingling.

But that was only one of his problems. He also had to figure out how to fix oatmeal with Conan in one arm, then eat it with the baby trying to grab the spoon.

How the hell did mothers and fathers, whichever stayed home with Junior all day, cope?

How had Annabel done it?

His respect for her was growing by leaps and bounds.

He could, of course, call her and ask her. But he didn't want to. Maybe he was too stubborn. Maybe he had too much pride. But he didn't want to go running for help at the first sign of difficulty.

"We can manage, can't we, fella?" he asked Conan.

Conan burped.

Carter considered the matter, and tried to visualize Frances with Jason. Of course, he knew Jason had slept sometimes. But just as clearly he knew that Jason had demanded his share of Frances's time and attention. And during all that time and all that attention, surely at least occasionally she'd had the use of her arms. How else could she have written two more books?

She'd had some sort of sling that snuggled Jason against her body in sort of reverse papoose fashion, keeping him close and leaving her hands free.

Well, Maeve hadn't provided any such gear, but Carter was nothing if not resourceful.

"I can create something useful out of damned little," his father had boasted to him as, throughout Carter's formative years, one enterprise after another prospered under strict MacKenzie tending.

"So can I," Carter muttered, less to Conan than to himself. He scavenged through Frances's drawers for material that would do the trick.

But he couldn't work on it immediately because Conan was awake and wanted attention.

"You're spoiled. You know that?" Carter told the baby in his arms.

They had a bottle of juice and some cereal. Carter took him down to see the goats and up the hill to inspect the sheep. He came back with the intention of putting Conan down for a morning nap.

But Conan wasn't sleepy. He batted the bottle out of Carter's hands, he wriggled in Carter's arms, he giggled, he bounced.

That was when Carter had gone deep into his subconscious to dredge up every nursery rhyme he knew.

So far they'd done at least twenty run-throughs of "The Grand Old Duke of York," twice that many of "Pat-a-Cake" and "This Little Pig Went to Market."

"How about '99 Bottles of Beer on the Wall'?" he asked the cheerful cherub.

Conan grinned at him.

Carter grimaced in return. He shifted in the chair, feeling itchy and irritable. Was parenthood paling so quickly?

But when he acknowledged the problem, it seemed less one of parenthood than of his jeans.

They hadn't felt quite right for a couple of hours. He moved to ease the scratchy discomfort. It didn't help.

He sighed and got back out of the chair again, pacing around the room, showing Conan the photographs on the sideboard. "This is Jack," he said. "And this is Frances. This is Jason. You'd like him." He went on at length for another half an hour, then he carried Conan upstairs and sat down in the rocker in Jason's room.

This time Conan went out like a light.

And this time Carter didn't sit solemnly for almost two hours admiring the child in his arms. He got up and carefully settled the baby on his stomach in the crib. Then he tucked a tiny quilt around him and, with one last backward glance, he stole out of the room.

He'd never been a whiz with a needle and thread. Still, he'd been a bachelor living on his own for half of his life. He could sew on a button if he needed to. The principle was the same, wasn't it? How hard could it be?

Of course, he couldn't try out his invention until Conan woke up, but once he did, the baby fit neatly and securely in the sling.

Carter grinned down at the silky hair and the warm cheek pressed against his chest. "Look, kid. Both hands." He waved them in front of Conan's face.

He climbed up on the roof that way. It was a little harder going up the ladder. And once he got there, he had to make sure he had all the shingles, nails and tools he needed before he settled down, because he couldn't scramble around with the ease he'd been used to.

But it worked!

"Take that, Dad," he muttered and hammered a shingle into place.

That's where they were when Leif appeared that afternoon.

He waved at Carter from the top of the hill, then loped down and climbed the ladder. It wasn't until he reached the top that he stopped and stared. "Cripes! It is a baby! Where'd you get it?"

Carter positioned another shingle. "On the porch." He took in Leif's disbelieving expression and added, "Would I lie to you?"

Leif grinned. "Maybe. Whose is it?"

"Somebody named Maeve."

"I know her! She used to come to see Frances. She was sorta cool." He peered again at the baby. "Cripes. She's like only a year older'n Libby. How come she brought it to you?"

"She thought she was bringing him to Frances. She's got some problems to work out."

"You gonna keep him?"

"For now."

"You know what to do with babies?" Leif was skeptical.

"More or less."

"You're pretty brave, Carter. Or pretty stupid."

Carter grinned ruefully. "Thanks."

"What's his name?"

"Conan."

Leif laughed and took another long look at the baby, then at Carter. "You're gonna have your hands full. Bring him over tonight. Show Ma. She'll flip."

"I've got a date." Even as he said it, he realized he also had a problem. Wondering if Marilee Newman liked children had suddenly become more than an academic question. He wondered what she'd think of going out as a threesome.

"Who with?"

Carter told him.

Leif's eyes got big. "Wow. She's foxy."

"She's what?"

Leif reddened. "Aw, you know. She's got big...an' she's real...and her eyes..."

"It's business."

"I thought you said it was a date."

"Date to talk about business."

"Yeah, sure." Leif was having none of it. "So, who's baby-sitting?"

"I haven't thought about it," he admitted.

"I will—at our house. If Ma's there. Ten bucks. What'd'ya say?"

"*Ten* bucks! You shyster!"

"Children are our most precious resource." Leif gave him a cheeky grin.

"I took you to Boston and I didn't charge your mother a cent!"

"She gave me money and told me not to impose on you."

"I bought your dinner and your ticket to the game."

"Yeah. Well, okay. Tonight it's on the house." Leif cocked his head. "Did you really think I was gonna charge you?"

"I never know what you Archers are going to do," Carter grumbled.

"Campbell. I'm a Campbell." Leif corrected. "Ma's an Archer."

Of course. A woman as stubborn and independent as Annabel Archer wouldn't ally herself with any man. Carter shifted irritably and scratched. Conan began to grumble a little, sucking on his fist, making a grizzling sound.

"I think he's hungry," Leif said.

"Probably," Carter agreed. "Let's call it a day."

"You wanta come see the fort me and Roger built by the old mill?"

"Not today. Gotta feed my friend here."

"Tomorrow?"

"Yeah, okay."

All the time he was mashing a banana for Conan, he considered his options: he could call off his meeting with Marilee; he could take Conan with him; he could get Leif—and thereby Annabel—to baby-sit.

He eliminated the second at once. Even he wasn't a big enough idiot to take a baby on a first date. He set Leif to feeding Conan while he went to call Marilee.

But she was in a meeting.

"May I take a message?" the secretary asked.

Carter couldn't imagine explaining over the phone that he'd come up with a baby overnight. He sighed. So much for options.

"Leif," he said. "You've got a job."

"WHAT DO YOU MEAN, you're baby-sitting for Carter?" The thought stopped her cold. Annabel knew Leif wasn't kidding. She could see that from the expression on his face.

"He found a baby on the porch this morning. It's Maeve's."

"Oh, heavens." But her feelings of sympathy for Maeve were overshadowed by a shaft of pure relief that the child was not Carter's.

"He's got a date tonight," Leif went right on. "With Marilee Newman. So we're going to baby-sit. Neat, huh?"

Annabel sat down.

Leif looked at her oddly. "You don't mind, do you, Ma?" he asked a little worriedly now.

She dredged up a smile. "Of course not." What she minded was that Carter was going out with Marilee Newman.

She tried to talk herself out of caring. Why should she? And why shouldn't he? she asked herself. It had been her own idea, for heaven's sake. She'd given him Marilee's name!

But try as she might, she couldn't face the prospect with complete equanimity. She kept remembering the picture of him with Libby and Leif, kept thinking about how frightened she had been, how tempted she had been the moment he'd come back to throw her arms around him and hang on tight.

No, she thought. Oh, no.

He was going out with Marilee Newman.

She drew a careful breath. "I'm looking forward to it."

She was, too, after a fashion. She was curious about how Carter had handled this unexpected windfall. She remembered saying to him just last night, "When you have a child," never thinking it would be so soon.

Not that it would last, of course. But she knew how much he liked children. She'd seen it with Libby and Leif, with Jason. Marilee Newman was the right age to be thinking about starting a family. She wondered if that was what Carter had in mind.

"Does Carter like the baby?" she asked Leif.

Her son looked at her as if she were out of her mind. "Like him? I guess! He made him this pouch an' everything."

Annabel amused herself with visions of Carter as a marsupial until he arrived on their doorstep, when she found out she wasn't far wrong.

She opened the door to find him standing there in jeans and a crewneck sweater, dark green, the same color as his eyes. His hair was brushed, his loafers shined. And wrapped around his middle was some sort of cloth contraption from which she could see poking out little bits of snugly wrapped baby.

"Amazing," she muttered. He looked so fatherly, so natural.

"What?" Carter sounded defensive.

She shook her head, smiling. "Nothing. Come in. I understand you've become a father."

"Only temporarily." He sounded almost regretful. "He's Maeve's. Did Leif tell you?"

"Yes. But not why she left it with Frances. At least, I presume she intended it for Frances and not you."

"She did. But we're not doing so bad, are we, fella?" Carter bent his head and spoke in a soft voice to the baby.

Annabel, watching him, felt a quickening stab of something—Envy? Jealousy?—she didn't know.

"Maeve and her husband or boyfriend—she doesn't say which—are having some problems and need a little time and space. Hence, Conan. I appreciate you taking him on such short notice."

"I had more notice than you did."

"Yeah, well . . . these things happen."

He didn't seem at all upset by his unexpected fatherhood. In fact, he seemed unwilling to hand the baby over. Only when Annabel asked, "What time is your date?" did he glance at his watch, grimace, then begin undoing the straps.

Annabel moved to help him, easing the baby out of its snug pouch and cradling it in her arms. It felt so familiar, so natural. It had been so long. She stepped away quickly, trying to squelch the urgent maternal feelings growing inside her.

"Leif said he'd take him back over to Frances's at bedtime," Carter was saying. "I brought along some food and a bottle. Also diapers and a clean stretch suit. An extra pair of plastic pants. And a rattle." He put each object in turn on the table.

"You're very thorough."

He gave her a strained smile. "I'm trying. I hope he doesn't give you any trouble."

Annabel shook her head and smiled at the baby in her arms. "He won't."

"You can call me. At Rossi's."

"I doubt if Marilee would appreciate a phone call in the middle of a date."

Carter looked uncomfortable. "It's okay," he insisted. "I hope we won't need to."

"Yeah, well, me, too." He shifted his weight from side to side again, as if something was bothering him.

Didn't he trust her? Annabel wondered. "I do know how to take care of babies, Carter."

He gave her a rueful grin. "Yeah. Better than I do, I'm sure. It's just...just..." He shrugged, hesitated, then backed out the door. "I'll go. Thanks."

Annabel, with the baby, walked him to the door, watched him go down the steps, felt an odd little tugging ache somewhere deep inside her. "No problem," she said. "We'll enjoy it," she said. "Have...a good time."

MARILEE NEWMAN was the woman of his dreams. The one he'd been waiting for all his life. Somewhere back in his subconscious, years ago, he'd dreamed her up—tall, slim, with long blond hair, sculpted cheekbones, classic jawline, full mouth with supremely kissable lips.

She was already at Rossi's when he arrived. Perched on a bar stool, sipping a club soda, her grape-colored wool skirt hiked up just enough to give him a glimpse of a tiny bit of thigh, her wavy hair curving to cup her cheek, she made his heart kick over, made the itch he'd been feeling all day grow worse. And worse yet when she looked him up and down and smiled.

Thank God he hadn't brought Conan. First things first.

He smiled. "Ms. Newman?"

"If we're going to have dinner together, I think you'd better call me Marilee." Her voice was slightly huskier in person than it had been on the phone, less businesslike, more caressing.

And she had a dimple, too, God help him. Just the tiniest indentation in one cheek appeared as she moved to make room for him at the bar.

Carter drew a steadying breath and held out his hand, enjoying to the hilt the warm, firm pressure of hers. "Marilee. I'm glad to meet you. At last."

One curving eyebrow lifted. "At last?"

"I feel as if I've been waiting all my life." If Annabel could hear him, she'd be gagging on her carrot juice.

Marilee laughed. "Better and better. Tell me about this property you want to buy and what you want to do with it. Tell me about you."

Carter could make small talk with the best of them. He was never averse to offering a personal anecdote or two. He ordered a Scotch. They moved from the bar to their table, with Marilee alternately offering sound purchasing advice and at the same time asking Carter questions about his background.

He tried to answer. He kept thinking about Conan. And Annabel. Was he taking his bottle? Would she remember to burp him? Had he left her enough diapers?

"And after Berkeley, what?" Marilee asked him.

"Huh? Oh, I spent a year traveling." Working his way around the globe, taking whatever jobs he could find, infuriating his father who wanted him to come home and get to work.

"Sounds like fun," Marilee said. "You must've been a regular rolling stone."

"I guess." The thought depressed him. He didn't want to roll. He wanted to settle down. He tried to focus on Marilee. She was beautiful, all right. And intelligent. Savvy. Was she really the one?

Had he remembered to give Annabel the jar of peaches?

"—leaving New York?"

"What?" He looked up, startled.

Marilee was looking expectantly at him. "Thought I'd lost you," she chided. "I just wondered if you were really serious about leaving New York."

Was he? He didn't know. He'd always lived in cities. They were comfortable as long as you knew the ropes. But he had to admit he'd rather enjoyed the last week. "I like Boone's Corner," he said, surprising himself.

Marilee smiled at him. "Good."

The food at Rossi's was good, the conversation better. It was serious, yet at times downright playful. Clearly Marilee Newman wasn't averse to a little flirtation. Nor, it seemed, was she averse to getting to know Carter better.

He tried his best to get to know her. It was perverse, he told himself, that when the right woman finally came along, he would find himself preoccupied by a baby and the world's most irritating woman. He shifted uncomfortably, trying to ease the continual itch that had been plaguing him all day.

He must have done something right, though, for after dinner, when he thought she'd want to hop in her car and leave, instead she suggested that they continue their conversation at an inn.

"There's a great piano bar. We could forget real-estate law and just talk. Like you said—" her lower lip jutted slightly, tempting him "—get to know each other."

"You don't have to be in court early?" he asked.

"Not until ten."

So they went to the piano bar. The conversation all but stopped, however. The piano was soft and moody and, the moment they got there, Marilee took his hand and said, "Let's dance."

What was a guy to do?

She was tall and she fit into his arms as if she belonged there. Her lips were bare inches from his.

Kiss me, they urged him. And he would have, wanting to see if her kisses would set him on fire the way Annabel's had. But the gentle press of her body against his set off a fiery feeling that wouldn't quit.

Carter was used to fiery feelings when it came to beautiful women, but this one was getting out of hand.

It had been building all day, nagging, itching, even before his proximity to Marilee. He didn't know what the hell was causing it. He only knew that Marilee made it worse.

She could make it better, too, he thought ruefully. But not tonight.

They danced three dances. He couldn't last any longer.

"I, uh, need to get home," he said when the music finally stopped.

Marilee cocked her head and gave him a teasing smile. "Got to get up early to work on the roof tomorrow?"

Carter flushed. "They're predicting rain in the afternoon." He didn't know whether they were or not.

Marilee sighed. "Fair enough." She picked up her coat from the back of the chair and Carter helped her into it. "Will I see you again?"

"Do you want to?"

"Oh, yes."

He smiled. "Dinner on Wednesday?"

His life would probably be back to normal by Wednesday. Maeve would probably have retrieved Conan by then, and this ridiculous itch—whatever it was—would be gone.

"I'll look forward to it," she said as he walked her to her car.

"Same time, same place?"

"Oh, I know a better place," Marilee said, her dimple returning to tantalize him. "Mine."

Carter wanted to scratch. He gritted his teeth. "Sounds great. I'll bring some wine."

"And you can help cook." The dimple deepened.

"I'll cook with you any day, Miz Newman," he drawled.

She laughed that husky, sexy laugh and blew him a kiss. "Till Wednesday."

ANNABEL WAS NOT sentimental.

She did not cry at weddings. She had let her children race off to kindergarten without a moment's qualm.

And if she'd kept the best of their baby clothes, it was more a matter of frugality and the fear that if she got rid of them, somehow God would find a way to get her pregnant again, than of a need to remember the days when Leif and Libby were so small.

So she couldn't understand this fascination with Conan.

But fascinated she was. Besotted, more like.

Why else would she have insisted on feeding him his bottle when Leif was perfectly capable of doing it? Why else would she have played pat-a-cake when she should have been poking cloves in oranges and saving up money to shingle her house? Why else would she have told Leif that she would carry the baby back to Frances's and stay with him until Carter got back?

Why else, except to recapture those moments when she had felt young and strong, steady and sensible, calm and collected, as if she had all the answers to the meaning of life?

Well, she might be doing it because of Carter.

If she was honest, there was that.

Carter MacKenzie.

She couldn't seem to get away from him. It was odd— annoying—how much time she spent thinking about a man she didn't even want to like.

She owed the whole direction of her life to Carter MacKenzie, and he hadn't a clue. Even now he was oblivious to it, wandering on through his own, dating this woman and that one. Lost, Frances said. Searching, Frances told her.

While he had inadvertently set Annabel on a course toward the best years she'd ever known.

She looked down at Conan, sound asleep in her arms. She stroked his petal-soft cheek and crooned lullabies to him. She remembered Libby as a babe in arms, recalled the chaos that had been her life then, of Mark's despair and flight, and still the comfort and sense of rightness she'd found holding her daughter close late at night.

She thought about Leif, born five years later into very different circumstances, to parents who'd weathered plenty of storms and had found faith in each other again.

She thought about Mark. About loving him and losing him. About finding and losing again.

She thought about the years since. Nine of them. Long years in some ways. Mere hours, in others, it seemed.

She was thirty-six now. Twice the age she'd been when Libby was born. Not twice as smart or twice as clever. Just twice as old.

And, she thought ruefully, sometimes she feared she knew no more about where her life was going than Libby knew about hers.

She knew the folly of dreaming. Of false hopes.

But as she looked down at Conan, snug and secure in her arms, she knew one thing. She had no real regrets. Her father had always expected her to, had waited all these years for her to admit she was wrong, to come back home.

But she hadn't been wrong. She still wasn't.

She had loved Mark. She loved her children. If Mark had lived, there would have been more.

"Babies like you," she said to Conan.

She looked down at the tiny child and a smile curved her mouth. "Just like you."

No, she didn't regret it a bit. She'd do it all over again.

Chapter Seven

Carter took the front steps in one bound, listening, as he had been since he'd opened the door of the Blazer, for sounds of Conan screaming.

All was quiet.

He slowed then, proceeding more cautiously, not wanting to wake the baby—not wanting to wake Leif, either, if the boy had fallen asleep. It was past eleven and high time he was home in bed.

Carter knew he should have called, should have told Leif he'd be late. But he'd had no idea when Marilee had suggested the inn with the piano bar that it would be so far or that it would take so long.

He eased open the door and crept into the entry, slipping off his shoes before he padded into the dimly lit living room.

Annabel was asleep on the couch.

He stopped dead and stared.

She lay with her head pillowed on one arm, her gingery hair spread out against the arm of the couch, her body curled beneath the soft sea-colored shawl. Her lashes lay like half-moons against her cheeks. He'd never noticed before how long and thick her lashes were. He'd never had the chance, he mused. Usually her eyes were wide open and flashing amber fire at him.

But her eyes were shut now, and he allowed himself a moment to appreciate her long-lashed beauty for the first time. He also appreciated her lips, slightly parted, full and soft and reminding him of the night he'd arrived, the night he'd kissed her.

He made a soft, strangled sound. Annabel woke up.

"Oh!" She blinked, sat up, rubbed her eyes and started to stand, but she did so too quickly and she lost her balance, sinking back onto the sofa.

"You okay?"

"Fine." Her voice sounded soft and rusty, quite unlike the customary drill-sergeant responses he expected from her.

He smiled.

"I just fell asleep a moment ago," she said, standing again, this time managing to stay upright. With one foot she was groping around on the floor for her shoes.

"I'm sorry I'm so late."

She stopped groping and gave him a sidelong glance. "I trust you had a good time." Her voice was getting back to normal. Starchy and disapproving.

He stiffened. "I did. I can't figure out why you put her fourth on your list." He tried to sound outraged as he took a step back. He was too susceptible tonight, too much in the mood for things that would never happen. And he itched. Still.

"I put her fourth because I didn't know her, that's all." Annabel found one shoe, stuffed her foot in it, then felt for the other. "I'm glad you liked her," she said tersely.

"You don't sound glad."

Annabel gave an inarticulate mutter. "I'm thrilled." She glanced at her watch. "Good grief. What'd you do, have a seven-course meal?"

"We went dancing. A discreet little piano bar. I didn't know Vermont had such interesting places."

"Trust you to find them." She bent down and was reaching under the sofa for her other shoe. In seconds she'd be gone.

"Did Conan behave?" he asked quickly.

"Oh, yes. He was a lamb. He ate his peaches and drank his bottle. We played games and Leif wrestled with him...." Her starchiness faded even as she spoke.

"Leif wrestled with him?"

"Oh, you know. Little-boy stuff. Lots of noise and not much else. Like you and Jack this summer."

Carter scowled at her. "That was not little-boy stuff."

"Oh, right." Annabel had found her other shoe and was heading for the door.

"I'll walk you home."

"Don't be ridiculous."

"It's close to midnight. You're a woman out alone."

"In the middle of the woods. This is not a discreet piano bar full of men on the make. Who do you think is going to jump me? Arnold?"

"I'll walk you home."

"Don't be an idiot, Carter," she said gruffly. "I'll be fine." And giving his cheek a condescending pat, she opened the door and walked out without looking back.

Carter stared after her. "You're a bossy witch, you know that?"

She turned, grinned, gave him a little wave. "You'd better believe it."

He watched her until she was across the yard and starting up the slope, until he had almost lost her in darkness. "Annabel?"

"What?" Her voice floated back to him.

" . . . Thanks."

HE HAD THIS FAINT mottled red rash in places he'd rather not associate with rashes. He had a baby who thought 2:00 a.m. was playtime. He paced the floor. And hummed. He played the guitar. And sang. He did pat-a-cake and peek-aboo and thought he'd lose his mind.

He tried to focus his thoughts on more pleasant topics: Marilee's throaty laugh and long legs, the way she had smiled at him, had said that next time they'd eat at her place. He remembered far more vividly Annabel asleep under her shawl, Annabel starchy and disapproving, Annabel's spitfire response.

He itched. He scratched.

"Come on, Conan," he pleaded. "We've got a long day tomorrow. Miles and miles of roof."

Finally at 3:00 a.m., when Carter had very nearly given up hope, Conan smiled, closed his eyes and went back to sleep.

"Thank God."

He had a new appreciation of why Jack sometimes looked bleary-eyed in the mornings. He sank back against the cool sheets and shut his eyes, reached down and scratched.

A million impressions kaleidoscoped in his mind, inundating him, spinning around, becoming a whirling mass of emotions, sensations, thoughts. He tried to stop them, order them, sort them: Conan in the box, Conan on the roof, Conan in his arms, smiling; Leif handing him the shingles, Leif feeding the baby; Marilee laughing, Marilee looking deep into his eyes while they danced; Annabel.

In the end, oddly, there was only that one.

Annabel.

"CARTER CALLED," Jack told Frances when she came in from walking Jason in the park.

"Anything new?"

"Two things. First, he's met his idea of the perfect woman."

"Ah." Her smile widened.

Jack grinned. "Her name is Marilee Newman."

"What? Who? Who in heaven's name is Marilee Newman?"

"Some lawyer from Gaithersburg. Annabel gave him her name." He almost laughed at the look on Frances's face.

But then the look changed, became thoughtful, then slyly knowledgeable. Frances nodded her head, smiled smugly.

Jack gave her a worried glance. "What?" he demanded.

"Defense mechanism."

"Huh?"

"Never mind. What's the other bit of news?"

"Oh." He wasn't sure whether he ought to grin about this bit or not. "He's become a father."

Frances just stared.

"Remember Maeve—"

"Maeve?" Frances was shocked. "No! He couldn't have! Carter would never—"

"Relax. *He* didn't do anything. Except find Maeve's baby on the doorstep. *Our* doorstep. She's taken off after her boyfriend or husband or whatever he is, and baby was a burden. She left him for you. Carter's got him.''

Frances grinned. ''I'll bet he's doing fine. Isn't he?''

''As a matter of fact, he seems to be. He was enjoying it.''

''I knew it.''

''You really think they'll be okay? The two of them?'' Jack didn't feel all that confident himself.

''I think they'll be fine.''

''What about Maeve?''

''She's a pretty bright girl. She obviously thinks she can work things out, and if Carter is willing to hang on to the baby while she tries, why not? They deserve a chance. All of them.''

''And you don't think you should maybe...step in? Arrange things?''

''Oh, no.'' Frances shook her head. ''I wouldn't have the faintest idea how things should work out for them.''

''Not like you do with Carter and Annabel?'' Jack teased.

''No,'' she said. ''Not at all like that.''

SO HE'D DINED and danced with Marilee Newman. He liked her. He was probably even taking her out again.

Annabel accompanied all these enthusiastic thoughts by banging her mixing bowls down on the counter and slamming the silverware drawer. She also reached over and changed the tape in her stereo. She'd started with Beethoven, gone on to Waylon before nine, and now at ten-thirty she knew if she was going to get anything done today, she'd moped long enough. She needed stimulation.

''How about this?'' she said to Goliath.

He shot off the counter at the first crash of John Philip Sousa.

"Sorry," she said to his departing tail. "But it's time for desperate measures."

Ten times, at least, she had reached for the phone to call and see how Conan was, to find out if he'd slept through the night, if he'd taken all of his bottle, if he was awake then and, if so, what he was doing.

Nine times, thank heavens, she'd put the receiver down without making the connection. The tenth she made herself dial Aaron Leggett, instead.

"I was wondering," she said without preamble, "if you would like to go see the Woody Allen movie in Gaithersburg tonight?"

Aaron stuttered for at least ten seconds before saying, "S-sure."

"Shall I meet you there?"

"I'll pick you up. We can have dinner."

Annabel thought that dinner might be too much, then thought it might not be nearly enough. "Why not?" she said recklessly.

"See you at five-thirty," Aaron said.

Annabel put the phone down and found that she breathed a little easier. Until five seconds had passed and she found that the sight of Arnie, looking grumpy in the pasture, made her think she should take him down to Frances's. And that made her think about Carter and . . .

"Stop it," she said to herself aloud.

She didn't want to think about Carter. He was well and truly taken care of at last.

He was plenty busy now with Conan and with the roof and with Marilee Newman. He wouldn't be at a loose end. All his available time was taken up.

She needn't worry about him being around disconcerting her anymore. She needn't worry about Frances's meddling.

If she needed to worry about anything, Annabel decided, she needed to worry about why she cared.

ALL DAY it had been getting worse.

The itching.

The scratching.

The rash.

He'd expected to get up in the morning and find it gone. It was still there, less red than when he'd showered the night before, but there, all right, from somewhere just south of his navel down to the tops of his thighs. Carter scowled at it, wondering what Milly would say if he showed it to her.

Probably tell him it was a psychosomatic allergic reaction to fatherhood or some ridiculous thing.

He'd never ask her in any case. He might on occasion bare his soul for Milly's inspection, but he'd be damned if he'd bare the rest of him!

Still, he had to do something. It nagged at him continually, made him quick-tempered and irritable, made it nearly impossible to sit up there and work on the roof for any length of time, made him squirm even when he was stretched out on the sofa giving Conan a bottle.

And every time he checked it, hoping against hope that it was lessening, growing fainter, he found it getting worse. Redder. Blotchier.

Leif came over after school so they could go see the fort he and Roger had built.

"You ready to go?"

The very thought of walking all that way made him wince. "Taking Conan might be a hassle. We could wait until—"

"It's no problem. Not with that sling thing you made. I'll carry him."

"It's almost time for his nap."

Leif stared down at Conan, lying on his back in the middle of a blanket, giggling, wide-eyed. Leif shrugged. "We can wait."

Carter managed a surreptitious scratch, then sighed. "Never mind. We'll go now."

The walk was less than a mile. Another day it would have been marvelous. The trees were at the height of autumn color and the day was clear and bright, warm in the direct sun but blessedly cool in the shade of the trees. They followed a narrow path behind Frances's property, then across the back of Annabel's. They went over three stone walls, up a hillside, along the side of the stream. Leif chattered. Conan gurgled. Carter itched.

He'd never had anything like it save the time he'd been cutting trees on his father's place in New Jersey and had got poison ivy all over his arms. This wasn't poison ivy— not unless he'd been shinnying up trees naked in his sleep.

By the time they got back, he was frantic. He handed Leif a bottle of milk. "Feed him this and put him down in the crib, will you? I'm going to grab a shower."

Still scratching, Carter escaped up the stairs. By the time he came back down, Conan was asleep and Leif was reading a magazine.

"Thought you'd have gone," Carter said, glancing at his watch. "Didn't you say your mother wanted you home by 5:30?"

"Not tonight. I can stay as late as I want. It's just me and Lib. Ma's going out."

Carter scowled. "With who?"

"Whom. With Aaron. Who else?"

"What for? Where? Why?"

"Dunno. She doesn't usually. She says she doesn't want to encourage him."

"She doesn't want to marry him?"

Leif made a strangling sound. "Gimme a break."

Carter grinned his relief. "So eat with me. Libby, too." He'd prefer it, actually. Having some company might take his mind off the red blotchiness that was driving him nuts.

Wishful thinking.

He didn't actually think Libby and Leif noticed his distraction. Even Libby, who professed no interest in babies, took a turn at giving Conan a bottle and playing peekaboo with him.

"He is kinda cute. It might be kinda neat to have a baby around."

"You're a little young."

"Maeve's only a year older," Libby countered, following him into the bedroom where he put a sleeping Conan into his crib.

"And you think she's doing a bang-up job, do you?" He bent and dropped a light kiss on Conan's ear, then turned and left the room, shutting off the light.

Libby followed, sighing. "I guess not."

"It's hard to be a parent when you're just a kid yourself."

"But if you meet the right guy—"

"It isn't only the people, Libby. It's the situation, the timing. It's all got to be right. Don't rush."

Libby looked up at him, her eyes, so like her mother's, wide and bright. "Don't get serious, you mean?"

Carter felt like an elderly uncle. "Something like that."

"About you?"

"You were interested in an old man like me?"

Libby laughed. She punched his arm lightly. "Oh, Carter."

He rubbed it. "I'm flattered."

"You are not." She started down the steps alongside him, then caught his arm, stopping him. "What about you? Are you ever going to get serious?"

"I try to now and then."

"Not that kind of serious, idiot. About a girl. A woman."

"Sure. When the time's right. If the right one comes along."

"When is it right? What makes the right one? How will you know?"

Trust a seventeen-year-old to ask the question of a lifetime. He gave a helpless shrug.

"What do you want in a wife?"

He didn't think he'd ever had a conversation like this with anyone, even Milly. He looked at Libby, wondering what she would ask next, wondering how he could even begin to answer the questions she'd already posed.

There was Diane, of course, whom he'd thought he loved. She'd said he didn't, and at the time he couldn't see it, but in retrospect, he was beginning to see that she was right.

He'd loved what Jack and Frances had—the sharing, the closeness, the commitment, the warmth. He wanted that for himself. And Diane seemed the best person to have it with.

But it wouldn't have worked. He liked Diane, maybe even loved her the way he loved Milly. He liked the way Marilee Newman looked. He liked her smile, her sexy laugh.

But real love? Honest-to-God enduring, adult love?

Love that made you want to laugh and cry, dance and sing, love that made life seem brighter, warmer, holier? Love that called forth the absolute best that a person had to give and made the world a better place?

"I don't know," he said at last.

The look she gave him bordered on exasperation. "Well, really, Carter. How can you expect to find the right woman if you don't have any idea what you're looking for?"

He raked a hand through his hair, then mustered a grin. "Don't you have to do your math?"

"Not tonight. Honestly, Carter, how can you be so good at math and so bad at life?"

He stopped grinning. It wasn't really funny.

"Men." Libby sighed and shook her head. "Come on, Leif. We've got to go."

"Half an hour," Leif promised. "I'm reading *Road and Track*."

"Leif—"

"Let him finish," Carter said. "I'll send him along shortly."

Libby opened her mouth to protest then shrugged. "Okay. But if he's still there when Ma gets home..."

It wasn't to let Leif finish the article that Carter wanted him to stay. It was because he wanted a favor.

"Listen," he said when Leif had finished the article and was putting on his jacket. "You know those potions your mother makes? The ointments and stuff? Does she have any for rashes?"

"Rashes?" Leif frowned. "Like poison ivy? Probably. She's got stuff for everything unless it's really bad. Then she sends us to the doctor."

"Could you bring some over?"

"Sure. After school tomorrow."

"How about tonight?"

Leif's eyes widened a fraction. "Tonight? Yeah, I guess."

"Thanks. You're a pal."

He almost gave up. It was close to ten-thirty when at last he heard the knock on the door. He strode quickly out from the kitchen and jerked it open.

"I thought you weren't—*Annabel?*"

Her cheeks were flushed with the cold. Her hair was flying in untamed wildness. She rushed right past him into the living room. "Let me see this rash."

WHY WAS HE STARING at her like that?

He looked almost horrified. Panicky. And here she'd been giving him credit for being such a surprisingly experienced hand at surrogate fatherhood.

Or, Annabel thought, maybe he wasn't panicking unnecessarily. Maybe Conan was really ill.

"Let me see the rash. Before I know what to do, I need to see it. Is it keeping him awake? Does he cry? He didn't have any rash last night." She said this last almost accusingly.

Carter just looked at her. There was a line of color along his cheekbones.

"Oh, for heaven's sake," she said when he still didn't speak. "Never mind. Frances says Jack goes nuts when Jason runs the tiniest fever. I suppose you're the same. I'll take care of it myself."

She flung off her coat and headed up the stairs. Conan wasn't crying at least. She'd reached the doorway when Carter cleared his throat.

"Annabel." His voice sounded ragged.

She turned, her hand on the knob.

"It isn't Conan."

"What?"

"It isn't Conan that has the rash." Pause. "It's me."

"You?"

He glared at her. "Babies aren't the only people who get rashes, you know."

"I know that. I—Leif said you needed ointment for a rash. He said Conan. I thought he said Conan. Did he say Conan?" She felt like a fool.

"Sorry," she said. She would have gone right back down the stairs but he was standing on them, cutting off her avenue of escape. "I misunderstood."

They stared at each other. Neither moved. From the other side of the door Annabel heard Conan sucking softly in his sleep.

"I was worried about Conan. I thought he was sick."

"He's fine. D'you want to see him a minute? Since you're here, I mean."

"That'd be nice."

He motioned for her to open the door, and together they crept softly into the room. Conan was sound asleep, his fist in his mouth, his face turned toward the wall.

Annabel leaned over and peered down at him, marveling at his beauty, at his innocence and trust. She remembered other babies, other nights. When Carter came to stand next to her, their hands brushed.

Quickly Annabel stepped back. "Thank you." She moved quietly toward the door. "He's lovely."

Carter nodded. "I hope Maeve and Jerry can make a future for him."

"Me, too."

They looked at each other then and smiled. In complete accord for once, Annabel thought, amazed.

"So. Let's see if we can help you."

Carter blinked. "Huh?"

"Show me your rash," she said.

SHE WASN'T LOOKING at him as she spoke. She'd clattered down the steps and had gone to get something out of the pocket of her coat. "What is it?" she asked him over her shoulder. "Poison ivy? Contact dermatitis? Athlete's foot?"

"Uh—well—"

She had two jars in her hand. She was setting out some small vials of powder. When he still stammered, she turned and looked at him expectantly.

"Carter?"

No one had ever called Carter MacKenzie bashful. Women had never complained that he was reticent about shedding his clothes in front of them.

But now?

Here?

In front of God and Annabel Archer?

He wanted to die.

Annabel seemed to realize this. She also seemed to realize he wasn't just going to push up his sleeve or reach down and slip off his shoe.

She looked faintly alarmed. "It's . . . ?"

He nodded. He could almost see her become professional, detached.

She swallowed.

He did, too. It became a war between his pride and his rash.

His pride surrendered. He dropped his pants.

ANNABEL FELT, for all the world, as if she were a doe trapped in the headlights of an oncoming car.

She couldn't move. Could only stare. And what she was seeing wasn't the rash.

"So what is it? And how do I get rid of it?"

Annabel pulled herself together. "I...er...the light isn't good right here. Could you, um, maybe come over and lie down on the couch?"

Carter gave her a fulminating glare.

She switched on the reading lamp and stood waiting. "I can't see it over there."

He gritted his teeth and somewhat clumsily he made his way over and stretched out on the couch. Annabel focused the light. She could see the rash very well now. She could see considerably more than the rash. She took a slow, steadying breath, then forced herself to concentrate on the medical aspect of the sight before her.

It looked red and itchy and basically unhappy. It went from an inch or two below his navel to the tops of his thighs. And it seemed to go right around...

"Is it on your, er, bottom, too?"

"Yes."

"And how long have you had it?"

"Couple of days."

She glanced at the sparkling white briefs pushed down below his knees. "New underwear?"

He scowled. "What? No."

She reached down and plucked the fabric between her fingers. "No? They look whiter than white."

"Thank your daughter the laundress."

"Libby washed them?"

"She washes all my clothes. Remember? It's her mission in life."

"I see."

She was seeing a hell of a lot, Carter thought grimly. He'd never felt more exposed in his life. Serve her right if he had some airborne venereal disease. He looked away at the far side of the room. "So what is it?" he demanded.

"It looks," Annabel said mildly, "like diaper rash."

His humiliation was complete. He glared at her, outraged.

She was grinning, damn her. "Contact dermatitis, Carter. Your skin's probably become irritated by whatever detergent Libby's using."

"But it's not in my shirts. Or my jeans."

"Maybe it's bleach."

"I'm allergic to bleach!"

"There you are, then."

Carter said a rude word. He said several of them. Then he sat up and started to pull up his pants.

Annabel moved out of his way. "You go run the bath water. I'll get the oatmeal."

"What in hell do you want to eat oatmeal for?"

"I don't want to eat it. You're going to take a bath in it."

"Annabel," he protested.

"I thought you ran a health-and-wellness store. Don't you know anything?"

"I don't know anything about bathing in oatmeal, for cripes' sake. Is that brought to us by the same people who think we want to wash our hair in wheat germ and honey?"

"Probably," she said, but she was on her way to the kitchen and there was nothing he could do but head up the stairs to comply.

He ran the bathwater and waited, scratching. Finally, unable to stand it, he stripped off his clothes and got in.

He no more than got into the tub, than the door opened and she walked right in.

"Hey!"

"What? Oh, am I supposed to close my eyes now?"

He scowled. "I suppose you're used to walking into men's bathrooms."

"Sure. I do it all the time. Here." She dropped a cheesecloth bag filled with oatmeal into the bath water. "Sorry it took so long. I had to find some way to confine the oatmeal. Swish this around. It should take some of the itching away if you sit there awhile. I'll take care of these." These were his underpants. She picked them up, waved them at him and vanished out the door.

She was right about the oatmeal. He swished it around and, after a while, it did seem to help. But the water was cool to begin with and he was getting goose bumps just sitting there, so he pulled the plug, got out and dried off carefully, trying not to start up the itching again.

Then, towel wrapped around his waist, he opened the door and padded into the bedroom.

Annabel was already there.

"Here. You can wear this." It was red and flannel and it didn't look promising.

"What is it?"

"Jack's nightshirt."

"Jack's *nightshirt? Jack's* nightshirt? Jack wears nightshirts?"

"Not ordinarily, I understand. But Frances got him one. For research purposes." Her face was absolutely straight, except for a momentary twitch of one corner of her mouth.

Carter muttered under his breath.

"Well, you don't seem to have anything suitable." Annabel cast a scathing glance at his belongings. "And you can't sleep in your underwear. It's in the wash. It'll have to go through at least twice, then be line dried tomorrow." She held out the nightshirt again.

"I sleep naked."

"Fine." She shrugged indifferently. "Come on, then."

"Come on? Why, Annabel Archer, I thought you'd never ask."

Chapter Eight

It was the challenge in his words that did it.

If he hadn't given her that seductive grin and almost taunted her—dared her—she would have simply handed him the ointment and walked away.

Heaven knew it was her first instinct.

But she couldn't.

It was odd, Annabel thought, the way life twisted and turned on itself, letting you walk away from situations, allowing you to believe you'd survived without confrontation, permitting you the false belief that you'd escape unscathed.

And then, whatever you'd run away from was back, staring—or in the present case, leering—you in the face.

And it was equally odd the things you thought of when it did.

Right now, for instance, faced with Carter MacKenzie wrapped in a towel, she was thinking of her father and Erik Erikson.

On the surface, not too likely. But if she analyzed it, which for a few moments she did, it made perfect sense.

Edward Lodge Archer met life head-on. Always had. Always would. And it galled him no end that his only child, Annabel, was such a wimp.

"You've got to get back on the damned horse, girl," he railed at her when his attempt to put his eight-year-old daughter on the most spirited horse in his stable had ended with Annabel in the dust.

But Annabel hadn't got back on. She'd mutely shaken her head and stumbled away. She'd never liked horses that much anyway.

She'd done the same thing when he'd taken her waterskiing. Plowing headfirst into the water wasn't Annabel's idea of fun. So what if you eventually got good enough to skim along at breakneck speeds, thumping madly along behind a maniac boat driver? If that didn't thrill you, why go through the pain?

And when someone clearly didn't want to dance with you at a yacht-club dance, when someone made it abundantly clear, in fact, that he thought you were the biggest turkey there, why force him—and yourself—into a clearly unpleasant situation?

What was wrong with avoiding problems?

Edward Archer and Erik Erikson knew.

You had to face problems to come away the conqueror, according to Edward Lodge Archer.

You had to pass through each successive stage of life before you could move on to the next one, wrote psychologist Erikson. No skipping. Ever. You stuck right where you were until you went through each and every one.

Annabel looked at Carter, at the low-slung towel. She knew now exactly what was underneath it. But she couldn't walk away yet. The gauntlet had been flung down.

Obviously Carter MacKenzie was a stage she was destined not to miss.

"Very funny," she said. "Now lie down so I can put this on you."

The seductive leer vanished in a flash. "Put what on me?"

"Ointment. It's what you asked for, isn't it?"

Something flickered in his gaze for just a moment...panic, apprehension? Annabel wasn't certain. But whatever it was, she was glad of it. If he was even slightly off balance, so much the better. Better the two of them than just her.

Carter seemed to grind his teeth.

Annabel waited, determined.

"Right," he said.

HE NEVER THOUGHT she'd do it.

One more time he'd misjudged Annabel Archer, he thought grimly as he lay facedown on the bed and felt the first touch of her fingers as they spread the cool cream against his fiery skin.

The gentleness of her touch almost made him moan. He swallowed hard.

"What is it? What sort of cream?" He needed to talk, to ramble incoherently, anything to forestall the inevitable physical response building inside him.

"Calendula cream." Her voice was husky. There seemed to be a vibrato in it when she spoke, or maybe he just imagined it. He didn't know anymore. Didn't even know his own name.

Her fingers were working a kind of magic on him. They moved rhythmically, soothingly over his tender hips and buttocks, then slipped down to stroke between his legs, not soothing him at all.

"Did you make it?" His voice was ragged.

"Yes." There was a slight catch in hers, too. "Does it help?"

"Yeah." But he thought the cure was likely worse than the disease. He fought down the urge to whimper.

Her fingers moved on, sending soft shivers through him, making him crazy. Finally they stopped, came to rest lightly on his hip. "You can . . . roll over now."

He went rigid.

Roll over?

God! Didn't she realize? He looked up at her.

She was peering down at him, apprehension in her wide dark eyes. "Carter?" She sounded a little worried.

She wasn't the only one.

He shut his own eyes. There was no way on earth he could roll over. Not without disgracing himself entirely. Or not without reaching for her, taking her, making her a part of him.

Make love to Annabel Archer?

How incredible was that?

But damn it, he wanted to! Wanted *her!*

And Annabel? Did she want it? Yeah, sure. One move and she'd give him a bloody nose. Or worse.

His fingers curled into fists against the sheet. He sucked in a breath and bit down on his lip.

"Go away, Annabel," he muttered into the pillow.

"I'm not—"

"Go away!"

"You don't want . . . ?"

He lifted his head and turned his glowering gaze on her. "Oh, yes, Annabel," he bit out. "I damned well do!"

He didn't move, just watched as she stood, then set the jar on the table by the bed.

She looked down at him, her gaze making him burn as it traveled with incredible slowness up the length of his body until at last once more their eyes momentarily locked.

She smiled, a faint and oddly wistful smile as she backed away. But the most disconcerting thing of all came when she turned and left the room.

Had he really heard her whisper, "Me, too?"

"DID YOU EVER HAVE a midlife crisis?" Annabel asked Sister Bertha the next morning. They had been making a new batch of goat's milk soap since seven o'clock, a project that required more than one set of hands. And while Bert discoursed at length on most of the important issues in the world, Annabel replied in monosyllables, if at all.

To Annabel, after last night, the most important issue in the world was what she felt about Carter MacKenzie and, more important, what she was going to do about it.

She had been determined to face him, to touch him, and to walk away unscathed. And she had walked away, all right.

But unscathed?

Dream on, sweetie, she told herself.

Whatever God and Erik Erikson had in mind for her in the Carter MacKenzie stage, it was obvious she wasn't through it yet.

"A midlife crisis?" Bert laughed as she poured the soap into the molds. "Did I ever! But they didn't call it a midlife crisis in those days. They called it Vatican II."

"I'm not sure it's the same thing."

"Of course it is," Bert said briskly. "It's a matter of confronting who you thought you were, learning who you really are and where you're really going with your life."

Yes, it was that, all right. "But I thought I already knew," Annabel said a bit plaintively.

"And...?"

"Now I don't."

"Carter."

Annabel looked at her sharply. "How did you know?"

"I've got eyes."

Self-conscious, uncomfortable to know she'd been so obvious, Annabel made a production of tapping the molds gently on the counter to release air bubbles. But finally she had to ask, "What do you see?"

"That you're interested." Pause. "And he is, too."

"Interested? In me? I don't think so."

Bert tsked. "Look again."

But Annabel shook her head. Even if he'd actually almost said he wanted to make love with her last night, she knew very well that it wasn't because he loved her. It was merely a physical response to her touching him. When she thought about it now, she could feel the blood burn in her cheeks.

How had she dared?

She was lucky he hadn't pushed the issue. Or had she been wishing he would? Was that what was behind her recklessness? Had she been hoping he'd take the matter out of her hands, leave her no choice?

The very thought made her wince. It was so very much against her principles, so totally against everything she had ever claimed to believe about the way relationships ought to be conducted between women and men.

What had Bert just said? That going through a midlife crisis was a matter of confronting who you thought you were, learning who you really are...

Annabel gave a little moan.

"Something wrong?" Bert asked.

"No. Not at all. Just . . . thinking."

She did a lot of thinking that day, about herself, about the past, the present and the future. About Carter.

She wished she had someone to talk to about it. About him. She wished now that she'd confided in Frances the first time Jack had brought Carter to the house. But she hadn't. What was the point? she'd asked herself. Why rake up past disasters?

And, indeed, at the time there had seemed little point. Especially since Carter clearly had no recollection of her.

Afterward, even when she saw him again at Thanksgiving or at Jason's baptism, she had said nothing.

She never thought she'd be subjected to him on virtually a daily basis. She never thought Frances would dream of matchmaking. And she certainly never thought that her reactions to Carter would have remained the same.

Was it natural perversity, she wondered, that made her so constantly aware of him—as aware now as she had been that fateful night at Marblehead?

She could remember it all so well, as if it were yesterday, not nineteen years before.

She hadn't wanted to be there at all. The yacht club was one of her father's bailiwicks. It had nothing to do with her.

She didn't like yachts any more than she liked waterskiing. Nor did she like going to dances where she stood on the sidelines thinking about the book she'd rather have been home reading while she watched other girls twirl competently around the room.

All in all, to Edward Archer she must have been a most unsatisfactory child.

She was a dreamer, given by fate into the hands of a doer. And while her mother might have felt a modicum of sympathy for the unsuitable daughter she had given birth to, Christina Archer had no power to protect her daughter from Edward's plans. Indeed, why should she want to?

It wasn't as if Edward abused the child. It wasn't even as if he didn't care. Probably, Annabel thought now, he cared too much.

But whether he cared or not, he certainly didn't understand her, didn't want to try.

He never accepted that she found little joy in the social whirl that was his life and breath. He never understood that what he found inspiring, to his daughter produced only dread.

Most importantly, he never saw that she wasn't every young man's ideal.

"You'll be the belle of the ball, my Annabel," he told her, with unpardonable optimism, the evening of the Marblehead affair.

He took in his tall, gangly daughter, her long gingery hair crimped and twisted into an uncharacteristic halo of curls, her curvy figure accentuated in a frilled and flounced, rose-colored gown her ever-hopeful mother had chosen, and nodded his head in approval.

Annabel merely shook hers. She knew better. There were girls who attracted the boys the way honey pots did bees. There were others who, in the words of one of her more perceptive teachers, might "find the right man someday."

Implied, but not stated, was that someday wouldn't be soon.

Annabel didn't care. She knew that someday her prince would come. She was quite confident that she would know him when he did.

She was willing to wait, even if her father was not.

Marblehead, as far as Edward Archer was concerned, was Annabel's launching pad. After an indifferent, inauspicious—not to say totally disastrous, in his eyes—childhood, she would redeem herself here.

Being a debutante was, happily for Annabel, passé. Few of the girls she knew were obliged to go through the continuous round of parties, teas and formal dances that had brought women of earlier generations into society's folds.

But just because she didn't have to go through the formal rigmarole, she didn't get off scot-free.

On the contrary, her father made it quite clear that, either at Marblehead or one of the several other dances she was going to that year, she would meet the man who would, a few years hence, marry her. Under Edward's careful tutelage, he would take over Archer Industries and, of course, provide Edward Archer with the requisite handsome grandchildren, thereby insuring the succession.

Annabel doubted it sincerely.

Of course, she didn't tell her father that. She never told her father anything. One didn't talk to Edward Archer. One only listened and, at the appropriate moment, nodded one's assent.

She expected a boring evening. She was prepared for nothing more than a duty dance with her father, another with Michael Peters, the son of her father's golfing crony, a few glasses of watered-down punch and a couple of tasteless cucumber sandwiches.

And then she saw Carter MacKenzie.

Love bloomed.

Well, not love precisely. Even Annabel wasn't enough of a romantic to believe in that.

But infatuation, certainly. Interest. Heightened awareness. A tingling. A sense of something momentous about to occur.

Years before she had expected him, her prince was here.

He was laughing, his head thrown back, a lively grin on his handsome face.

Yes, Annabel thought. Oh, yes.

But it was his liveliness more than his good looks that attracted her. Handsome young men in tuxes, their manners as polished as their shoes, were a dime a dozen in

Annabel's stuffy world. But this one made a difference to the very air.

The room had seemed flat and stale until he'd come in. Now there was life, excitement—promise—in the air.

"Who is he?" she asked Lolly Talbot, one of the twirlers who would undoubtedly know.

Lolly looked. "Carter MacKenzie. Daddy's in oil. Chemicals. Steel or something. New York, Palm Beach, Cape Cod. Good catch."

Annabel wasn't fishing. She wouldn't have cared had he been destitute. It was the inner man who mattered, not how many companies his father ran or how many mansions he owned.

She looked at Carter again, who was now being introduced to somebody's mother, and saw that the laughter had vanished. He was looking polite and slightly bored, but there was still that energy in him, leashed now, controlled. As if he wasn't really interested, as if he was but waiting . . . waiting . . .

Like her.

She wanted to dance with him, to talk to him. She wanted to know what made him laugh, what made him frown, what would make his heart sing the way hers had the moment he came into the room.

She hadn't the slightest hope of doing so. Unless . . .

He was dancing with Wendy Ferguson. The same Wendy Ferguson who had copied Annabel's sociology homework for an entire semester. The same Wendy Ferguson who would have been caught smoking before chapel had Annabel not deliberately crashed into her and knocked the cigarette into the pond. The same Wendy Ferguson who spent the weekend with Willy Carstairs last March and told her parents she was with Annabel Archer.

Wendy owed her. A lot.

She got up, moved over near to where Carter was standing and tried to look as if she were having such a good time that he should come and share it with her.

He didn't.

She followed him to the punch bowl and waited for him to see her and fall under her spell the way she had fallen under his. But he only edged past her in the crush, then tripped over her feet on the way back.

He did, however, give her a glance and vague smile.

Annabel stood, rooted, smiling back at where he'd been.

"Do take a cup and move along, dear," said one of the matrons irritably. Sighing, Annabel did.

But as the evening wore on and he never approached her, she grew more and more desperate. She felt as if she were Cinderella at the ball, watching midnight come ever closer and never getting a chance at the prince.

She knew—just knew—if the dance passed without her getting to know Carter MacKenzie, her life would be irrevocably different.

She sought out Wendy Ferguson in the powder room.

"You want to dance with Carter? Why?"

But even if she'd been inclined to, Annabel couldn't have answered that. "M-my father," she offered after a moment. "He'll think I haven't been making an effort."

"Whatever."

They left the powder room separately, Wendy first. When Annabel came back into the ballroom she spied Wendy across the floor, talking earnestly to Carter MacKenzie.

While Annabel watched and tried to appear not to, she saw Carter frown and scan the room. Wendy turned and nodded her head in Annabel's direction. Carter looked right at her.

Self-conscious, Annabel pivoted slightly and tried to look bright, zestful, interesting, as if she were deeply involved in the discussion about tropical fish between the two Harvard juniors who were standing right there ignoring her.

The music started up again. Couples moved out onto the floor. Annabel lost sight of Wendy and Carter, but she knew the deed had been done.

Now she only had to wait.

She made herself as conspicuous as possible, standing instead of sitting, smiling vacantly and tapping her foot in time to the music. But Carter MacKenzie never materialized in front of her. She didn't see him anywhere.

She waited through three more dances. In vain. The evening was drawing to a close. The lights were dimming, the music becoming softer and more romantic with each piece.

And then she knew. He was waiting for the last dance. The special one.

He had seen her and he had known, just as she had, that they would need more time than a simple dance with each other. They would need hours and hours. Days. Was a lifetime too much to hope for?

"We'll wait for you out front after," her mother whispered in her ear.

"Don't."

Christina Archer blinked. "But—"

"It's all right." Annabel fabricated a story. "I'm going with Wendy. We . . . we arranged it a little while ago."

"Wendy Ferguson? But I thought she and Willy Carstairs were . . ."

"Oh, well, they are," Annabel said brightly. "We all are. Going out for a postdance breakfast, and then back to Wendy's. I'll be fine, Mama. Really."

And Christina, relieved at last that her ugly-duckling daughter had found some friends to go out with, could only smile and give her consent. "Well, of course, darling. I'll tell your father. He'll be so pleased."

Of course he would. But whether Edward Archer was pleased or not didn't matter to Annabel in the least.

She spotted Carter just then, going into the alcove that led to the rest rooms. She didn't know if he'd seen her or not. She gave her mother's hand a quick squeeze and headed off in his direction.

She stopped just outside the alcove, determined not to go after him, but quite equally determined to be readily available when he reappeared.

She didn't lean against the wall. She didn't sit down. She stood quite straight and tall, waiting, dreaming.

In mere minutes, she told herself. In scant seconds . . .

"The things one does for mothers." She heard his voice around the corner, coming closer as he replied to another gruff masculine one. "I told her no. God knows I didn't want to come."

"Pretty slim pickings," his friend grumbled.

"Not a looker among 'em," Carter agreed. "I said I'd dance with Wendy and Bitsy, but that's it."

"What about that girl Wendy asked you to dance with?"

Carter snorted. "The gingerbread girl? The one with the Orphan Annie hair and the dress that looked like it was made for Petunia Pig? No way. A guy's gotta have some standards."

He came around the corner then—face-to-face with Annabel Archer.

She didn't move. Didn't blink.

He opened his mouth, closed it, swallowed, ducked past.

And Annabel fled, cursing her romantic idiocy, into the cool silence of the soft April night.

Minutes later she met Mark.

IT WAS ODD, she thought now, how wrong—and how right—she'd been that night. Right about the fact that Carter would change her life from that day forward; totally wrong about the means through which he would do so.

For instead of finding in him the man of her dreams, she had fled the suddenly oppressive building and run smack into Mark, who worked there, one of the minions in charge of maintaining the grounds.

Mark Campbell had no fortune in chemicals, no future in steel. And his only connection to oil, he'd told her with a grin, was a father who ran a filling station in Indianapolis.

But Annabel could talk to him, could relax with him. And, as the hours wore on, she let down her defenses and became herself with him.

In fact, she spent the night with him, cuddled in his arms in the bunk of some rich man's yacht.

It had been a reaction to her rejection by Carter, certainly. But as crushed as Annabel had been by Carter's words, she wouldn't have gone as far as she had if there hadn't been something wonderfully right between herself and Mark.

It was the day she left childhood irrevocably behind, the start of a course of action that had ruptured her ties with her family and had brought her here.

Face-to-face with Carter once more.

But now she was a woman, an adult with her feet planted firmly on the ground. She wasn't angry or hurt by

Carter anymore. In fact, damn it to hell, she actually liked him.

But Annabel was no longer a dreamer. She entertained no illusions.

Carter could still affect her, no doubt about that. He still called forth in her that same shivery awareness that he'd been able to elicit almost nineteen years ago.

He also seemed to feel some sort of awareness himself.

Where would it lead? Annabel wondered.

To bed?

It was a mark of her years, she guessed, that allowed her to consider such a possibility dispassionately.

Would she do it? she asked herself.

It might be the only way to get through her preoccupation with him—the stage of her life that was Carter MacKenzie.

Yes, she imagined it could lead to that.

One thing she knew it would never lead to—happily ever after.

Sometimes Annabel might still be a fool, but she'd never be a big enough fool to believe that.

CONAN SLEPT through the night.

Carter didn't. He spent it twisting and turning, writhing and restless. He cursed himself for his idiocy. Could rolling over and exposing his desire for her possibly have been any worse than this?

"Me, too," she'd said.

Or had she?

God, he wished he knew!

He was still awake at Conan's first mutterings shortly past six. He got up, naked and shivering in the early October morning, groping about for something to wear. His underwear was, of course, in the washer. The thought of wearing his jeans without it made him wince. Jack's nightshirt lay on the dresser. He remembered Annabel holding it out to him, challenging him.

He remembered his challenge back to her.

And her response. Her touch.

The memory stirred him. He shivered again. Ached a bit. He reached for the nightshirt and tugged it over his head, then went to get the baby.

He moved in a sort of daze—warming milk for Conan, changing him, then carrying the baby back upstairs, crooning to him softly all the while. It was too early to get up. He was too tired. He crawled into bed and cradled Conan close, nuzzling the baby's soft hair as he fed him his bottle. He wondered what Milly would say if she could see him now.

Lying back against the pillows, he closed his eyes. He felt bleary and disoriented, frustrated and sleepy.

But for the first time in months he felt challenged. Alive.

Chapter Nine

Annabel knocked, but no one answered.

She waited, then opened the door. "Carter," she called, but still no one came.

His Blazer was parked right where it had been last night. He couldn't have gone far.

She and Bert had finished with the soap half an hour ago, and Bert, promising to be back to wrap the bars on Thursday, had headed home.

It was almost eleven, and Annabel had more than enough to do. She had orders for wreaths that needed making, ornaments to fashion, goldenrod to pick, a dozen Christmas centerpieces to start. She should be starting to think about them, getting some ideas in her mind, planning.

But in her mind all she saw was Carter.

All she could think about was Carter.

She wanted to see him. She didn't want to see him.

She needed to talk to him. She never wanted to talk to him again.

It had taken her only a few minutes after Bert's departure to know that she wasn't going to get anything done until she faced him again.

Besides, she had promised to hang out the wash. She was as bad as Libby, trying to come up with an excuse!

Now, of course, it was so late that she had no doubt he'd hung the wash out himself. But when she came over the hill, she saw no string of underwear flapping on the line. No one answered her knock. No one came to her call.

She called again, then walked in, curious, frowning.

She looked in the kitchen for signs of habitation, found none except a pan of now-cool water on the stove, which earlier he might have used to heat Conan's bottle.

A faint gurgling sound made her turn and retrace her steps into the living room. "Carter?"

Another gurgle. A coo. From up the stairs.

He hadn't left the baby alone, had he?

She took the stairs two at a time and hurried into Jason's room. Conan wasn't there.

Just as quickly she walked down the hall to the other bedroom and stopped quite still.

Conan lay on his back, waving his arms, kicking his feet. He was perfectly safe, fenced in by a wall and a huddled comforter.

And under the comforter, sleeping soundly, was Carter.

He was curled up, his reddish-brown hair tousled and drifting across his forehead, one red flannel-clad arm tucked under his head, the other still loosely grasping the empty bottle he'd been feeding to Conan. So—she smiled—he'd put on the nightshirt after all.

She moved closer, bemused, and simply stood there, taking advantage of the opportunity to study him. Were there, in his sleeping features, vestiges of the boy he'd been?

His mobile mouth was softened, lips parted, reminding her of a younger Carter. His high cheekbones and slightly beaky, once broken nose were the same, as well. Tiny lines fanned out from his eyes, aging him, but not unattractively.

It was his eyes that were different. And that was because now dark lashes hooded their normal mocking green.

Last night, she remembered, she had seen a different look in them.

Desire.

She had felt it herself then, felt the stirring of it again now as she stood here simply looking at him.

However long her ill-begotten attraction lasted, it had certainly survived the night.

Conan kicked again, burbling, smiling at her, and she smiled at him, wondering how long he'd been awake. Not long enough to wake Carter, that was clear. He still hadn't moved.

Had he had as restless a night as she'd had?

Probably worse, she reflected, recalling the red itchy skin that had plagued him as well as the frustration she'd heard in his ragged voice.

She reached across Carter's sleeping form and scooped the baby into her arms.

"Come along, laddie," she said softly. "We'll get you changed and fed, then you can help me hang out the laundry."

The next hour seemed rather like a déjà vu to Annabel. The sloppy spooning up of baby cereal with its accompaniment of drools and dribbles, kicks and lunges was so familiar, so comfortable. It came back as naturally as if she still did it every day of her life.

She rinsed out the bowl, then hummed as she put the laundry into the basket. Balancing Conan on one hip and the basket on the other, she went outside.

The day was clear and cool, warm enough for shirt-sleeves in the sunshine, but Annabel was glad of a sweater when she stood in the shade, and glad she had dressed Conan in a furry jacket that Jason had outgrown.

She set the basket on the ground, then tied Conan against her middle with the sling Carter had made. She moved from the basket to the line, back and forth, making Conan giggle when she swooped down to grab another piece to hang on the line.

"You like that, do you?" she said to him, laughing a bit herself, bending her head to drop a light kiss on the top of his. She danced him around the yard, doing chain steps and double steps, making him crow with glee. And when she stopped, he hiccupped and looked surprised, then giggled again.

Annabel gave him a gentle hug.

That was the problem, she thought, with having had her children when she was scarcely more than a child herself. She'd never fully appreciated them.

Oh, she'd enjoyed them enough, had played right along with them. But she had also been so worried about doing a good job, about being a responsible mother so that no one could possibly say she wasn't—making sure they ate the right vegetables and didn't watch the wrong television shows—that she'd missed some of the sheer joy that came with relaxing a bit, sitting back and sharing their enthusiasm in simply being alive.

She heard a scraping sound behind her. "Good morning. Or is it afternoon?"

She turned, startled, and looked up.

Carter had opened the bedroom window and was leaning on the sill, his hair tousled, his chest and arms still covered in red flannel as if he'd come straight from bed.

Annabel licked suddenly parched lips, clutched Conan against her front as if he were a shield.

Carter was smiling at her, a hint of amusement in his gaze. She wondered how long he'd been watching her.

She felt faintly foolish that he might have seen her antics, then deliberately shrugged it off. A sense of fatalism took its place.

"Qué será será," she muttered under her breath. Then she met his gaze. "It's morning—barely—sleepyhead," she replied, and she couldn't resist smiling, too.

"How about breakfast?"

"Conan's already eaten."

"I meant us."

Us.

Nineteen years ago Annabel would have swooned over the very thought.

Don't, she cautioned herself. "That sounds...fine." She tried to sound positive, upbeat, cheerful.

Carter grinned. "Don't sound so worried. I can cook."

It wasn't his cooking she was worried about.

HE'D WATCHED HER for a good five minutes before he opened the window and spoke to her.

He'd seen the bounces, the turns, the swoops and the flourishes. He'd watched her gingery hair glint almost bronze in the sunshine as Annabel Archer swirled herself and Conan around the yard.

It was an Annabel he might very well have denied existed a few days ago. She certainly bore no resemblance to the one he'd first met. Where was the stiff, judgmental woman who'd always looked down her nose at him, who made him feel as if he were a schoolboy, and not a particularly well-behaved one, either?

He didn't feel especially well behaved at the moment, come to that. If he hadn't been wearing this damned nightshirt and nothing else, he might have gone down and joined in.

Which would have got him where?

He grimaced. Precisely, he thought.

There was no telling where, given their history, he and Annabel might end up.

But he was beginning to think bed might not be such a bad place to start.

THE THING TO DO, Annabel told herself, was to be matter-of-fact, sensible.

She was attracted to him. She should admit it.

Yeah, sure, she thought, and have Carter say that was nice but he sure as hell wasn't attracted to her.

If she was going to admit anything, she thought, she ought to admit to herself that his rejection of nineteen years ago could still hurt.

But was he the same man he'd been nineteen years ago? Heaven knew she was not the same woman.

She watched him now, flipping pancakes with aplomb, not the least bit self-conscious that she should be sitting there while he wandered around the kitchen in Jack's nightshirt.

She couldn't imagine his eighteen-year-old self doing any such thing. So maybe he wasn't the same man, she conceded. But that didn't make his reaction any more predictable.

Her own was becoming disgustingly predictable. The simple sight of those hairy calves peeking out below the hem had her remembering last night, remembering the strong length of his legs, the bony knees, the muscular thighs, the . . .

And she'd berated Libby!

HE WISHED TO GOD she would stop watching him.

Of course, he acknowledged, there wasn't a lot else in the kitchen of consuming interest.

Conan had, fifteen minutes before, drifted off into his morning nap. The morning paper had been read, the table set, the orange juice poured.

He was the only thing moving, as he flipped pancakes and shifted from one foot to the other on the bare wood floor.

So Annabel watched him.

He was glad the floor was cold. It made his feet cold, which in turn provided a certain amount of coolness to his calves. He wished like hell the coolness would reach further up. He wished he had put on his jeans, underwear or not.

He needed . . .

He wanted . . .

He looked around desperately. Out of the window he spied Arnold with one of Frances's nannies doing precisely what he wanted to be doing with Annabel. It was the last straw.

He scraped up the half-cooked pancakes and slapped them onto the plate. He carried them across the room, holding them strategically as he went. He stuck them right in front of Annabel.

"Dig in. Don't wait."

"But—"

"I'll be right back."

Annabel took in the heightened color in his face, the hastiness of his departure and frowned.

A few minutes later he reappeared, this time dressed in jeans and a flannel shirt. A line of color still ran along his cheekbones and he didn't say a word, just went straight to the griddle and, ignoring her, poured out more puddles of batter.

She watched him, intrigued, wondering...

Was she having the same effect on him that he had on her? Was he as attracted to her as she was to him?

If so, were they ever going to be able to get on with their lives unless they got past it?

A younger Annabel wouldn't have done it.

A less frantic Annabel would never have dared.

But this Annabel was thirty-six and desperate.

She wanted her sanity back. She wanted her sense of focus and direction, her calm and peaceful life.

"Carter," she said to his back, "do you think maybe we should just forget the pancakes and go to bed?"

IF HE LIVED TO BE A hundred, Carter was sure he'd never win a bet on the next words to come out of Annabel Archer's mouth.

Heaven help him, he'd have lost a bundle on those.

For a moment he didn't even realize that he was pouring batter all over the griddle, the stove and the tops of his toes.

"Here," Annabel said. "You're making a mess and a half. Let me do that if you're so desperate for pancakes." She whisked the bowl and spoon out of his hands, set them aside, mopped up his spill efficiently and poured neat little round puddles of her own.

He watched numbly, mind reeling.

She glanced at him, her hands on her hips. "Don't look so shocked." Her chin came up; there was a note of challenge in her voice.

"No. Of—of course not. I just...just..." He looked at her dazedly and shook his head.

Annabel sighed and flipped the pancakes. "This is all Frances's fault."

"Frances? What's she got to do with it?"

"The kiss," Annabel said sweetly.

"It was just a kiss."

"It was a setup!"

He stared at her.

"Don't you realize it yet? This is all her fault. She created this situation. She threw us together and then challenged us. It was like someone saying, 'Don't think of elephants. Whatever you do, don't think of elephants!'"

Carter grinned. "'Whatever you do, don't think about going to bed with Carter MacKenzie'? That sort of thing?"

Annabel's flush deepened. "Exactly." She turned back to the pancakes, scraped them into a pile and dumped them onto the plate, then thrust them at him. "Here. Eat."

He took the plate, held it a moment, then let his eyes rove slowly down the line of her nose, past the thin-pressed lips, the stubborn jaw. His gaze slid leisurely over the swell of her breasts, the line of her legs. He set the plate on the counter.

"I think I'd rather go to bed."

ANNABEL HOPED he couldn't notice that her knees quaked as he followed her up the stairs. She hoped he couldn't tell from her flushed cheeks and damp palms how really nervous she was.

Had she really suggested going to bed with Carter MacKenzie? Out of the clear blue? Just like that?

Yes.

And had he taken her up on it? Just like that?

Right again.

Oh, Annabel, what a big mouth you have!

She shut her eyes, her fingers tightened on the banister. It wasn't too late to turn back, she told herself.

She didn't really want to go to bed with Carter MacKenzie, did she? She didn't really want to know intimately the man who had been the source of her humiliation all those years ago, did she?

Yes.

She wanted to know him, *needed* to know him, to solve the mystery of his attraction and get back to the important things in life.

And did she want him to know her?

Her palms were damp, her cheeks flushed. The very thought frightened her. Once more her knees trembled. She chewed on her lip.

Perhaps Conan would cry, the phone would ring, Arnold would come rampaging up onto the front porch.

She took the steps slowly, deliberately, stalling. But there was no rescue, only the sound of Carter's bare feet on the floor behind her, only the heat of his body when she paused in the doorway to the bedroom.

"Second thoughts?"

The barest hint of challenge, real or imagined, was enough to send her right on through. "Of course not," she lied. But at the side of the bed, she stopped once more.

It was so big, so broad, so rumpled. As if it had already known a night of passion, of love.

It won't be love, she told herself. It was a scientific inquiry, an exploration of phenomena. Nothing more.

Quickly she reached down and picked up the nightshirt Carter had discarded. She folded it automatically, smoothed it against her breasts, held it like a shield against her.

Carter reached out and lifted it from her hands, setting it on the dresser. His own fingers lingered, smoothing it, too. Then slowly he turned to face her.

His eyes were so green, so deep. It didn't seem fair that a man so shallow should have such wonderful eyes. Or was he really shallow? She wasn't sure anymore.

He wasn't smiling. He looked, if anything, even more serious than she did. As if he didn't want to be here any more than she did. As if he were just performing a duty. The thought made Annabel wince.

"What's wrong?" he asked her.

"Nothing."

"You always act like this when you go to bed with someone?"

"I don't often just 'go to bed' with someone."

"I didn't mean . . ."

"It was perfectly obvious what you meant."

They glared at each other. Annabel could see a pulse ticking in Carter's temple. His lips were a hard line. Her own lips were pressed together tightly.

He sighed and thrust his fingers through his hair. "So do you want to or not?"

"How charming. Is this the way *you* always act when you go to bed with someone?"

"Cripes, Archer, I don't know whether to strangle you or kiss you."

She shrugged. "Don't ask me."

"Ah, hell," Carter muttered and reached for her.

He didn't strangle her, but he might as well have. He robbed her of all her air.

He'd kissed her before. Twice. Three times. Annabel didn't remember.

They weren't all that memorable, she'd told herself. Carter MacKenzie was no great shakes as a kisser.

Think again, sweetheart, her reeling mind managed to convey before she lost all coherent thought.

This was no quick peck, no brotherly buss. His lips met hers with a hunger that astonished her. They asked for— no, demanded—a response.

And Annabel, lost to propriety, rationality and simple common sense, gave him one. She couldn't help it.

Her fingers came up to close on the soft flannel of his shirt. Her hips surged forward to press against his. And her lips opened, parting under the urgent quest of his tongue, tasting of him with the same eagerness with which he tasted her.

When he pulled back, she was speechless.

"That," Carter said hoarsely, "is the way I act when I go to bed with someone."

Annabel swallowed again.

"Shall I continue?" His soft voice challenged her. "Or not?"

Are you woman enough?

He didn't say the words. Annabel heard them loud and clear.

"Yes."

Her fingers fumbled with the hem of her sweater. Carter couldn't seem to get his shirt buttons undone. He muttered his frustration.

"Let me." Annabel reached for them at the same time his fingers touched her sweater.

"I'll help you," he said.

They stopped, stared at each other for an instant, offered hesitant smiles.

Annabel unbuttoned his shirt. Carter eased the sweater over her head.

He had much better luck with the buttons on her shirt than he'd had on his own. Annabel stood mutely while he worked, but her fingers came up to rest softly against his now-bare chest.

He skimmed the shirt off her shoulders, letting it drop to the floor. Annabel bent automatically to pick up both his shirt and her own.

Carter took them and tossed them aside. Then he stood, silent, wetting his lips as he gazed down at her breasts inside the ivory lace.

Annabel was not ordinarily given to frilly underwear. Sturdy, not sensuous, was generally the order of her day. Who was she going to do a striptease for? she asked Libby when her daughter suggested some sexier lingerie.

Libby took matters into her own hands. For Christmas last year Annabel had opened a gaily wrapped ivory lace bra, her size, not Libby's 32A.

She glanced down at it now self-consciously.

Carter reached behind her and undid the hook, then drew it forward, letting the straps slide down her arms, his fingers following, the backs of his hands brushing her arms, the tips of his fingers gliding lightly over her breasts.

Annabel looked away, then ventured a quick glance back at him. He looked utterly serious, intent. The bra fell to the floor.

Annabel didn't pick it up.

With slow deliberation Carter leaned forward and touched his lips to hers.

This kiss was totally different. Slow and sensual. A quiet start, then steamy, seeking. Simmering. Smoldering.

It set off an answering heat in Annabel that started somewhere deep inside and curled downward into the center of her, making her burn. She felt a shudder run through her.

Carter pulled back. His eyes were dark, the skin on his cheeks taut and flushed. He was breathing quickly. His fingers went to the top button of his jeans. Annabel saw a fine tremor in his hands as they tried to open it.

"Please. I want to."

Was that her voice? Her words? Had she dared say such a thing?

Carter's hands dropped to his sides. His fingers clenched lightly. His hooded eyes watched her. He held his breath.

Annabel did, too.

She moved closer, slipped her hand lightly beneath his waistband and eased it open. Her fingers brushed his hard belly and the line of silky hair that arrowed down his abdomen. She felt him tense as she moved on to the next button... and the next.

She undid them all with studious concentration, then hooked her thumbs in the belt loops and gave a gentle tug. The jeans slid down his hips to his knees. He kicked them off.

He wasn't wearing any underwear.

It was nothing she hadn't seen before. He was the same man he'd been last night. He even had the same rash, although it was slightly fainter now.

But last night he'd been discomfited, irritable, tetchy. Today he was aroused. By her.

Annabel couldn't stop looking at him.

"My turn." Carter's voice was ragged.

She blinked, momentarily disoriented, then lifted her eyes to meet his, all her nervousness returning as she realized what he intended.

He bent his head. His fingers went to the snap on her jeans and popped it easily. Annabel started to take a breath, but his hands didn't move away. They remained, the backs of his fingers brushing lightly to and fro across her belly, fanning the flames within her, making her ache.

She'd thought she would hate for him to undress her, to expose her body to his gaze. Now she only wanted him to hurry.

But he wouldn't. His fingers were maddeningly slow as they plucked at the tab of the zipper, then lowered it. They were painstakingly gentle as they slid inside the denim and pushed the fabric down her hips.

She tried to kick them off as he had done, but hers were cut narrower and she couldn't shed them without help.

Carter dropped to his knees, skimming his hands down her thighs and calves, taking the denim with them, lifting her feet one at a time. The calluses on his fingertips made the soles of her feet tingle. Off balance, Annabel tottered, then righted herself by catching hold of his head.

It was the first time she'd ever touched his hair. Her fingers curled in its thickness. She felt the silky softness of it brush her thighs. She trembled.

Then he settled back on his heels and his hands slid slowly back up her legs.

Annabel waited, tense, scarcely breathing, expecting his fingers to continue their climb, to hook in the waistband on her panties and slip them down.

Instead one finger lightly traced the leg opening, then another did the same. He lifted his head and looked up at her. She swallowed. His fingers continued their light tracery, moved slowly, teasingly up until they'd slipped under the cloth barrier. Touched her. Knew her. Learned of her readiness, her need.

Annabel's fingers clenched in his hair.

In mere seconds he peeled off the last barrier to her nakedness, and bore her back onto the bed. His eyes glittered green fire now. The skin was taut across his cheekbones, his breathing came shallow and quick.

She lay in his embrace, reveling in the feel of his firm, hair-roughened flesh, in the sinewy strength of his arms as he pulled her against him, kissing her eyes, her cheeks, her hair.

At eighteen she'd had the barest notion, the faintest fantasies of what going to bed with Carter MacKenzie would be like.

At thirty-six she found that reality was beyond compare.

He was as impatient as she was, but controlled. He let his hands rove her body with excruciating thoroughness, stroking, inciting, making her yearn for more.

Her own hands sought him just as eagerly, skating lightly over his ribs, learning the rough strength of his thighs, then at last, finding the center of his desire.

A tremor shook him. He bit his lip, groaned and shifted so that he knelt between her legs, ready.

And Annabel was ready, too. She held him gently to draw him to her, but he shook his head.

"Not yet." His voice cracked. His fingers trailed down the smoothness of her belly, touched the soft hair at the apex of her thighs, slipped beyond it.

Annabel sucked in her breath, held perfectly still...then melted under the rhythmic, knowing stroke of his fingers.

Her own fingers trembled, reached out and clenched handfuls of the sheet. Her back arched. She gasped. "Carter!"

He came to her then. Hot. Hungry.

She welcomed him, opened for him, savoring his silken strength as he slid inside, meeting his thrust, arching into it, making him groan.

His weight rested on his arms. They shook. He shut his eyes, then opened them again.

And Annabel met his gaze. She loosened her hold on the sheet and lifted her hands, setting them lightly against his back, smoothing him, stroking him, learning the feel of the bunch and flex of his muscles under her touch.

She tried to be analytical, objective.

She tried to fathom her attraction, his mystery.

She couldn't begin to.

She was lost.

Lost in the hunger of his gaze, in the sweet slip of his body into hers, in the hunger and passion that flamed between them. Her fingers clenched against his buttocks, her toes curled. She tossed her head from side to side.

And all the while Carter moved. Slowly at first, then faster. Finally frantic, desperate. Wanting. Needing. "Anna...bel!"

Annabel was with him, meeting him, feeling the explosion growing inside her. One last thrust and then a shudder. Her body splintered, her mind reeled.

Carter collapsed against her, trembling, his back slick with sweat, his breath hot and quick against her shoulder.

As her own breathing slowed, as she gathered her scattered wits about her, tried to muster all those logical, objective, analytical thoughts, attempted to put Carter MacKenzie behind her, Annabel really only knew one thing.

She hadn't got over him in the least.

Chapter Ten

Making love with Annabel Archer wasn't what he'd expected.

Not at all.

He'd expected complaisance, competence, a cool, composed coupling. Nothing to write home about.

He'd burned. Gone up in flames, more like.

And so had Annabel Archer—he thought.

But if she had been as affected as he'd been, why, Carter asked himself, had she so blithely bounded out of bed to fetch Conan the moment he yelled?

Why had she hummed with such carefree exuberance while she changed him?

Why had she left again right after, giving Carter just a nonchalant goodbye wave and nothing more?

He needed to think.

Strapping Conan against his chest, he clambered back up onto the roof and set to work. The sunshine warmed his back as he worked. Conan gurgled and burbled, wriggling and cooing.

Normally Carter would have stopped work and bounced the baby on his knees, tickling him and reciting the nonsense rhymes that seemed to lurk somewhere in his memory ready for recall at a moment's notice.

Today he didn't even think about Conan. The baby was there, a part of the environment. But nothing more. Carter moved rhythmically along, laying the shingles and hammering, his mind consumed with Annabel.

Annabel in bed. Annabel making love. Annabel kissing him, holding him tight.

But other Annabels, too. The one who good-naturedly listened to Leif's innumerable knock-knock jokes, who could act pleased about the gift of a pair of ridiculous jeans. The Annabel who hung out the clothes while dancing with the baby, who crooned lullabies and cooked Chinese and dealt masterfully with goats. The Annabel who could spit fire at him and argue with him, then love him with such intensity he'd burned.

It didn't make sense.

Maybe he was having a relapse.

He wondered if he ought to call Milly.

And tell her what? That he'd made love with a woman for the first time in months and now he couldn't stop thinking about her?

What's wrong with that? Milly would ask him.

And Carter wasn't even sure there was something wrong. But he'd never felt quite like this after making love before—as if some fundamental chord deep inside him had, for the first time in his life, been touched.

And by Annabel Archer?

Good grief.

He worked like a demon all afternoon, stopping only when Conan fell asleep, and then only long enough to tuck the baby into the crib before heading back to the roof once again.

But even physical labor and lots of it didn't settle his mind. Or his loins.

He still had the rash, of course, and it still itched, though less than it had, thank goodness. He did his best to attribute his state of unrest to that.

Carter was only ever marginally successful at lying to himself. This wasn't one of those times.

He wondered when he'd see Annabel again. Would she come back over this evening? Did he dare just sort of casually drop in on her?

The thought made him laugh. To think that he was actually plotting ways to be in her company. It boggled the mind.

He thought about Frances. Had she really been trying to match him up with Annabel as Annabel had claimed?

Obviously Annabel thought the idea preposterous.

Carter found her reaction annoyed him. Was he as unlikely a marriage prospect as all that?

The phone was ringing when he got down off the roof. Annabel?

He hurried to answer it.

"Carter." The voice was undeniably female, actually quite sexy. "It's Marilee," she said after a moment when he didn't reply.

"Oh, right! Marilee! How are you?"

"Looking forward to Wednesday," she said in that throaty voice of hers.

"Wednesday?" He couldn't get a grip on it.

"Dinner. You didn't forget!"

"No. Not at all."

"Well, I called to tell you I'm doing chicken marengo, so if you still want to bring the wine, get a white."

He felt like saying he couldn't come. He didn't want to. Not now. Not after loving Annabel.

Why not? he asked himself irritably. It wasn't as if Annabel really gave a damn about him. She'd been positively cavalier in the aftermath. She'd practically sprung out of bed to get Conan. She'd scarcely spared him a glance when she left.

"Carter?"

"Er, sure. Fine." Pause. "Can I bring anything else?"

"Just yourself." Another throaty chuckle. "You don't know how much I'm looking forward to it."

He hung the receiver up slowly, trying to sort things out. It made sense to go out with Marilee, he thought. She was gorgeous, talented, witty—everything he'd ever wanted, ever dreamed of.

And Annabel?

What about his relationship with her?

They were adults. Consenting adults.

LIFE, ANNABEL TOLD herself, hadn't changed a bit. She still had work to do, children to raise, goats to tend. She had pomanders to poke and a siding job to save for. Her oven was just as dirty as it had been last night, and if she needed to keep her feet on the ground, she could always contemplate how many hours it would take to clean it.

But she couldn't help smiling. A lot.

It was foolishness—this business with Carter—and she knew it.

There was no future in it. She knew that, too.

But it was fun. It was different. It was lovely, charming, sexy, beautiful.

It had been far too long since her life had held all those things together.

As long as she remembered that, as long as she saw their lovemaking as a lark, an affair and nothing more, she could handle it.

Like the series of allergy shots she remembered from childhood, developing a resistance to Carter would apparently take some time. It would, she thought with a smile, be a blessed sight more pleasant a way to develop resistance than the allergy shots had been.

She knew it wouldn't last. She was a big girl now. She didn't believe in fairy tales. Goodness knew, Carter was no knight in shining armor, no prince come to rescue her from her dreadful plight.

Her plight wasn't all that dreadful. In fact, life was damn good.

Making love with Carter—however briefly—just made it better.

In the afternoon she took Eb's standing order down to the shop and helped restock his shelves. She took Leif to Gaithersburg for his trombone lesson and picked up Libby to go to the dentist.

She did the laundry, dyed soaps and untangled Arnold from the thicket behind the barn. The washing machine overflowed. She called the plumber, went back and got Libby from the dentist, picked up Ernie and Bert's order at the bakery, dropped it off, then shopped for the groceries for supper. The washing machine cost $84.70. The parts wouldn't be in until next Thursday. Maybe the plumber could come back a week from Monday. He'd have to see.

A normal, average day.

But better than wonderful really because while she shelved and drove and wrapped and dropped and coped, she remembered her morning with Carter.

She smiled.

She cooked lasagna for supper, the kids' favorite. She made a chocolate cake.

"Chocolate? Not carrot?" asked Libby. "What's the occasion?"

Annabel smiled.

It wasn't until Libby was tucked up with forty pages of government to read and outline, until Leif had finished his homework and gone to sleep, until she had mopped up the water in the basement and had decided, by brief experimentation, on a natural cranberry dye as a possible coloring agent for the soap, that she actually sat down, put her feet up on the hassock, closed her eyes and wondered what Carter was doing at that very moment.

A few seconds later when the phone rang, she found out.

"Where've you been?"

Just the sound of his voice set off tiny nerve endings all along her spine. She flexed her toes. "Don't ask."

"Why? What happened?"

"Nothing out of the ordinary. Not since this morning anyway," she added, still smiling.

"Shall we do it again?"

"We could, I suppose."

"When?" His eagerness was flattering, heady. Dangerous.

Annabel opened her eyes.

Deliberately she grounded herself in the holey sneakers under the table, the trig book on the counter, the comfortable bulk of Goliath curled in the best chair in the house.

Those were the things that would last. Not her affair with Carter MacKenzie.

"You could make a house call," he suggested. "Put a little more ointment on my rash."

A tempting thought. "I can't," Annabel said. What would she tell Libby if she suddenly took off?

There was another pause. "Chicken, Annabel?"

She sat up straight. "Like hell!"

CARTER WAITED. And waited.

She never came.

Finally, sometime just past one, he gave up, climbed the stairs, checked on a soundly slumbering Conan and fell frustrated into his bed.

He was exhausted. He couldn't sleep. Images of Annabel played with his mind, teasing him, touching him. His rash bothered him, but he was too tired to get up and put the ointment on it.

So he lay there and itched—and wished.

His dreams, when he finally managed to sleep, were vivid and erotic. They did everything to him that Annabel wasn't there to do, except to satisfy him. Until the last.

The last dream was different. Gentler. Cool at first, as if a soft breeze caressed his heated skin. Then soft. Her fingers playing with his toes, then moving on to his calves, smoothing and stroking, brushing lightly against the backs of his knees, sliding slowly up under the hem of the nightshirt to caress his thighs.

He twisted under her touch, moaned at the injustice of it, knowing it was a dream. But still her touches went on. Feathery light. Maddeningly slow. Driving him to the brink.

He fought his way to consciousness and flipped over, furious with himself.

In the soft morning light, Annabel sat on the edge of the bed, smiling at him, all ginger hair and golden freckles.

He blinked. Blinked again. Made a little disbelieving sound at the back of his throat.

The comforter had been shoved to the foot of the bed and he lay covered only by the nightshirt. Annabel's finger traced tiny circles on his knee. "I'm making a house call."

He reached for her, but she pulled back, still smiling, and shook her head. "You're the patient, remember?"

"And what are you?" His voice was rusty.

"The doctor, of course."

Carter hesitated, then slowly let his arms fall to his sides. He watched her warily as she got up and reached for the jar of cream on the nightstand, then came back to kneel at the foot of the bed between his legs.

She picked up his left foot, flexing his knee as she settled the foot in her lap.

"I don't have a rash on my toes!"

"The best doctors are the most thorough, Carter. Who knows what I might find?"

She found that he was ticklish. He squirmed as her fingers explored his toes, as her nails traced gentle lines along the sole of his foot, scratching lightly, first on his left foot, then on his right.

"Annabel!"

She touched a finger to her lips. "Shh. You'll wake the baby."

Even as she spoke her hands moved on, circling his ankles, then tripping lightly up his calves. She leaned forward and kissed his kneecaps.

He jerked at the touch of her tongue. "What the—"

"Just testing reflexes. I didn't bring my hammer."

His fingers twisted in the sheet. "Annabel," he warned, but still she ignored him, her fingers edging beneath the hem of the nightshirt, lifting it, pushing it up until she exposed the beginnings of the rash at the top of his thighs.

"Ah, yes." One finger trailed lightly along the bottom edge of the redness. "I begin to see the problem."

"You can't possibly see the problem!"

She gave a light laugh. Her fingers strayed briefly beneath the bunched-up nightshirt, finding and acknowledging the true source of his distress.

''We'll get to that,'' she promised, her fingers leaving him, their absence making him ache. She edged up closer so that she sat between his knees. ''First things first.''

Her fingers dipped into the jar, then began to spread the cream along the tops of his thighs. It was so cool and blissful at the same time that it made him feel hotter and hungrier than ever. He bit his lower lip, watched her from beneath hooded lids.

She looked so serious, so intent, her head bent, her eyes cast down as she watched her fingers move, noting his response to them. Only the faint tremor in her touch gave her away. His own body was perilously close to giving everything away.

''Annabel!'' He muttered her name again, tensing, resisting the sensations she was arousing.

She lifted her head, smiled at him. ''I think I missed my calling. I had no idea a doctor's life could be so interesting.''

''We could make it a lot more interesting,'' he said huskily.

A gingery brow arched. ''Oh? How?''

''Let me take your clothes off.''

''Oh, no. We couldn't do that. I'm the doctor. Doctors don't take their clothes off. That wouldn't be fair.''

''Not fair? This is fair?''

''You don't like it?'' Her hands stilled, then pulled back.

''Annabel!'' Her name whistled through his clenched teeth. His hips arched, seeking.

She took hold of the nightshirt again, easing it clear up so that now it bunched around his waist, exposing him totally. He was on fire. She didn't touch him.

He tried to lie still, not to squirm. She was frowning now, bending her head closer, then she lifted her gaze and met his, her expression quite grave.

"Goodness," she said quite solemnly, "have you had that swelling long?"

"Too damned long," Carter growled, the last threads of his control beginning to unravel as her soft fingers touched him once more.

Annabel made a tsking sound. "Dear me. It looks serious."

"It *is* serious!"

"Perhaps I should call for a second opinion."

"Not on your life, lady. You're the doctor. You know what to do about it." And please, he thought, desperate, aching, his whole body rigid under the gentle brush of her fingers. *Please do it. Do it now!*

She bent slowly and brushed a kiss across his lips.

"I think I have just the remedy on hand." With quick efficient movements, she set the jar of cream aside, reached up and stripped off her shirt, slid out of her jeans and came to him, giving him hungry kisses, nipping at his nose, his chin, his ears.

And Carter, who had never in his life been so ready for loving, gave himself up to it. To her.

He kissed her fiercely, ferociously, unable to get enough of her. His arms went around her, drawing her down so that now she straddled him. With his hands, with his hips, with everything in him, he urged her to complete their union.

And the second she did, he felt as if he had come home, as if this embrace was the one he had been looking for, this the haven he had been seeking, the love he'd always hoped for and despaired ever to find.

His climax hit him so swiftly, so fiercely that he felt a moment's panic that he had gone too fast, taken everything for himself, leaving Annabel behind. But it wasn't so.

She was with him, her body as consumed by the force of their union as his.

After, he felt her lift her head and kiss his chest, then look him in the eyes. "What do you think?" she asked huskily. "Are you cured?"

Not nearly, Carter thought. And when she sank against his chest, he kissed her hair and held her close and wondered how he could have been so blind.

GREAT SEX, Annabel decided, could blow your mind. She'd never realized.

Sex with Mark had been lovely. It had been warm and tender—once, that is, they'd figured each other out. But it had never completely shattered her, had never left her reeling the way she reeled under Carter's touch.

She sat in the rocker in the living room, cradling Conan in her arms, giving him a bottle, smiling at him, smiling at the memories of the past hour and a half, at the thought of Carter's naked body under the shower right now upstairs.

It was dangerous the way she was coming to feel about Carter, the way she wanted to be with him, to touch him, to feel him tense under her fingers, to feel the hunger of his lips on hers. It was like playing with explosives. A good way to get hurt.

The moment she thought it, she denied it.

Love would hurt. If she loved Carter, it would hurt. She didn't. She was simply, briefly, enjoying him.

And a good thing, too, she thought moments later when the telephone rang.

"Is this Frances? This is Marilee Newman," the voice said at her answer. "Tell Carter I've changed my mind. I'm making beef Wellington tomorrow night. If he hasn't already got the wine, tell him to get a red. Thanks." She rang off without giving Annabel a chance to reply.

Annabel sat quite still. She looked down at Conan, listened yet again to the running water upstairs. Her throat felt funny. Kind of tight.

If she'd *loved* him, she would have cared.

It was ever such a good thing she did not.

Conan finished his bottle and batted it aside. Annabel heard the water shut off, heard Carter's footsteps making the floor creak overhead as he moved around the bathroom.

The door opened and he padded down the hall. Moments later he came down the steps and smiled that bewitching smile.

"I washed all the ointment off in the shower. I don't suppose you'd like to maybe... apply another dose?" His grin beguiled her.

Annabel shook her head. She swallowed carefully. "Can't. Conan wouldn't approve. You can do it yourself."

"More fun when you do it."

For a fleeting moment she wished—oh, God, she wished—it had been more than lust, more than great sex between them.

But it wasn't. Wouldn't ever be.

"I agree," she said. "But that's the breaks." She got up and carried Conan with her into the kitchen to wash out his bottle. "By the way," she said over her shoulder. "Marilee Newman called. She said to tell you to bring a red wine instead." She waited half a second before adding, "Do you by any chance need a baby-sitter?"

Probably she was a fool for asking, but she had to show him that it didn't matter—that *he* didn't matter. She wouldn't let him hurt her again. The problem was hers, not his. He'd never pretended to love her.

She concentrated on the bottle, running the water, swishing it around, rinsing it again.

"Er, yeah, I guess," she finally heard him say behind her. She turned to see Carter standing in the doorway to the kitchen. He wasn't smiling.

"What time?"

"Um, about six. Shall I bring him over?"

"Sure. At bedtime I'll bring him back here." She dumped out the water and set the bottle on the counter upside down, then handed Conan to Carter. "I've really got to be going," she said, wiping her hands on the sides of her jeans. "Lots to do."

Carter followed her to the door. "You don't mind? Baby-sitting while I . . . while I . . ."

"Go out with Marilee? Heavens no. It was my idea, wasn't it?"

HE WENT OUT WITH MARILEE. He smiled at her jokes, he praised her cooking, he brought red wine instead of white. He made a deliberate effort to enjoy himself. She was a charming woman—even more charming than she'd been the first time he'd met her.

He didn't care.

He was thinking about Annabel, remembering her blasé attitude, her easy dismissal of his date, the nonchalance with which she'd greeted him earlier in the evening, taken Conan from his arms and given him a blithe smile.

"Have a wonderful evening," she'd said.

"I will," he'd answered with gritted teeth. If she didn't care, neither would he.

Nice try, Carter, he told himself ruefully.

"What? What did you say?" he asked Marilee. It was the fifth time he'd lost the thread of the conversation since they'd left the table and adjourned with brandy glasses to sit on the sofa in front of the fire.

He turned to her, gave her a game smile and tried to look interested.

"It doesn't matter," she said lightly, curling her feet underneath her, smiling at him. "I was just talking real estate. Were you really thinking of buying property up here?" she asked him, a speculative look on her face. "Or was it just a ploy?"

"Er," Carter said. "Um..."

"I thought so." She leaned toward him and brushed her lips across his. "I'm so glad."

He sat up straight, blinked several times, eased his collar away from the back of his neck. "Yeah, me, too."

"Collar too tight?" Marilee's fingers were eager to solve the problem.

"N-no. It's fine." Carter pulled back. "You know," he glanced at his watch, "I really should be going now. You have to get up and go to work tomorrow."

"It's early yet."

"Yeah, well, it isn't just for you. I— There's this baby."

Marilee's eyes got huge. "You have a baby?"

"No. Not I—but—"

But he'd seen enough of Marilee to know that mentioning the circumstances of his acquaintance with Conan would not be a good idea. Marilee would doubtless find Maeve's behavior reprehensible. She was a good lawyer, a thorough one. She might even know of a law against it. Child abandonment came to mind.

"I promised to baby-sit," Carter lied. "I nearly forgot."

"At this hour? For who?"

"Er, no one you know. And like you said, it's early yet."
He got to his feet and plucked his jacket off the back of the
armchair, shrugging into it.

Marilee looked at him with a mixture of hurt and sus-
picion. Carter felt vaguely guilty. He should have begged
off, should never have come at all.

It was all Annabel's fault that he had. If she hadn't been
so damned cheerful about his going out with Marilee ... if
she hadn't been so eager to baby-sit so he could—as if their
morning together had meant nothing more to her than a
good-time roll in the hay, so to speak—he would have
called Marilee and told her he couldn't make it.

Damn Annabel, he thought grimly.

He took hold of Marilee's hand. "Thanks for the wonderful dinner. I enjoyed it. You're a fantastic cook."

She smiled a little ruefully. "I'm glad you liked the dinner at least."

"I liked the company, too," he said. "I'm afraid I'm
just ... preoccupied tonight."

"Apparently." Marilee walked him to the door. "It's
been ... interesting, Carter."

It was his turn to look rueful. "You're being kind."

"Perhaps."

"I'm sorry."

"Me, too. But, hey—" she gave a little shrug "—that's
life. We're grown-ups, right? We know not everything goes
the way we want it to."

"Yeah," Carter said.

WE KNOW NOT EVERYTHING goes the way we want it to.

Her words echoed in his head as he walked to his car, as
he got in and started the engine, as he drove home to
Conan. And to Annabel, who didn't love him.

There was, he supposed, a certain amount of poetic justice in her casual approach to their intimacy.

Heaven knew he'd been casual enough for most of his life. It wasn't until he'd met Diane Bauer that he'd ever even considered a less-than-casual approach to women.

But Diane hadn't meant to him what Annabel did. He hadn't thought about her night and day. He hadn't dreamed of her, needed her, loved her.

Diane had told him he hadn't, but he hadn't really understood. Now he was beginning to.

Because for the very first time he thought it was happening to him.

He had, somehow or other, fallen in love with Annabel Archer. Without wanting, without knowing, certainly without trying.

But definitely with passion. With exuberance. And increasingly with every little corner of his soul.

And she thought he was a good lay.

Chapter Eleven

He was in a less-than-cheerful frame of mind when he got home.

He didn't know what to say, how to act. He flicked off the ignition and jerked open the car door. Stuffing the keys into his pocket, he strode toward the house.

Would she be smiling? Welcoming him with open arms? Ready for another tumble in the sheets?

The thought made him grit his teeth.

He didn't damned well *want* another roll in the sheets. No, that wasn't true. He wanted one, but he wanted it to matter. *He* wanted to matter.

To Annabel Archer?

Fat chance.

He banged the door open with unnecessary force, ready to make up a thousand lies about a wonderful evening with Marilee. So what if it wasn't true. She didn't have to know. A guy had to preserve his pride, didn't he?

But he never got to say a word.

Annabel was standing in the middle of the floor looking at him, stricken. Her face was blotchy, her freckles more pronounced than ever. Her eyes were decidedly red.

"What is it? What's wrong?"

For a moment she didn't speak, just shook her head, her lips pressed tightly together, her fingers knotting.

"Annabel!" He crossed the room and grabbed her by the arms. "Damn it! What happened? Is it Conan? Leif? Libby?"

He'd never seen her look like this. He didn't know what had happened, but whatever it was, he knew it was serious.

She seemed to stiffen under his touch. He could feel her begin to compose herself, pull her emotions in, straighten up, draw a deep breath.

"It's . . . my father . . . he's had a stroke." Her voice was almost steady. He felt her begin to shake, and he pulled her hard against him, holding her.

He didn't know anything about Annabel's father. She'd never mentioned him before. But from her reaction he decided they must be close.

"Is he—I mean, how . . . how bad . . . is he?"

"Bad," she said, her mouth against his jacket. "Mother would never have called me otherwise. He wouldn't have let her."

"He'd try to protect you from knowing?"

Annabel shook her head. "He wouldn't want me to know."

"Why not?"

She looked away, out the window into the darkness. "We don't . . . speak."

"Ever?"

"Not for nineteen years."

"My God." All his impressions changed in an instant. *Not speak for nineteen years?* He couldn't imagine it. He and his own father had yelled at each other every chance they got.

He suddenly realized how little he really knew about Annabel. She might have been found under a cabbage leaf for all he knew. And he wanted to know everything.

But now was not the time.

"What are you going to do?"

"I don't know." Her fingers twisted together. She bent her head.

"Should you go see him?"

"The shock would probably kill him."

Carter looked at her closely. There were tears on her eyelids, trembling, about to fall. She blinked rapidly.

"I doubt that," Carter said gently.

"You don't know my father."

Carter didn't think he wanted to. Anyone who could reduce Annabel Archer to tears sounded like a bastard and a half. "I know you."

She pressed her forehead against his shoulder, shaking her head. He held her, his lips brushing against her hair, wishing he could make the whole painful episode go away.

The phone rang. Carter gave her a quick hug and went to answer it.

It was Leif. "Is my ma still there? Did she tell you my grandmother called looking for her? Did she say why? Was that really my grandmother?"

"Yeah, she told me. Yeah, it was." Carter didn't know what else to say.

"What's going on?"

"She'll talk to you when she gets home."

"Is she . . . okay?"

"Yes." He wasn't sure it was the truth, but he'd do everything in his power to make it so. He hung up the phone and went back to Annabel.

"Leif," she guessed, her voice a monotone.

"He's worried about you."

"I'm fine. Everything will be fine." She reached for her coat. "I've got to go."

"I'll walk you back."

"Conan—"

"Conan will be fine."

"You don't know—"

"I know what my priorities are. I'm seeing you home."

They walked quickly, in silence. Annabel's hand was cold and dry in his. She didn't speak. Nor did Carter. He didn't know what to say or what to do. He needed to wait for her.

Leif was at the door when they arrived. "She called again. My grandmother." He seemed almost to test the word as he spoke it, as if he might have got it wrong.

Annabel's hand clenched around Carter's. "What'd she say?"

"To call her." Leif thrust a piece of paper at her. "This is the number."

Annabel snatched it and hurried to the phone. Carter followed her in and shut the door, leaning against it. Leif watched his mother punch out the number.

"What's wrong?" he asked Carter.

"Your grandfather's had a stroke."

"I didn't know I had a grandfather, either. Holy cow. Is he gonna die?"

"I don't know."

Annabel had got through and was talking now in a low, intense tone. Her face was pale, her freckles vivid.

"I hope not," Leif said. "Not when I just found out I got him."

Annabel's voice rose slightly. "I don't know! What'll he think if— I know, Mom. I know. But if he doesn't even *know* . . . yes." She bowed her head. "Yes. All right." Her voice faded almost to a whisper now. "All . . . right."

She let the receiver drop back onto the hook and stood staring at the floor. Then slowly she raised her eyes and met Leif's gaze.

Carter saw the boy hesitate, bite down on his lip.

"Oh, baby," Annabel said and in three steps came to take him in her arms. She buried her face in Leif's fair hair, hugged him close. Leif put his arms around her, held her.

Carter envied them their love.

Annabel lifted her head and met his eyes. "I have to go. I have to go, and I don't know how. It's been so long. Too long. But I can't let him go without...without trying."

Carter nodded. He understood. Oh, God, how well he understood! He wished he'd had the chance.

"I'll go with you."

SHE SHOULD HAVE SAID NO.

She should have had the guts to handle it on her own, shoulder her own burdens, fight her own fights.

She couldn't.

She needed Carter.

She needed his support, his calm, his steady presence, his wry humor.

She didn't think she could get through the next few days otherwise.

She had been stunned by her mother's phone call. Communication between Annabel and her parents had been virtually nonexistent since the night she'd announced she was marrying Mark.

Christina Archer, to give her credit, had tried to mend the breach between father and daughter. But she had no success. Edward Lodge Archer would tolerate no view other than his own, and his view was that Annabel had ultimately and completely let him down.

"Him or me" might be too simplistic a way to think about the choice her father had given her. Doubtless he had couched it in finer, more sophisticated terms. But ultimately it had come down to the same thing.

And for Annabel there had been no question.

She'd picked Mark and her unborn child.

"Go, then," Edward had said. "Marry him. Make your bed and lie in it. But don't come back to me as long as you have him. Don't expect me to save you from your folly. As long as you persist in this, I no longer have a daughter."

She'd never seen her parents after that night. She'd married and buried a husband. She'd given birth to two beautiful children. She'd supported herself and them for eighteen years. And she'd done it all without a word from Edward Archer.

Someday, she'd told herself, there would come a time to face the past, to test the pain, to see if the wound had healed.

But never had the time been now.

Never until tonight...until her mother's desperate phone call told Annabel that tomorrow might well be too late.

"Please come," Christina had said. "Don't let this go on between you."

And if he still refused to make peace with her?

Christina did not believe he would.

Annabel was less certain. She was afraid to contemplate the possibility.

But with Carter behind her, Carter's hand in hers, her father's ultimate rejection no longer had the power to terrify her.

Carter might not love her—she didn't expect him to love her—but at least he cared.

HE GOT UP at the crack of dawn, not even waiting for Conan's summons. He had his own gear packed and most of Conan's by the time the first warbles from the back bedroom were heard.

A clean diaper, a warm bottle and a quick change of clothes and Conan was ready to travel. Stowing the baby and the gear into the Blazer, he set off for Annabel's.

She was in a dither.

He'd never seen Annabel in a dither, indecisive, muttering, putting this into her bag, taking that out again. He didn't take time to appreciate the novelty of it.

"Hold Conan. I'll do it," he told her.

And while she sat on the couch, crooning softly to Conan, Carter packed for her. He also packed for Libby and Leif.

"What are you doing with all that?" she demanded when he reappeared coming down the steps carrying suitcases filled with their clothes.

"I don't need all that."

"It's not all yours. It's mine, Conan's, Libby's and Leif's."

"Libby's and Leif's? They're not coming!"

Carter just looked at her. "You think they're going to stay here?"

"If I tell them to. I'm their mother!"

"Exactly. And you love them and you want what's best for them."

He didn't have to argue very hard.

She pressed her lips together. "I don't want them hurt."

"No one will hurt them. I won't let anyone hurt them. I'll keep an eye on them while you're at the hospital. I don't know where you grew up, Annabel. I don't care. But I promise you, I can handle it."

She looked almost startled. But then she nodded, a tiny smile twisting her mouth. "I can't imagine anyone better equipped."

He didn't know what she meant by that.

He just bundled her and the baby into his car, called Bert and asked her to feed the goats and keep an eye on things, called Jack and Frances and left a message on their answering machine just in case Maeve contacted them about Conan, then went back and got into the car.

"Where are we going?"

"First to pick up the kids from school, then Boston."

He remembered Libby saying her mother had been born there. He remembered how little she wanted her children exposed to it. He supposed it must have something to do with the places she had lived growing up.

There were some rough parts in Boston. Some seedy neighborhoods, some less-than-savory streets. He thought he understood.

But when they arrived on the outskirts, Annabel aimed him through the suburbs, past the factories, beyond the row houses and the narrow dirty streets. They came into rolling wooded hills, lush lawns, palatial estates.

"This exit," she told him.

He frowned. There was nothing here save money and influence, Harvard accents and well-limbed family trees. He'd even been here himself a time or two, under duress, at somebody or other's dance or deb ball in the days before he'd learned the fascinating art of rebellion.

But he wasn't questioning Annabel now. He didn't have to. As they wove through the tree-shaded lanes, catching occasional glimpses of scrupulously manicured lawns and rambling Colonial-style mansions, the kids did it for him.

"You lived *here?*" Libby's tone was accusing as her eyes followed one after another of the curving driveways up into the wooded hillsides that protected most of the houses from view.

"Holy cow," Leif muttered. His head swiveled as he caught a glimpse of a three-story building set back into the hillside. "Look at that. Is it a house or a school?"

"A house, stupid," Libby said. "These are all houses. Aren't they, Mother?" There was just a hint of challenge in her voice.

"Yes."

Leif whistled.

Carter didn't say a word. He glanced over at the woman by his side, taking in her plaid flannel shirt, her faded jeans, her scuffed earth shoes. Earth Mother my foot, he thought, and reassessed everything he knew about Annabel Archer yet again.

"Take a right at the next drive," Annabel directed. Her fingers were knotted in her lap.

Carter slowed down. "This the road to the old homestead?"

She sighed. "I'm afraid it is."

"Are you okay?"

"Fine."

"You look like you're about to throw up."

"Thank you very much." But he saw the corner of her mouth twitch.

He grinned. "I'm a great flatterer."

Annabel's smile faded. "Not always."

"Huh?"

"Never mind."

He didn't have time to pursue the matter for they went around the curve in the road and there across a wide, shimmering pond, lay an immense three-story rose-colored Georgian brick with four gleaming white pillars.

Carter stopped the car.

"That was the house you grew up in?" asked Libby. Her eyes were like saucers as she looked from the house to her mother and back again.

"Yes."

"Hol-eeee cow," breathed Leif.

And Conan, who had slept like the proverbial baby since early in New Hampshire, opened his eyes at the sudden cessation of movement and looked around.

He gave a tiny whimper and started to cry.

ANNABEL KNEW precisely how he felt.

The first glimpse of Archer's Lodge—her father's pun on his middle name—was always intimidating to be sure.

But it wasn't the house that daunted Annabel. She knew about the cracks in the plaster, about which corner had settled and which chimney smoked.

It was the past that loomed before her, all the memories of expectations and failures, of battles lost and wars not won. And she wondered not for the first time why she had even bothered to come.

Nothing would have changed. Certainly not Edward Lodge Archer.

And to subject Libby and Leif to all this?

And for what?

Her fingers twisted in her lap. A strong warm hand covered them, squeezing them lightly, then just holding on.

She glanced over. Carter gave her a quick smile.

Oh, Carter. She wanted to put her arms around him and hang on, lay her head against his shoulder and cry.

He was being so strong, so steady. And she was taking such advantage of him.

She'd half expected a roar of outrage when he discovered where she'd lived, the circumstances in which she had grown up. She had knowingly misled him about her back-

ground ever since she'd met him. And she hadn't had the
strength to explain how things really were either last night
or this morning. She'd expected he would ask questions on
the way in, but he must have realized how fragile she felt.

He hadn't said a word.

Even now the look he gave her was solicitous as he simply asked, "Are you ready? Shall we go on?"

Annabel drew herself together, then nodded. "I don't
know if my mother is at the hospital or home. But the kids
can stay here while I go to the hospital."

"Don't we get to go to the hospital?" Leif asked.

"Not yet."

She might not totally be able to protect them any longer
from the knowledge of their grandfather's existence, but
she was going to do whatever she could to keep them from
experiencing the same sort of rejection she had felt as the
recipient of her father's cold, disapproving stare. She
wasn't taking them anywhere near him until she knew they
were welcome.

As Carter pulled up in front of the house, the door was
flung open. Disapproval was the last thing on the face of
the woman standing there.

"Mother." Annabel just stared at her, seeing the result
of nineteen years of sadness on a woman she remembered
as sunny and gay. She blinked back tears, then opened the
door slowly and got out.

This was, she realized, going to be harder than facing
her father would be. She could still get angry at him, could
easily justify her actions with him. She'd never been angry at her mother.

Christina Archer might have been weak, she might have
failed to overcome Edward's flat edict that Annabel was
henceforth banished, never to be permitted home again,
but she'd never said an unkind word about Mark, had

never berated Annabel for making her choice, had never said she no longer had a daughter.

But Annabel had acted as if she'd never had a mother. She'd hugged her hurt tight against her, refusing contact with the woman who had borne her. "Him or me," she'd said in effect.

And Christina had paid the price.

And now?

Annabel stood quite still, her throat aching, her eyes stinging. "Mom?"

"Annabel!" Her mother came down the steps two at a time to sweep her daughter into her arms.

"Oh, Mom." Annabel buried her face in her mother's hair, hugged her tightly, struggling to hang on to her composure. Losing.

It was several moments before she could step back and swipe at her eyes. "Come," she said when her mother, too, took a step back and looked up at her. "Meet your grandchildren."

Libby and Leif had stopped their oohing and ahhing and now sat in the back of the car, silent and unmoving. Libby held Conan in her arms, staring down at him, trying to look as if she wasn't paying attention to every word her mother said.

Annabel didn't blame her. She didn't blame Leif, either. Neither they nor she knew precisely what to expect.

Carter eased out from behind the wheel and opened the door for Libby, taking Conan from her, offering soft words of what Annabel could only guess was encouragement. Libby gave him the baby and got out to stand next to him. Leif came out the other side and stood holding the open car door.

"This is Libby," Annabel said quietly. "And this is Leif."

Christina reached Leif first, stopped in front of him and simply looked at the boy who was only an inch shorter than she, who had her own fair hair and freckled skin, yet who looked at her solemnly with Mark Campbell's blue eyes.

She smiled and held out trembling hands to him.

Leif took her hands in his, and that was all she needed. She drew him close and rested her cheek against his hair, then brushed her lips against his forehead, once and then again. "Oh, Leif, I'm so glad you've come."

It was a minute or more before she stepped back, still holding his hands, and looked over to meet her grand daughter's eyes.

Annabel watched grandmother and granddaughter and hurt for them both. Innocent victims of a father-daughter battle, they had never known the closeness they might otherwise have shared. Christina, she thought ruefully, would have loved a cheerleader.

Would she have changed things if she could? she asked herself. Had she stayed away after Mark died only for spite?

No.

She'd put the obituary announcement in the paper she knew her father read. If they had come to the funeral, if they'd sent flowers, even a card, she would have tried again, would have braved her father's scorn for her mother's love.

She'd never had a word.

She wasn't Edward's daughter for nothing. She wasn't going to beg. Not then. Not now.

But as she watched her mother's first hesitant steps toward the child whose very life had caused the rift, she wished there could have been another way.

"Libby," her mother breathed and held out her arms. "I'm so happy to see you at last."

For a long moment Libby hesitated. She was no fool. If she and her mother hadn't actually discussed the reasons for the breach between Annabel and her parents, it didn't mean Libby didn't suspect what it was.

Annabel knew she'd been wrong not to have talked to Libby before now, knew that very shortly she would have to. But in the meantime she hoped her daughter would give her grandmother a chance. She gave Libby an encouraging smile.

Libby gave her a faint one in return. Then she took one step, then another, and allowed herself to be enfolded in her grandmother's arms.

Then, still holding her granddaughter's hand, Christina looked at Carter. She hesitated a moment, then held out her hand to him.

"Mark," she said. "Thank you for coming."

Annabel stared. *Mark?*

She'd called Carter *Mark?* She didn't know? She'd never been told? All this time and Christina never even knew that much about her daughter's life?

Oh, God, Daddy, couldn't you at least have told her?

She shook her head. "This isn't Mark. Mark...died nine years ago."

Christina went white. "Died? But...I thought..." She looked from Annabel to Carter, shaking her head.

"This is Carter, Mom. Carter MacKenzie. He's a...a friend." She didn't know how else to describe him. "And this is Conan," she went on quickly, more from desperation than anything else.

"I...I see," Christina murmured, though in fact Annabel didn't think she saw much at all. How could she when for at least nine years she hadn't known the truth?

"How's Dad?" Annabel asked.

"I don't know. They don't tell me much. They say he's 'stable,' that he's 'resting comfortably,' is feeling 'as well as can be expected.' How can you tell?"

"I'll go now. Can the kids stay with you?"

"Of course. I'd be delighted." She beamed at her grandchildren, who gave her slightly wary smiles in return. "Come along, both of you."

"Isn't Carter staying?" Leif asked Annabel.

"I'm going with your mother," Carter said, and Annabel didn't realize how much she'd been counting on him until that moment.

"But—"

"Moral support," Carter said. "You'll get your turn. Will you take care of Conan till I get back?"

"Sure." Leif reached for the baby, handling him with an expertise that made Annabel smile. He gave his mother a worried look. "You okay, Mom?"

"Fine." She ruffled his hair, gave Libby's hand a squeeze, kissed the tip of Conan's nose. "We won't be long."

Carter unloaded Conan's car seat and the bag that contained his gear, handing it to Libby. "That'll do for now," he said. He went around and held the door open for Annabel.

She got back into the car and stared straight ahead.

THEY HARDLY SPOKE all the way to the hospital. Carter knew enough not to offer platitudes. Annabel apparently could think of nothing coherent to say. She seemed to retreat further and further from him the closer to the hospital they came.

When, at last, they arrived, she made no move to get out of the car. Her face was chalky white, her knuckles even whiter. She looked as if she were going to face a firing squad.

"You don't have to do this," Carter said.

"Yes. I do."

He understood what she meant. He didn't know everything that must have passed between her and her father, but he could guess.

He wished—oh, God, he wished—that he'd been given the same opportunity, that he'd been there on that golf course, that he could have told his own father that he loved him, that just once he could have heard those words from his father's lips.

"All right," he said. "Let's go." He got out and came around to join her, tucking her arm through his and pulling her against his side, needing to protect her in whatever way he could.

He kept her there while they walked down endless corridors, held her hand while she talked to this nurse and that one, felt her tremble beneath the touch of his fingers when at last a nurse pointed them toward a private room at the end of the hall.

She took three steps, then stopped; her fingers strangled his.

"It's okay," Carter said. "It'll be fine."

She shook her head and took a deep breath. He could see her struggling, could see the fear in her eyes.

"He's your father. He loves you."

Annabel bit her lip. Her fingers tightened on his and he squeezed hers in return.

"He does," Carter repeated. "He does." As if it were a mantra. And as he spoke, he drew her with him down the hall.

She came slowly but steadily, hesitating only for a moment outside the room, and with just the briefest glance at him, she pushed open the door.

Carter intended to stay where he was—not wanting to intrude—but when she didn't let go of his hand, he followed her in.

Annabel's father lay in a high bed next to the window. He was painfully pale, his cheeks sunken, his lips cracked. But Carter knew him now by name, by reputation and, even devastated by the stroke, Edward Lodge Archer was a formidable man.

He could have given old C.W. a run for his money, Carter thought. Probably had.

The old man's eyes were closed as they approached. Annabel stopped beside the bed and cleared her throat.

"Daddy?"

His eyes opened then, slowly. He focused. Frowned. His eyes were a glittering amber-hazel that reminded Carter of an agate marble he'd had as a child.

"Hello, Daddy." Annabel managed a smile.

Edward Lodge Archer's lips parted slightly. Carter could hear the labored intake of breath, then the wheeze as he spoke. "Go... away."

Chapter Twelve

She left. Turned and, without a backward glance or even the slightest hesitation, marched straight out the door and down the hall.

Carter stood staring after her, speechless.

He looked from the rigid waxen features of her father to the rapidly retreating back of the woman he loved.

"You bloody damned fool!" he yelled at her father "How could you say that?"

The nurses came on the run.

Carter didn't care. He'd had his fill of crusty old men, of opportunities lost, of chances never taken. He pulled away from the nurse who had hold of his arm and bent over the bed.

"She loves you, you blind idiot. She's your daughter, for God's sake!"

"Mr.—Mr.—Whatever your name is! Please, lower your voice!"

The nurse had his arm again, aided by another one. They were both dragging him toward the door.

"Come along. Let's go now. You really must behave. Mr. Archer is very ill!"

"He can damned well die for all I care!" Carter knew his voice was caroming off the walls. "As far as I'm concerned it'd be no big loss! But before he does he ought to think about making peace with his family. Not everyone gets to, damn it. Did you ever think about that, you old bastard? You're lucky you have the time!''

"That's enough." The nurses had him almost out the door now. "This is a hospital! You're disturbing the patients. If you don't leave quietly at once, we'll have to call security."

Carter took one last look at the man in the bed. The nurses pushed. He held fast. His eyes met Edward Archer's.

"Don't worry," he said. "I've said it all. There's nothing left to say."

SHE MUST'VE BEEN SITTING in the car a good five minutes before Carter came.

Of course, she could hardly have expected him to participate in her dramatic exit. He had no stake in what was going on between her and her father. He had simply been there for support.

No doubt that's what was taking so long. He was busy placating the nurses, being polite to her father, smoothing over the troubled waters she'd left behind.

Thank God for Carter.

She'd been right. Her father's rejection had hurt, but it wasn't devastating. Not with Carter there.

She looked up and saw him now, walking toward her, his hands stuffed into his pockets. His head was bent. He scuffed the leaves as he came. With every scuff of his foot, with every step he took, Annabel felt as if the clouds were lifting, as if the gloom was being swept aside.

Even the darkest clouds—even the deepest pain—went away when Carter was there.

He got into the car and rested his hands on the wheel for a long moment, then looked over at her. "I'm sorry."

"It's hardly your fault. I really shouldn't have expected anything else." She gave him the best smile she could manage.

"You deserve better," he said tersely.

"Heaven help us if we get what we deserve." She turned then and leaned toward him, kissing his cheek. "Thank you. I appreciate your being there."

"Will you?" Carter muttered enigmatically. "I wonder." He started the engine. "Where to?"

"Back to get the kids, I suppose. Then home."

"What about your mother?"

"My mother and I will talk."

Annabel didn't know what sort of understanding they would come to, what form their relationship would take. She only knew that from here on, it wouldn't be wholly determined by her father.

If her mother was willing to see her, there was no way she was going to let her father keep them apart.

Christina was, to say the least, disappointed when she heard about Annabel's encounter with her father. "Oh, my dear. I'm so sorry. I never thought..." She sighed and wrung her hands.

"Nothing's changed. He's a stubborn man, Mom. He doesn't want me there."

Christina pressed her lips together. "I had so hoped..."

"Don't. There's no point."

"I suppose not." Christina's gaze went to her grandchildren outside exploring the garden. Leif was swinging from a tree. Libby, with Conan in her arms, stood watching him. They were laughing.

There was no laughter in Christina's face as she turned to her daughter. "I don't want to lose them, Annabel. I don't want to lose you."

"You won't."

"But your father—I don't know what to do about your father."

"You can't do anything," Annabel said. "He did it himself."

Christina sighed. "I guess he did."

"If you want to see your grandchildren, you're always welcome. If you want to come and see me, I'll always want to see you," Annabel told her.

"Oh, my dear," Christina murmured and put her arms around Annabel, holding her close.

The phone rang and Annabel felt her mother jerk. Then, pulling herself together, Christina went to answer it.

"When?" Her fingers clenched on the receiver. "Now? I'll come right away." Christina dropped the receiver back onto the hook and looked at Annabel, anguished. "It's your father. They want me to come."

HE SHOULD HAVE KEPT his big mouth shut. There was always the chance that the old man might have come around if he hadn't shot off his mouth as if he were some raving lunatic. He should have been rational, sensible, coherent. All of the above.

Carter sighed, and stared at the white line curving through the Vermont mountains as he drove. When had he ever been any of the above?

That had always been his father's complaint.

"You never think," C.W. would bellow at him. "Never! You only feel!"

You're right about that, old man, Carter thought.

He felt like hell.

Why should that surprise him? Hell was exactly what he deserved.

He wondered if C.W. was chortling in the hereafter at the idea of his son finally agreeing with something he'd said.

Somebody might as well be getting some joy out of it. It wasn't going to be him—or from the look of things, Annabel.

He'd left her and the kids at her mother's, looking distraught.

"I can't leave," she'd told him. "What if...what if...?"

She didn't have to say it; he already knew the only *if* that mattered. If her father was dead, she could thank Carter for having been the one to dispatch him.

He didn't tell her that.

He couldn't have borne seeing the look on her face, the dismay, the disgust, the disdain.

Everything his father had always felt for him. In spades.

"I'd rather come home with you, but—"

He understood that she was just being kind, just saying thanks for having come along, not really aware of what a botch he'd made of things, not aware at all of what he'd done that was going to be the cause of even further pain.

For regardless of what she said, he knew her father's words this afternoon had hurt her.

He'd seen her instant of recoil, as if she'd been slapped. And then he'd seen her pull herself together, begin to rationalize, to pretend she didn't care.

He understood her reaction all too well. He'd done it often enough himself.

He also knew what a lie that facade of difference was.

"I understand," he told her.

He'd allowed himself one chaste kiss on her cheek. He'd given Libby a hug, and Leif one, too. Then he'd carried Conan out to the car and started the long, lonely trip back to Vermont.

"THERE WAS A MESSAGE on the machine when I got home," Frances said when Jack came in the door. "From Carter."

"How's the roof coming?"

"He says he can't work on it for a while."

"Why not?"

"He's gone to Boston. Taking Annabel home to her parents." She was smiling.

"I didn't know Annabel had parents."

"Neither did I. But you can hear it yourself. I kid you not."

"WHY COULDN'T CARTER stay?" Leif asked.

Annabel, distracted, pacing the hospital corridor she'd just walked out of scant hours ago, anticipating the worst, wished desperately she knew the answer to Leif's question.

She shook her head. "I don't know. The roof, I guess. Conan." *Marilee Newman.*

She didn't mention Marilee, of course. She might not be the actual reason that Carter had left.

All Annabel knew was that he had.

Ever since they'd driven away from the hospital she had felt him withdrawing from her, distancing himself.

Who could blame him? she thought grimly. She should never have pitched him into this mess. It could only embarrass him, make him regret they'd become friends.

It was better, anyway, that he'd left. If her mother came out with the news she expected, Annabel would never be able to brave it out. She'd go to pieces, she knew she would.

And Carter would have had to deal with that.

"Is he gonna die, Ma?" Leif asked. "Your father, I mean."

"I don't know."

"How come we've never met him?"

"Leif!" Libby admonished.

But Annabel took him by the hand, then reached for her daughter's, leading them both over to the orange plastic bench by the wall. "It's time we talked about that."

She didn't start at the beginning—she couldn't tell them about Carter—but she did start with her moonlit encounter with their father. She told them about Mark's warmth, his strength, his innocence as well as her own.

"We were children," she said simply. She looked at her daughter. "I wasn't any older than you."

"Oh, Ma." Libby's eyes brimmed.

"I don't want you to think I regret it," Annabel went on. "I don't. I never have. But it wasn't easy. Not for your father or for me."

"He left you, didn't he?" Libby asked.

Something else Annabel had never talked about—the four years when she had been alone.

"We were big responsibilities, you and me," she said to her daughter. "Heavy burdens for such a young man. He didn't know where to turn. He didn't have a job, didn't have any skills to speak of. I said we could manage with the sheep, the goats, a little farming, my herbs and things. We argued. He drove off. I didn't hear from him for a month. And then I got a postcard from Pensacola. He'd joined the navy."

"You got his picture in the album," Leif said. "In his uniform. I saw it."

Annabel remembered the day she had put it there. It was on Libby's second birthday. It had come the day before in her daughter's birthday card.

It was the first communication she'd had since Mark's postcard almost eighteen months before. The card, of course, was for Libby. In it he'd put a check. "I can't go shopping at sea," he'd written. "But it doesn't mean I've forgotten. Please get her something so she'll know her father loves her. And you."

Until then, Annabel hadn't hoped. After that she hadn't dared. Not at first anyway.

But on his next shore leave, Mark had come to see her. Theirs had been a tentative meeting. "I didn't know," he'd told her, "if you were even still out here. I thought you might have gone home to Mommy and Daddy."

Annabel hadn't even considered it. She hadn't wanted to face her father's certain rejection. She might be struggling to make ends meet, but she and Libby were doing all right. She liked her independence, liked being responsible and making ends meet, liked the feeling that she could make it on her own.

But she liked sharing life with Mark even better, and she told him so.

Uncle Sam did his part in making sure they didn't have a lot of time together until Libby was four and a half. But as soon as Mark was out of the service, he came to Vermont.

"Did you mean it?" he asked, and she knew from the hesitancy in his voice and the wary look in his eyes that he was afraid she might not.

"Oh, yes," Annabel had told him.

She smiled now at her son. "And then we had you."

"And your parents..." Libby began somewhat hesitantly "...they still never came around?"

"No. But," Annabel had to admit this, "I probably wouldn't have been very welcoming if they had."

"Because they hurt you."

"Yes. And I wanted to hurt them in return," Annabel replied. "And I think I hurt us all instead."

"It wasn't your fault," Leif said.

Annabel gave him a hug. "Thank you for saying so."

"It's true," he insisted. "They were rotten."

"But it was a long time ago," Annabel told him. "And we've all paid the price. We'll see your grandmother sometimes now. And I don't want it to come between you. The fault was mine and my father's. Not hers."

"She's nice," Leif allowed.

Libby nodded. "She is."

"I'm glad you like her," Annabel said.

"She said maybe she could come and see us sometime," Leif reported.

"Maybe she can."

"What about your father?"

But Annabel never got to answer that, for just then the nurse opened the door to his room.

"Ms. Archer? Come quickly. Please."

CONAN CRIED the last half hour of the trip. Carter's head ached, his nerves were shot, his emotions in tatters. He felt like crying, too.

When they finally pulled into Jack and Frances's yard and the yard light came on, he sagged against the steering wheel until Conan's yelling urged him on. It was all he could do to unload Conan's gear and his own. He set it on the porch, then turned to go back to get the baby.

Arnold came ambling around the corner of the barn.

"Damnation!"

Arnold cocked his head.

Conan was screaming his head off. Hungry, no doubt. Also very likely sopping wet.

Carter took a step off the porch. Arnold came a bit closer. He made no pretense of cropping the grass, showed no feigned interest in tree bark—his interest was all in Carter.

"It isn't as if you don't know me, you old reprobate," Carter muttered, coming slowly the rest of the way down the steps. "You see me every damned day."

Arnold stood still, his feet planted squarely, regarding the man who walked steadily toward the car.

"Don't tell me you haven't noticed," Carter went on. "I'm the one on the roof, the one you always check to see is there watching before you go after one of your girls in the pasture." He couldn't be sure, of course, that Arnold was deliberately flaunting his prowess with the ladies, but it was the interpretation Carter had early on given Arnold's glancing smirk in his direction.

"I'm impressed," he said now. "You're a damned sight more successful with females than I am." He had almost made it to the car now.

Arnold still watched.

Conan screamed.

"Maybe I should take lessons from you," Carter told the goat. He reached the car, opened the door and realized there was no way he was going to get Conan out of the car without exposing his backside to Arnold.

"So that's what you were waiting for," he muttered.

Oh, well. What the hell. What else could go wrong today?

Deliberately Carter turned his back on the goat and bent over Conan, unbuckling the strap that held his car seat in place. At every instant he was prepared to be catapulted forward from one of Arnold's powerful butts.

He felt a quiet, curious nudge to his elbow. He turned, car seat and screaming baby in his arms. Arnold was standing next to him, scowling as only a goat could scowl. He was regarding Conan with a mixture of goatish worry and distaste. Then he looked at Carter, his wide expressive eyes quizzical, not hostile in the least.

"He's hungry," Carter explained, and didn't think it odd that he should be offering explanations to a goat. "And wet. I have to change him." Cautiously he began to move toward the house.

Arnold walked right alongside him, keeping pace. When Carter went up on the porch, he did, too. When Carter balanced the car seat against his hip and opened the front door, Arnold stepped aside politely and waited. Carter went in and Arnold followed, nosing curiously around the house, then peering directly into the screaming baby's face when Carter set the car seat on the kitchen table.

Conan shut up abruptly.

Carter looked at Arnold, amazed. "How'd you do that?"

The goat belched and nuzzled Conan's belly, tugging at his blanket.

"Here now. Quit that." Carter cast about hastily for something to offer Arnold in place of the blanket. All he could find that was edible was a banana. Did goats eat bananas?

He held it in front of Arnold's face. Arnold nibbled at it delicately, then curled his lip and took a bigger bite.

"Right," Carter said. "Why don't you just come with me, then? Enjoy your banana on the porch."

He didn't imagine he had a snowball's chance in hell of getting Arnold to come along quietly, but apparently once the baby had stopped crying, the goat lost interest. He allowed Carter to slowly chivvy him out the door, across the yard and through the gate into the pasture with the nannies.

Carter had no idea if he was supposed to be there or not, but Leif wasn't around to ask. And there was no way he could take Arnold home.

He shut the gate and hung over it a moment, watching Arnold as he worked his way through the banana. "'Night, Arnie," he said.

Then he made his way back to Conan, shaking his head.

But it had to say something about the quality of his day, he thought as he was changing Conan, that the high point was not getting knocked on his rear by a goat.

Conan, changed, was a happier camper. He waved his arms and gurgled while Carter spooned cereal into his mouth. He blew oatmeal bubbles and they dribbled down his face. Carter wiped them off with the edge of the bib.

"You're a slob," he told Conan. "Your manners need work. Tomorrow you're going to have to do better. How can I let you out in the civilized world otherwise." He remembered his mother saying exactly the same words to him.

Conan made a distinct raspberry sound.

Carter smiled at him. "My feelings exactly." He finished feeding Conan, then put a bottle on to heat. He walked the baby around the kitchen as they waited, savoring the solid warmth of Conan's tiny body nestled against his chest, the weight of the baby's head as it came to rest on his shoulder, the soft sound of Conan sucking his thumb.

He picked up the bottle, dried it off and carried it and the baby into the living room. Only the one light beside the sofa was on. Carter sat in the rocker as far away from it as he could, settling in, relishing the dimness, the peace.

He didn't have much else to relish. Only Conan. The baby lay snuggled in his arms, one chubby hand pressed against the bottle, the other gripping the front of Carter's shirt.

Carter looked down into the dark watchful eyes, saw them cloud with sleep, fight to stay awake, then lose. The bottle slipped out of Conan's mouth. His lips moved, then stopped, remaining parted, almost smiling.

Carter continued to sit there, rocking. He couldn't just get up and carry the baby upstairs. He couldn't let go that easily. It was comforting, sitting there holding Conan and rocking. Carter needed comforting tonight.

He dozed there till well past eleven. He was roused by a knock on the door.

Annabel?

His heart leapt before he became rational and realized it couldn't possibly be. But then . . . who . . . ?

He got up carefully and moved to lay Conan, still sleeping, on the couch, buffering him with a pillow so he wouldn't roll off. Then, at the second knock, he went to answer the door.

It was a plump fair-haired girl about Libby's age. Behind her there stood a weedy-looking young man with wild hair.

"I'm Maeve," she said. "And this is Jerry."

HE DIDN'T NEED THIS.

God knew, on top of everything else that had happened today, Carter didn't need to confront Conan's wandering parents.

"Who're you?" Maeve demanded, apparently noting for the first time that he wasn't Jack.

"My name's MacKenzie. I'm a friend of the Neillandses. I'm putting on their roof."

"Where's my baby?" There was panic in Maeve's voice now. She pushed her way past him into the living room, stopping only when she spotted Conan asleep on the sofa.

"Is *this* where you've been keeping him?" she demanded, rounding on Carter, furious.

"No, by God, it's not where I've been keeping him," Carter snapped back at her. "But a hell of a lot you'd care anyway, going off and leaving him like that!"

"I thought Frances—"

"Think again. Frances and Jack are in New York. But did you think to inquire? You might have left Conan with anyone—with *no one*— dumping him on the porch like that! Like he's some kind of parcel!"

He should have been calm, should at least have not yelled. Heaven knew he should have learned his lesson by now. He plowed straight ahead. "He's fine, no thanks to you," he told the two of them harshly.

"I didn't mean . . ." Maeve said faintly. "I saw the car, and . . . I never thought . . ."

"Well, you need to start thinking," Carter told her in more modulated tones. "You have a child. Not just when you feel like having one, but all the time. And you have responsibilities toward that child."

"I know that." She met his eyes for just a moment, then looked away.

"It . . . was my fault." Jerry's voice was gruff.

Carter's gaze swung to fix on the boy.

Jerry rubbed a hand through his hair, making it stick up even farther. "I panicked. I ran. I lost my job and I didn't see how I could get another one. She . . . came after me. I'm coming back. I'll take care of him while she's working. It'll be okay. I'm going back to school, too. And I'll try to find part-time work. We worked it out."

"Nice for you," Carter said. "It might not have been so nice for Conan."

"I'm sorry," Maeve whispered.

"Me, too," Jerry said. He craned his neck, trying to catch a glimpse of the blanket-wrapped child. "Is he all right? Really?"

"He's fine," Carter said. "I just got him to sleep. I was holding him when you knocked."

Maeve started toward him, then hesitated, looking again at Carter. "Can I—"

"Go ahead."

She started to, then stepped back. "No. Jerry, you do it."

Jerry looked as if she'd asked him to wrestle Arnold to the death. But he gamely moved forward and bent to scoop Conan up in his arms.

Carter moved, too, wanting to push Jerry out of the way and show him how to pick up the child. He shoved his hands into his pockets, told his feet to stay welded to the floor.

Jerry bobbled the baby momentarily, then got a hold on him, rather as if he were a wide receiver and Conan a football. He peered down into his son's face, jiggling him, waking him.

Carter wanted to gnash his teeth.

"See, look. He remembers me." Jerry was beaming. He bent his head and nuzzled his nose against Conan's. "How ya doin', son?"

And Carter felt his throat close tight.

"I really am sorry," Maeve said to him. She put her hand on his arm so that he couldn't walk away. "I've always depended on Frances. She's meant so much to me. Like an aunt, I guess. I knew her when she taught at my school when I was just in junior high. She saw me getting involved with the wrong crowd and tried to steer me away. I didn't always listen, but I always knew she'd be there when I needed her." She colored slightly. "At least I expected she would. Thanks a lot, Mr. MacKenzie. You're really special, too."

Carter managed half a smile.

"Come on, Jerry," Maeve said. "We've bothered Mr. MacKenzie long enough. Where are Conan's things?" she asked Carter.

"I'll get them." He made his escape up the stairs to Jason's bedroom. He gathered up the small pile of Conan's clothing, his extra blanket, leaving behind only the footed sleeper Annabel had given him that had belonged to Leif. He stood for a moment looking down at the empty crib. His eyes stung.

He turned and walked quickly back down the steps where Maeve met him at the bottom. He piled everything into her arms. "His extra bottles are in the kitchen. Hang on, I'll get them."

He put the bottles, the jars of strained peaches and pears, the half-gone box of cereal into a grocery sack. He carried that back into the living room. Jerry was already putting Conan into the car.

Maeve stowed the sack in the back, then got into the passenger side and rolled down her window. "I don't know how to thank you," she said.

Carter leaned one hand on the car door and looked at the baby, wide-eyed and curious in the back seat. He looked back at Maeve. "I think you do."

"I'll take the best care of him in the world," she promised. "Would you like to...see him sometime?"

Carter hesitated. How much pain could a grown man stand? he wondered. But would not seeing Conan ever again be better?

"Yes."

Maeve patted his hand. "You can be his honorary uncle."

UNCLE CARTER.

He supposed there was justice in it. He supposed, if he looked hard enough, he could even find some small consolation. It was better, he told himself, than nothing.

But he couldn't muster up much enthusiasm, because right now nothing was exactly what he felt he had.

He'd done what Milly had suggested: he'd gone away, taken a look at his life. He'd discovered quite a lot of things about himself that he'd only just begun to suspect.

He would have been a good parent.

He'd first begun to consider the idea when he'd been entrusted with Jason, when Jack and Frances had smilingly but quite seriously bestowed on him what Jack called "godfatherhood." He'd confirmed that feeling in the past few weeks in his dealings with Leif and Libby. And with Conan.

He sat now in the rocker. Alone. In the dark.

And he remembered the solid warm body he'd held against his only a few short hours ago. He ached for the loss.

He ached for another loss more.

He knew he'd never really had Annabel Archer. She'd never loved him the way he'd grown to love her. But he missed her anyway. He wondered if she would even speak to him again when she found out what he'd done.

What could she say to the man who'd killed her father that he might conceivably want to hear?

Most of his adult life he'd found fault with his own father—especially with C.W.'s inability to form and maintain relationships. He knew now that he had no room to talk.

The old man had been right after all. Carter did screw up everything he touched.

He'd finish the roof. It'd take another day or so. Then he'd be off.

He'd go a long way away this time. To the farthest ends of the earth. Maybe join a monastery.

Not the Trappists. They lived in communities. The Carthusians would be better. They couldn't ruin relationships—they lived by themselves in little huts.

He could get a really good perspective on his life then, Carter thought. But he wouldn't have to look for what was missing. That he already knew.

Annabel.

The other half of his heart.

Chapter Thirteen

"Is he—" Annabel's eyes flew to her mother's. Christina, standing beside the hospital bed, one hand gripping the bed rail, looked very pale.

"He wants to talk to you."

Hesitantly, feeling as if she were negotiating a mine field rather than a linoleum floor, Annabel crossed the room.

Her father looked much as he had earlier, pale, waxen, a shadow of his former self. His eyes met hers as she approached, but he didn't speak until she was right next to his bed.

Then, with considerable effort, he raised himself slightly and his lips began to move. His voice was hoarse, ragged, and the words came out one at a time. *"Who... the...hell...was...that?"*

"Who? Who was what?"

"Man...yelled at...me."

Annabel could only stare at him.

His adam's apple was working in his throat. His left hand clutched fretfully at the sheets. "Man...with...you. Yelled...old bas...tard."

Annabel's mind was whirling, trying to make sense of what he was saying. His hazel eyes were snapping with impatience. That much hadn't changed a bit.

She shook her head. "Some man yelled at...you, Daddy?" She didn't think mental confusion was part of his diagnosis, but she had to admit, she didn't have the faintest idea what he was talking about.

"The man with you," the nurse told her. "He was, well, yelling at Mr. Archer."

"Carter?"

"'S'name?" her father demanded.

"The man who was with me was Carter MacKenzie, but surely you're mistaken! He wouldn't—"

Her father coughed weakly. His head sank back against the pillows. "Might've...known," he rasped.

Annabel stared at him. "What?"

"Brash...arrogant...know-it-all. Son...of...a...bitch." He stopped and took a breath. "Jus'...like...'is father."

THEY ARGUED, of course. How could you not argue with the man who called the man you loved a son of a bitch?

The man she loved?

Loved?

Well, yes, of course. It was crystal clear now, for all the good it did her.

But Annabel didn't even stop to think about that until after. She made some concessions to her father's health. With her mother looking on and the nurses alternately tittering and wringing their hands, she had to.

But she didn't let him get away with it.

She told him in no uncertain terms that Carter was a far better man than he had ever been, that Carter knew what it was to be a friend, a father.

"He loves children who aren't even his own," she told him finally. "Unconditionally."

Edward's jaw stiffened. He glared at her, then, slowly, his gaze slid away. His hand worked again fitfully on the sheet. "Was...wrong," he mumbled.

"What?"

"Said—" his voice broke with the effort "—I was...wrong." His eyes came back to meet hers. They weren't flashing anymore. They looked shadowy now, sad almost. "Shouldn't...have done...what I...did. Too hard."

Annabel stared at him, stunned. An apology from Edward Archer?

But he wasn't finished yet.

"He's right...y'know...M'Kenzie...said I got to...make peace. Tell...the truth 'fore s'too...late." He looked at her. "Sorry."

His hand clenched again. Annabel reached out and took it in her own. Their fingers curved around each other's. Annabel, mind reeling, throat aching, hung on.

"Anna...bel? Love...you."

Carter had accomplished this?

Carter had yelled at her father?

"Good...man," her father went on, his fingers slowly, weakly kneading hers. "Better'n...'is old man. More...fire. Guts."

"Yes."

"Marry him?"

"What?"

"Deaf?" The hazel eyes were snapping impatiently at her again. "Said...you going to...marry him?"

Don't I wish, Annabel thought. *Haven't I wished for years and years?* But she had nothing to offer Carter except a house with a mortgage, a goat who couldn't stand him, two children to drive him crazy and a wife who had neither youth nor beauty nor exceptional talents, whose only claim to his attention was that she'd imposed on him tremendously and that she'd dreamed about him for nigh on twenty years.

Carter wasn't interested in her. Not as a wife. He could have virtually any woman he wanted. Like Marilee Newman.

She gave her father's hand a gentle squeeze. "I'd like to, Daddy," she said with absolute honesty. "But I'm afraid Carter has other plans."

"You blew it," Jack told Frances cheerfully when she came in from taking Jason to the park.

His wife cocked her head. "I beg your pardon."

"Milly called while you were gone. Said she'd called Carter. He's back in Vermont, by the way. Roofing. She asked him how Annabel was. He hung up on her."

She didn't want to go and see him.

It would hurt. He would want to pick up where they'd left off in the bedroom earlier in the week—or he wouldn't.

And she didn't know which would be worse.

Because there was no way on earth she could go to bed with him now. Not loving him. Not knowing that he didn't love her. While she'd been able to keep the knowledge of her feelings at bay, she'd stood half a chance of not making a fool of herself.

No more.

And if he didn't want to—well, perversely enough, that would hurt, as well. It would mean he was moving on, ready now to find someone new. A woman he could really love, who would be able to start a marriage afresh, without encumbrances.

Marilee Newman?

A good bet. But if not her, then any one of a legion of women. Carter had always been good at finding women, she thought wryly. There'd never been any doubt about that.

Still, she had to go by and see him. Had to say thank you.

How did you thank a man who had given you back your father? What words could express the gratitude, the joy, the satisfaction Annabel felt?

She didn't know.

She only knew she had to try.

She was quiet and distracted all the time the kids were getting ready for school. They were kind and solicitous, careful with her, as if she were some fragile piece of porcelain, all too capable of being cracked.

She knew they thought she was suffering from the aftermath of the reunion with her father and mother, of the soul-baring talks that all of them had just shared.

She let them think it. Telling them how she felt about Carter, and more especially about the futility of those hopes, was more soul baring than she could stand.

She waited until they were safely on the school bus. She waited until Bert had come, wrapped soaps, chatted and gone. She waited until Aaron had stuck his head in and asked if she wanted to go to a movie and she had gently declined.

Finally she could wait no longer.

HE SAW HER the minute she came over the top of the hill. He was sitting on the roof, three rows away from being finished with the whole reason for his being here. And he had been hoping he would get done—and gone—before he had to talk to anyone else.

And here she came.

She looked remote, distracted, unhappy. What else? Her father had just died, hadn't he?

And even though the old man had sent her away with what was probably close to his dying breath, it didn't mean she'd be rejoicing. She'd probably heard from one of the nurses what had transpired.

She was probably coming to tell him off.

He didn't blame her a bit. All the same, he sat very still and hoped she wouldn't look up.

Dream on, sucker, he told himself an instant later when her eyes lifted and her step faltered. She picked her way down the rest of the trail, then crossed the yard, stopping where she could look up and see him.

"Carter?"

"I'm really busy. Gotta get this done before it rains." There was maybe one cloud in the sky. He set to hammering again, positioned another shingle, hammered some more, moved on.

When he glanced up again, she'd disappeared. He breathed easier.

"Fine," he heard her voice a moment later, and looked up to see her climbing onto the roof. "I'll talk to you up here."

He bit down on the nails he held between his teeth. He shrugged, facing the inevitable, wishing it would hurry up and be over. He wanted to say he was sorry about her father, sorry about his part in it, but he was too much of a coward. He set another nail and began to hammer.

"You did it, you know," Annabel said quietly.

So much for vain hopes. He shut his eyes. His knuckles went white around the hammer. He bowed his head and took a slow breath before he could look up again and meet her eyes.

She was smiling. Not a thousand-watt grin, but still a smile.

He didn't understand. He shook his head. "I didn't mean—"

"You gave him back to me."

Now he really was confused. He sat back on the roof and spat the nails into his palms. "I don't know what you mean. I lost it in there. I yelled my bloody head off, said things I don't even want to think about now and—"

"And got through to him."

"I . . . killed him."

She started, laid a hand on his knee. He flinched and she drew back abruptly. "On the contrary. I think you brought him back to life."

Carter stared at her. "That—that phone call. From the hospital . . . Didn't he . . . didn't he die?"

Annabel shook her head. "He made the nurse call my mother, wanted her over there right that minute. She thought it was the end, too. So did I, so the kids and I went with her and hung about in the hall. He wanted her to find me." She stared off into space for a moment, then smiled again, that same gentle smile.

"He thought he'd driven me away for good, and wanted me back. Wanted to 'make his peace,' with me. That's what he told me when they let me in." Her gaze met his. "Because of you."

Carter sat very still, letting the words sink in. His jaw tightened, his throat felt blocked. He hadn't killed him, then? His yelling had actually done more good than harm?

"He said you were a brash, know-it-all son of a bitch, just like your father."

"*What?*"

Annabel shrugged. "That's what he said. He seemed pleased."

Carter wasn't. He was horrified. "I'm like my old man?"

"That's what he said. Except that you were better. He said you had more—more fire. More guts."

Carter digested that. It mollified his feelings a bit. There was a certain amount of truth to Edward Archer's assertions, God help him. He'd never wanted to acknowledge it before, but now he had to.

He and C.W. were both stubborn, both opinionated, both passionate in their beliefs. That was why they'd gone head-to-head so often. Less similar men might have found ways to accommodate each other.

It wasn't the first time he'd heard it said, either.

Even Milly had told him so. "One jackass braying at another" was the way she'd described them.

But he'd ignored her. What did sisters know?

Besides, he'd been jealous of her, if he was going to admit the truth. Milly had always been able to twist their father around her little finger, had always been able to smile and get good grades and say the right thing. And Carter had always yelled and fought and then pretended it didn't matter.

Just like his old man.

"I thought I'd killed him," he said to Annabel now. "I really thought I'd done him in." He felt weak with relief. She wouldn't hate him now. Was that enough?

He sighed and placed another nail. It would have to be. There was certainly nothing encouraging in the way she was looking at him, nothing that might give him the faintest hope that she'd come to see him as being more than a physical significance in her life.

And he couldn't be that. Not the way he felt.

It would kill him.

"Thanks for telling me," he said and began to hammer again, hard, expecting her to go.

Please God, she had to. She wasn't going to sit there and come on to him, torment him, expect him to make love to her, was she?

But she made no move to leave.

"Where's Conan?" she asked after a moment. "He surely can't be sleeping through all this hammering."

"He's gone. Maeve and Jerry came. Took him," he said through the nails in his mouth. He bent his head, concentrating on the shingling.

"Oh, Carter." She sounded as sad as he felt. She put her hand out again, as if she would have touched him. But then she jerked it back. "I'm so sorry. I know how much you'll miss him."

"Yeah," he said gruffly. "But, hell, that's the way things go. He had to go back."

"Did they settle things?"

"They damned well better have! I told 'em he's a baby, not some parcel they can just set aside whenever they don't feel like dealing with him! I told 'em—" He stopped abruptly, embarrassed by his vehemence.

"You were right," Annabel said gently. "I hope they take it as well as my father did."

He hammered in another nail. For Conan. Pounding some sense into his parents' heads. "It's great being right about everybody else's life," he said bitterly. "I feel like some damned oracle."

"You're a perceptive man. Sensitive. Caring."

Too damned caring, Carter thought.

"You were good for Conan. You were good for Libby and Leif. You'll . . . be a good father someday, Carter."

"No."

"Doesn't . . . doesn't Marilee want any kids?"

"Marilee?" He frowned at Annabel. "What's she got to do with it?"

Annabel shook her head. "I—I thought . . . You said she was so wonderful! You went out with her after . . . after we—" She broke off, looking away, the color high across her cheekbones.

"I didn't want to!"

She looked at him then. "Why not?"

"After making love with you I'm supposed to want to go out with somebody else?"

"She called. She said you had a date."

"Yeah, made days before... before—" Oh, hell, why was he doing this? Why was he opening his mouth? Telling her things he didn't want to tell her?

"—before we made love," she said quietly.

He looked out over the wooded pasture, at the brightly colored trees, the brilliant blue of the sky. He looked down at the toes of his sneakers, at the roof between his feet.

"Did it... matter?" She sounded doubtful.

"Hell, yes!" He couldn't stop himself. He would never learn. There was no hope. "It mattered to me. It sure as hell didn't matter to you!"

"*What?*"

"You didn't give a damn," Carter insisted, his teeth biting down on the nails. "You bloody offered to baby-sit!"

"Well, what was I supposed to do? You had a date!"

They glared at each other.

Then Carter set down his hammer. He spat out the nails. He turned on his knees and faced her squarely with far more confidence than he felt. "Do I matter, Annabel?"

He felt time stop.

Then Annabel's eyes met his, warm and unguarded. Infinitely gentle. "Oh, yes."

He didn't know if he believed in fairy tales or not. He didn't know if he was dreaming some impossible dream and might at any moment awaken. He only knew it was the answer to his prayers.

He reached for her, pulled her into his arms and knew a sense of relief when she came so willingly, putting her own arms around him, holding him, kissing his jaw, his cheeks, his ears.

Then Carter kissed her. He kissed her with everything he had in him—all the hurt and all the sadness and all the thwarted hopes, and all the joy and all the gladness and all the satisfaction that came from finding at last his heart's desire.

"I love you," he whispered.

And Annabel shook her head. "I don't believe it."

So he had to show her again. And this time, when he pulled back and asked, "Do you believe it now?" she nodded shakily.

"I—I want to," she said. Her voice wobbled, sounded tight, as if her throat hurt.

"Please believe it. I've never said anything truer in my life."

Annabel smiled, a watery smile. "And we know you tell the truth at all costs, don't we?"

Carter winced. "I should learn to keep my mouth shut."

"I don't think so," Annabel told him, and proceeded to show him one reason why he shouldn't.

"You're shameless," he told her. He was laughing and trembling at the same time.

"Possibly," Annabel said. "But I don't do that with just any man. Only with you. Because I love you, too."

He didn't realize how badly he'd needed to hear the words until she said them.

He couldn't remember anyone—save perhaps his mother—ever having said them to him. They seemed rare and beautiful, and Annabel must have sensed it because she laid her hand on his cheek, touching her lips lightly to his.

"I've loved you forever," she told him. "Almost twenty years."

He didn't know what she meant. "Twenty years? You were a child."

"We were both children. And besides being a child, I was a bit of a romantic fool."

"What are you talking about? Twenty years? We only met maybe three years ago, because of Jack. And you hated my guts from the first moment you saw me."

"Ah, yes," she admitted. "But that was because it wasn't really the first moment." She blushed and looked down. "I've never told anyone else this. I probably shouldn't even tell you. It makes me sound like an idiot."

"Tell me."

"It was at a dance at Marblehead. I was seventeen. Gawky. Tongue-tied. Bookish. A dreamer. I should have stayed at home, but Daddy insisted I go. To meet my prince, he said. If not there, then at some other dance shortly thereafter. He was always a bit unrealistic when it came to his expectations for me." She made a wry face. "It must have rubbed off on me because I had unrealistic expectations of my own the moment you walked in. I was convinced you were my prince." She gave a self-conscious laugh. "You thought otherwise obviously."

"Oh, God." Carter felt the blood drain from his face. "You? You were her? The gingerbread lady?"

"'With the Orphan Annie hair and the Petunia Pig dress,'" Annabel quoted. "Yes. And my only hope of salvation has been believing you didn't remember it at all. And you do!" She almost wailed this last.

Carter rubbed a hand against the back of his neck. "I ought to remember. My mother overheard me, too. Gave me holy hell all the way back to New York. Told me I was rude, inconsiderate, obnoxious, hateful and a few thousand other things equally as bad."

He looked right at Annabel, seeing for the first time a remote resemblance to that awkward young girl. "My mother was right. I was rude, inconsiderate and obnoxious. I'm sorry."

She put out a hand, brushed his hair away from his forehead, touched his cheek. "I think I've recovered from the trauma," she told him softly. "It was childishness on both our parts. I shouldn't have been such a ninny."

He kissed her. "Forgive me?"

"Oh, yes. In fact I owe you."

"For your father, you mean?"

"And for Mark. I ran out of the dance straight into his arms. Fell in love. Got pregnant. Married him. I owe you the past nineteen years of my life."

"Good God."

"They've been good years, Carter."

"I hope the rest of them will be even better," he told her unsteadily. "Will you . . . marry me?"

He waited a long time for her answer.

An interminable time.

He sat very still, his head bent. He remembered when he'd asked Diane. Her gentle smile, her tender touch, her soft "Oh, Carter, I can't." He relived it all now, didn't know what he'd do if it happened again.

"Are you sure, Carter?"

His head snapped up. "You think I'm asking for the hell of it?"

"But I'm old!"

He laughed "No older than I am."

"I've got kids."

"I've noticed."

"An unfriendly goat. A cat. Responsibilities."

"Commitments. Yes, I know. I envy you your responsibilities, Annabel." He took her hands in his. "I want to share them. All of them. Will you let me?"

Her eyes seemed to become suddenly brighter, brimming with tears. "Oh, Carter. Oh, heavens, yes!"

She launched herself at him, practically knocking them both off the roof. Only a hand out to stop their headlong tumble saved them. And then he was kissing her again, and salvation seemed assured.

"Carter," she said when they'd stopped to breathe, "would you like to have a baby?"

He went quite still. He hadn't really thought about it, hadn't dared. Even when he was mentally rearranging the world according to his own desires, he'd never got Annabel pregnant. "Would you?" he asked hoarsely.

She nodded. "Maybe it's silly, but I was such a child when Libby was born, I hardly got a chance to enjoy her. And with Leif I was a widow so soon after... I love babies, Carter. I loved having Conan. I might be too old, but—"

"Stop with this old business." He'd felt old himself only hours ago. He didn't feel it anymore. He felt as if all possibilities were open to him. He felt young, untried, new. Amazing, he thought, what love could do.

"We're not old. We've got a lifetime ahead of us, Annabel. And I'd—" his voice wobbled "—I'd love to have a baby with you." He kissed her lingeringly. "Or two."

Annabel, starry-eyed, smiled at him. "You're such an optimist."

"I have my reasons." Carter hugged her close. "We might think about going down now. Perhaps getting started."

"We can't."

Carter felt a sudden alarm. "Why not?"

"Look." Annabel pointed down into the yard. Arnold was staring up at them. He wasn't wearing a lead. "I don't know if I can keep him away from you."

"Don't worry. Arnold will approve. He and I have an understanding."

Annabel cocked her head quizzically.

Carter grinned. "Over the past few weeks we've taught each other a thing or two."

FRANCES LOVED a good wedding.

It was so satisfying seeing people who belonged together realize what she'd known all along.

"Nice, wasn't it?"

"Different," Jack conceded. "I can't believe they let the goat in the house for the reception. I guess I'm lucky you didn't bring the sheep to ours."

"You wouldn't have noticed if I had," Frances said, snuggling back against him in their bed.

"Probably not."

"I don't think Carter and Annabel noticed, either. They had eyes only for each other."

Jack grunted.

Frances tucked his arm up against her breasts and turned her head to brush a kiss across his lips.

"I told you so," she said.

HE WAS BORN the following August.

He weighed eight pounds three ounces, was twenty-one inches long. And what hair he had was red.

"What else did you expect?" Annabel asked her husband, who simply looked at her with tears of joy in his eyes and shook his head.

"He's beautiful," he told her, stroking her cheek. "You're beautiful."

And Annabel, who had months ago stopped arguing with him about that, smiled and kissed his hand. Then she looked down at the baby in her arms, whose dark blue eyes seemed already to have a hint of green as he tried to focus on her.

"Welcome to the world," she told him softly. "Welcome home, Carter William MacKenzie, the fifth."

She heard Carter's sharp intake of breath, prepared herself for the explosion, for the adamant rejection of the name, of saddling their son with the generations of baggage that went with it.

She heard him swallow and saw his hand drop to rest lightly on the baby's red hair.

"All right," Carter said. Then he lifted his gaze and smiled at her. "But he's going to be his own person."

In his eyes she saw that the battle was over, that love had won. "Of course," Annabel said and touched her lips to his. "I thought we'd call him Joe."

HE CROSSED TIME FOR HER

Captain Richard Colter rode the high seas, brandished a sword and pillaged treasure ships. A swashbuckling privateer, he was a man with voracious appetites and a lust for living. And in the eighteenth century, any woman swooned at his feet for the favor of his wild passion. History had it that Captain Richard Colter went down with his ship, the *Black Cutter,* in a dazzling sea battle off the Florida coast in 1792.

Then what was he doing washed ashore on a Key West beach in 1992—alive?

MARGARET ST. GEORGE brings you an extraspecial love story next month, about an extraordinary man who would do anything for the woman he loved:

#462 THE PIRATE AND HIS LADY
by Margaret St. George
November 1992

When love is meant to be, nothing can stand in its way . . . not even time.

Don't miss American Romance
#462 THE PIRATE AND HIS LADY.
It's a love story you'll never forget.

PAL

HARLEQUIN

A M E R I C A N ◆ R O M A N C E ®

A Calendar of Romance

American Romance's yearlong celebration continues.... Join your favorite authors as they celebrate love set against the special times each month throughout 1992.

Next month... Mix one man and one woman, two matchmaking moms, three young boys and 50,000 turkeys and you have a recipe for an uproarious Thanksgiving. It'll be a holiday that Luke, Darcy and the Calloway turkey farm will never forget!

NOVEMBER

S	M	T	W	T	F	S
1	2	3				7
8	9					
22	23	24	25	26	27	28
29	30					

#461
COUNT YOUR BLESSINGS
by Kathy Clark

Read all the Calendar of Romance titles!